AIRSHIP 27 PRODUCTIONS

™

Caged Fury
© 2022 R.A. Jones

Published by Airship 27 Productions
www.airship27.com
www.airship27hangar.com

Interior illustrations © 2022 Neil Foster
Cover illustration © 2022 Chris Rawding

Editor: Ron Fortier
Associate Editor: Gordon Dymowski
Marketing and Promotions Manager: Michael Vance
Production designer: Rob Davis.

ISBN: 978-1-953589-35-4

Printed in the United States of America

10 9 8 7 6 5 4 3 2 1

CAGED FURY

R.A. Jones

Chapter 1

Jason Mankiller was undoubtedly the only passenger who was *hoping* the stage would be held up.

The rugged and isolated foothills along the Colorado and New Mexico borders had proven to be fertile grounds for such felonious activity. One pair of outlaws in particular had begun making something of a habit of waylaying coaches belonging to the Russell and Ludlow Stage Line that served this region.

Their action had become the source of growing financial concern to the stage line—and had resulted in said company offering a substantial reward for the two suspects. To underscore the sincerity of the bounty, it was offered for the bandits' apprehension *Dead or Alive*.

That's what had brought Mankiller to the region.

Having discovered a natural aptitude for gunplay and an innate ability as a tracker of human predators, he had found the role of the bounty hunter to be one that suited him well. It paid far better than the $30 and found of a typical cowhand and was not nearly so like to break back and soul, as was the lot of a farmer.

Bounty hunting did carry a far greater risk to life and limb, of course. But the hellish, blood-soaked battlegrounds of the War Between the States had left Mankiller with a fatalistic indifference to such.

Not that he didn't still carry wounds, physical and otherwise, from the horrible conflict now ten years behind him. But the scars were of wounds no longer felt, and the nightmares he kept to himself. Like all who successfully survived immersion in the cauldron of war, he had come out tougher, more resilient.

Harder.

Like most of their kind, the stage robbers he hunted were too lazy and too stupid to wander far from the pattern of their thievery in either location or method. Every hold-up attributed to them thus far had occurred within a roughly ten square mile area in this region.

A couple of waylays had taken place outside that boundary in recent weeks, but Mankiller lent reports of them little credence. False attributions were common in the West; had Jesse James and his gang in truth committed all the robberies credited to them at various times and places, poor Jesse would have been required either to possess the speed of winged Mercury or have been triplets.

That still left plenty of territory, plenty of trails for Jason to cover in his manhunt. Hoping to increase the odds of encountering the thieving pair he sought, he had taken to booking passage on random runs of the stage line. This was his fourth such jaunt.

In addition to its driver and accompanying shotgun messenger, the creaking Concord carried five passengers on this day. Next to Mankiller sat a portly and somewhat slovenly whiskey drummer possessed of the noteworthy ability to actually sleep, and rather soundly at that, despite the noise, dust and continual rough bouncing of the coach as it made its way up a winding ridge.

Across from the bounty hunter sat a man and two women. The fellow looked even younger than Mankiller himself. From the way he held the hand of the still younger woman beside him and the loving looks they frequently exchanged, Jason took them to be a married couple, probably newly so.

Directly across from him sat an elderly woman of nearly fifty by her severe looks. Frequently holding a faded lace kerchief to her nose and mouth to protect from the worst of the trail dust, she mostly avoided making eye contact with Mankiller. On those occasions when she did, her gaze betrayed a combination of fear and revulsion.

Jason thought nothing of it; his countenance often invoked such reactions, from both the innocent and the guilty.

Most distinctive about his rugged countenance was a red *tattoo* that ran down the left side of his face, from the outer corner of his eye to the bottom of his high cheekbone. A "present" from some of his fellow soldiers, drunkenly celebrating after his nigh legendary heroics at the Battle of Gettysburg, the scarlet rivulet had given him a grim appellation of growing and spreading fame.

The Man Who Cries Blood.

He didn't bother to smile at the older woman when he caught her casting furtive glances in his direction; experience had taught him that any such effort to put her mind at ease would be futile.

"What's wrong?" she asked no one in particular as she now felt the jostling coach roll to a jerking halt.

"Prob'ly nothing, ma'am," Jason tried to assure her. "Even with a six-up like ours, this is a heavy load to pull. The driver most likely is just giving the horses a chance to blow a little now that we've reached the top of the rise."

He realized he'd spoken too soon when a single gunshot rang out.

A sudden movement seen through a window of the coach's left side caught Mankiller's eye. He knew with grim certainty it was the toppling body of their shotgun messenger.

A moment later, the right side door of the coach was roughly jerked open. Standing there was a slovenly cutthroat holding a pistol aimed at the passengers.

"Ever'body out," he barked in a voice made hoarse by tobacco and rotgut whiskey.

Amazingly, the whiskey drummer had remained blissfully asleep through all the uproar. He snorted and sputtered awake only after Mankiller gave him a nudge in the ribs with his elbow.

"Nice and slow," the highwayman commanded, backing up slightly. "Keep yer hands where I can see 'em."

They all did as ordered, Mankiller first. When he offered a helping hand to assist the older woman down, she pointedly refused it.

"Are any of you heeled?" the robber demanded.

"What?" the whiskey drummer replied, not familiar with the term.

"Guns!" the robber barked harshly. "Are any of ya carryin' guns?"

The question was met with blank stares from all but Jason Mankiller.

"I am," he said calmly.

"Let's see it," the robber snapped, taking yet another wary step back.

Slowly and deliberately, Jason pulled aside the left side of the gray corduroy jacket he was wearing to reveal the Colt's .45 revolver nestled in a cross-draw holster on his left hip.

"Take it out—real, real slow, mister. Two fingers. Then toss it away."

Jason did so without argument or hesitance.

"Hey!" a new voice called down from above.

The voice belonged to the highwayman's partner in crime. A thin man with the menacing eyes of a snake, he was standing astride the boot of the coach. Beside him, hands in the air and frozen in place, sat the coach driver.

"Climb on up here and give me a hand with this strongbox," Snake-Eyes said. His partners turned away from the passengers to comply.

This was the moment for which Mankiller had been waiting.

With a smooth and barely detectable movement, he slipped his right hand under and around the back of his coat. Tucked into the waistband of his trousers was a second gun: a Colt's "Storekeeper." Its short, 3.5-inch barrel made it idea for concealment. The bounty hunter's fingers wrapped easily around its butt and pulled it free.

He chose as his first target the man farthest away and thus requiring more deliberate aiming. The pistol barked and bucked in his hand. Though it dispelled only .38 caliber slugs, it was more than powerful enough to do the job when in the hands of an expert.

A look of stunned horror twisted the face of the outlaw standing atop the coach. A bright red flower of blood blossomed from the base of his throat as he was hurled backward into thin air.

Caught flat-footed, his partner on the ground turned back toward the passengers—only to find himself staring down the short barrel of Mankiller's cocked pistol.

The sound of the ensuing shot did not have time to register on his senses before the fired slug burrowed its way into the middle of his forehead. His knees collapsed beneath him and his heart pumped its last as he crumpled to the dust.

Taking no chances, Mankiller kicked away the outlaw's dropped firearm, then quickly raced around the back of the coach to the other side. His pistol was cocked and aimed at the highwayman who had fallen there, but even a quick glance assured him this outlaw too was dead.

"Sweet day in the mornin'!" The words almost came out as a loud sigh from the astounded coach driver, whose empty hands were still held aloft.

"I never seen nothin' like that in all my born days!"

Mankiller, now kneeling beside the still body of the fallen shotgun messenger, looked up at the driver.

"There was nothing I could do to save your friend," he said. "He's gone."

"He was a good man," the driver replied, lowering his arms at last.

"I'm sure he was."

"What'll we do now?" the driver asked.

"With your help, we'll heave the bodies up to the top of the coach and take 'em to the next town."

The driver looked at his quizzically. "I'm all for doin' right by Earl, there," he said, referencing the slain shotgun messenger.

"But why not just leave them other two bastards for the buzzards?"

"Because they're money in the bank for me," Mankiller replied his voice coldly even.

"Eh?" The stage driver squinted at Mankiller, seeing him and his distinctive tattoo clearly for the first time; then his eyes opened wide in recognition.

"Yer *him*, ain'tcha? The bounty killer."

"I am."

The driver continued to stare at him for a long moment before shrugging his shoulders and starting to climb down from his box.

"Fair enough. You saved the strongbox and mebbe my bacon, too. That's worth a little liftin' and totin'."

The grisly chore was achieved by tying a rope under the armpits of each corpse; Mankiller and the driver then stood atop the stage and hoisted each body up in turn. When the final corpse was stretched out, Jason used the rope to secure them to the roof.

"Give me a couple more minutes," Mankiller said to the driver, after lightly dropping down to the ground.

"Make it quick," the old salt replied. "We're far enough behind schedule as it is."

The bounty hunter pushed his way through some nearby underbrush that lay in the direction from which he assumed the shot had been fired that took out the shotgun messenger.

When he returned a short time later, he was leading the slain outlaws' horses, which he tied onto the back of the coach.

Opening one of the passenger doors, he started to climb aboard, only to pull up short. The whiskey drummer had, not surprisingly, already fallen back asleep again; his robust body slumped to one side. The young married couple clung tightly to each other, eyeing Mankiller with as much fear as they had displayed in the face of the outlaws. The look of revulsion on the face of the older woman was even more intense than before.

"You mind if I ride up top with you?" he called up to the driver.

"Can you handle a shotgun?"

Mankiller looked at him as if he was a child.

"'Course ya can. Never mind. Come on up; we need ta get this show on the road!"

Jason made a point of tipping his hat courteously to the older woman before slamming the door shut and climbing up onto the boot of the coach.

He felt he would definitely be in better company with the driver and the three corpses.

Chapter 2

The town of Low Water was little more than a wide spot in the road. Almost all of its buildings were spaced tightly along either side of his lone and main street. Built on a slight north-south incline, it allowed for good drainage when the rains came. At the moment, the dirt street was dry, dusty and hard packed.

Inside the relative coolness of his office, Marshal Blue Thorpe was enjoying a cup of coffee.

He'd been a hard man in his younger days, not overly tall but well muscled. Time and the relative ease of his current position had softened him considerably, if only in the physical sense. There was a slight flabbiness around his middle now, fighting to escape the bounds of his waistband.

As the midday stage rolled into town and pulled to a rocking halt before the express office across the street and down a ways from the jail, Thorpe glanced at his office wall clock. This coach usually made it here closer to on schedule than seemed to be the case today. He stepped closer to the window to take a better look.

The lawman choked slightly on his next sip of coffee, coughing as the hot liquid slid down the wrong pipe.

He'd never before laid eyes on the lean man who nimbly dropped down from the boot of the stagecoach, but he instantly recognized him. The reputation of the bounty hunter with the blood red tattoo had begun to spread fairly widely, as the tally of outlaws bodies left in his wake grew ever larger.

Thorpe saw the express office clerk coming running around from the opposite side of the coach and begin a rather animated conversation with Mankiller. At last, the clerk turned slightly and pointed in the direction of the jail and marshal's office.

"Dan'l!" Thorpe shouted, spinning away from the window.

Outside, Jason Mankiller was once again explaining to the clerk the circumstances leading up to the grisly sight of three stiffening bodies arriving on the midday stage.

"He's tellin' it to ya straight, Homer," the driver said, stepping out of the express office with a roasted beef sandwich in one hand and a steaming tin cup of coffee in the other.

"Now, I gotta get movin'. We're burnin' daylight!" He cast a respectful glance at Mankiller. "You comin' with us?"

"No," Jason replied. "I've got to take care of business here."

"Good luck to ya, then."

"Oh, mister?" a soft voice called to Jason tentatively. He turned to see the young married woman leaning slightly out of the coach window.

"I'm sorry we didn't thank you for what you did," she said rather anxiously. "Those creatures might have killed us, too." She reached out and took his hand for just a moment, squeezing it lightly. Her husband looked out over her shoulder and graced Jason with a tentative smile and nod of his head.

"Glad I could be of help," Mankiller said, tipping his hat. He barely had time to step back away from the wheels of the Concord as the driver yelled at his lead horses and flicked one on the ear with his whip, causing them to leap forward with the coach in tow.

Arrangements were made to take the bodies of the shotgun messenger and the two outlaws to the town's barber, who also served as its undertaker.

Mankiller then took the slain highwaymen's horses to the livery stable at one end of town before turning his sights and his footsteps in the direction of the marshal's office.

He opened the front door to see a young man seated behind a battered desk. He was leaned back in his chair, hands held together and resting on his belly, eyes closed as if preparing to take a nap. At the sound of Mankiller's boots on the wooden floor, he opened one eye lazily.

"You the marshal?" Jason asked with puzzlement.

"Me? Naw. I'm Dan Green. I'm Marshal Thorpe's chief deputy."

"Ah." And, one would hope, a relative. How else to explain putting such an obviously…challenged individual in such a position?

Mankiller casually glanced around the office. "Is the marshal around?"

"Not just now. He had ta go meet with the mayor."

"Mmm. Any idea when he'll be back?"

"When they's finished, I reckon. He said it'd prob'ly be 'bout an hour. Can I he'p ya?"

Mankiller did not voice his opinion that the young deputy appeared to lack sufficient intelligence to give a typical goose a run for its money.

"That's all right, Deputy Green. I'll just grab a bite to eat and come back a little later." He turned toward the door.

"Could I have yer name?" the deputy inquired. "So's I can tell Marshal Thorpe who was lookin' fer 'im?"

"It's Jason Mankiller."

Deputy Green grabbed a sheet of paper and a pencil. Touching the point of the lead to his tongue, he began to laboriously print the bounty hunter's name. It took him nearly a full minute to do so, and when he glanced back up he wore the slanted grin of one who had just achieved a noteworthy accomplishment.

"Where's a good place to eat around here?" Jason then asked. The young lawman seemed to need to think far longer and harder than should have been required for such a simple question, given that the entire town was only about a quarter of a mile long and surely didn't boast of many eateries.

"I ain't sure just how *good* you'd call 'em," he said at last, looking as though he had made a Solomonic decision. "If yer wantin' a beer or whiskey to wash it down, the saloon can fix you up with a steak that usually ain't too old or tough."

"Right now, all I want is food."

"Ah. Then you'd best go to the Blue Bird Café. Just cross the street, turn right and foller yer nose."

"Obliged." Mankiller tipped his hat, stepped outside and shook his head.

He had indeed enjoyed better cooking than he encountered at the small café; but having spent his share of days on the trail and in army or cattle camps, Mankiller had most certainly experienced his share of far worse. The steak he was served was thick and mostly chewable, and the portion of fried potatoes that came with it was generous.

He took his time with the meal, lingering over a small pot of what turned out to be quite good coffee. Mostly because of this, when he rose to leave he left a ten-cent tip behind.

He availed himself of a toothpick as he leisurely strolled back to the town jail. When he opened the door and stepped inside, he immediately noted that a different lawman was now seated behind the desk. An older man he was, and wider of girth, with thick moustaches drooping wearily down each side of his mouth. His hands were beneath the desktop, presumably resting in his lap.

Something about him seemed vaguely familiar, but Jason couldn't put his finger on why this was so.

"You the marshal?" he asked.

"I am. Blue Thorpe's the name."

"Marshal Thorpe. My name is Jason Mankiller."

"Oh, I know who you are, right enough," Thorpe replied rather harshly. "Can't be no mistaking that face."

"I suppose not," Jason replied, feeling he'd just been insulted but thinking it best be ignored.

"I've got business with you," he continued.

"And I got business with you."

An ominous metallic click came to Mankiller's ears: one with which he was all too frighteningly familiar.

Keeping both hands away from his sides, he slowly swiveled his head.

The deputy to whom he had spoken earlier had stepped out of the back area of the jail, where the cells were most likely located.

He was holding a single-barreled shotgun in both hands, threateningly aiming it at Mankiller's midsection.

A second, softer metallic click brought Jason's head back around. Marshal Thorpe had lifted his right hand out from under the desk. In it rested a revolver that had doubtless been secreted there all along.

"Unbuckle yer gunbelt and let it drop to the floor," Thorpe demanded.

"What's going on here?" the stunned bounty hunter asked, even as he complied and dropped his weapon.

"What's goin' on is that you're under arrest, mister," Thorpe replied in an icy voice.

"Arrest? For what?"

"The folks hereabouts don't take kindly to *murder*," came the reply.

"Murder? You got the wrong man, marshal. I've never murdered anybody!"

Thorpe rose rather ponderously to his feet, his gun barrel never wavering as it pointed at Mankiller.

"Yeah? Well, sir, we got two dead men over ta the undertaker's who might care to argue that point with you—if they was able."

At these words, the bounty hunter relaxed slightly. "Is that what this is about?" he said. "You got it all wrong, marshal. There's a third body laying there, too. He's the shotgun messenger who was killed by the other two."

"So you say."

"It's true. They're a couple of wanted hold-up men. That's why I brought the bodies in—to claim the reward offered for them."

"Again...so you say."

"I don't just say it," Mankiller snapped, feeling his hackles rise. "I can prove it."

"You'll get yer chance ta do just that," Marshal Thorpe said, waving his pistol to indicate he wanted Mankiller to move toward the row of cells at the back of the building. "At yer trial."

"Trial? There shouldn't need to be no trial!"

Thorpe's face split with a greasy smile. "Would ya rather we just hung ya *without* a trial?"

Mankiller said no more until the barred door of the cell into which he was ushered clanged shut behind him.

"Am I at least gonna be allowed to have a *lawyer*?" he asked.

"Sure," Thorpe replied, leaning in close to the bars. "You *know* one?"

Mankiller reflexively took a step back away from the lawman; not from fear, but because that nagging feeling that he had indeed seen this man before also led him to believe that Thorpe posed a clear danger to him, beyond merely incarcerating him.

"After I had my dinner," the bounty hunter said with measured tones, "on my way over here I did happen to notice a lawyer's shingle on a building across the way. If I recollect right, the name on it was Carter Frain."

"Frain?" Thorpe repeated, the disdain in his voice clear. "Son, I wouldn't trust that Easterner to keep me from hangin' for spittin' on the sidewalk!"

That was all the recommendation Jason needed.

"I think I'll take my chances," he said. "Do you think you could get word to him that I'd like to retain his services?"

"I'd be purely de-lighted," Thorpe replied. "Right after I tell the undertaker to start buildin' a *fourth* coffin."

Chapter 3

Two hours later, just as Jason Mankiller had begun to think that no effort had been made to fetch him legal counsel, he heard the door between the cell block and the outer office of the jail swing open.

Deputy Dan Green passed through it, escorting a well-dressed man who appeared to be in his late twenties. Short and slight of frame, his mostly blond hair was slicked and neatly combed, while a pair of eyeglasses rested atop his slender nose. He carried a leather briefcase in both hands and appeared to be as excited as a five-year-old boy at his first County Fair.

"Mr. Mankiller?" he said in a refined but sturdy voice. "I'm Carter Frain. You sent for me."

"Pleased to meet you," Mankiller said, extending his right hand through the bars of his cell and shaking that of the attorney.

"I s'pect you'll have your hands full if you agree to take me on as a client," he said bluntly.

"That may be so," Frain replied. "But I'm willing to make a go of it if you're willing to let me."

"Consider yourself hired," Mankiller said with no hesitation, trusting his usually reliable instincts when it came to passing quick judgment on the quality of a man's character. He then turned his head to glare at the somewhat slack-jawed deputy who was still standing close by with his arms leisurely folded over his chest.

"I believe I'm entitled to talk to my lawyer in *private*," Jason said pointedly. The deputy responded with a harsh grunting sound, a measure of his low intellect, but did exit the block, closing the door to the office behind him.

The young lawyer pulled up a three-legged stool and took a seat on the opposite side of the bars restraining Mankiller. From inside his briefcase he withdrew a notepad and pencil.

"Why don't we start by you simply telling me, as best you can, what led up to your arrest," he instructed. "Don't leave anything out, even if it seems small and unimportant to you. You can sometimes hang a solid defense on a nail you wouldn't think could support a picture frame."

For the next half-hour, Jason recounted the events of that day as nearly as he could recall. Lawyer Frain interrupted a time or two to seek clarification, but otherwise simply listened whilst furiously scribbling away with his pencil. Even when Mankiller concluded his tale Frain continued to take down notes for a few minutes before looking up at his client.

"I did a little asking around at the express office before coming over here," he told Jason.

"Without even knowing if I would hire you as my attorney?"

Frain smiled thinly. "Without knowing if I would *accept* you as a client." Mankiller chuckled softly, certain now he had chosen his representation wisely.

"Anyway, I talked to Homer Pertwee—the stage office manager. He told me what you had told him about the incident and it matches precisely the account you just relayed to me."

Jason realized that, by asking for his story, the attorney had been in part testing his truthfulness, looking for any changes or inconsistencies in Mankiller's retelling. Rather than being offended by this tactic, Mankiller was impressed by the attorney's canny acumen.

"Mr. Pertwee's testimony will be helpful," Frain continued, "but is of course only hearsay; he didn't actually witness what happened during the holdup."

"No, but there's five other people who *did*," Jason asserted. "Besides me, that is; and none of them would have reason that I know of to lie about what went down."

"Of course," Frain nodded. "Unfortunately, they have all left town to continue on their respective journeys."

"Can we get them back to testify?"

"I doubt it. But, small as Low Water is, it does have a telegraph office. I can telegraph the authorities farther down the line; ask them to question the passengers and take sworn depositions from them. That should be enough to satisfy the court.

"And if the driver follows his usual route, he should pass back through here within a week. With him to bear witness on the stand and the depositions read into the record, we should be able to prove to any reasonable jury that you acted within the constraints of the law."

Mankiller nodded. "I think I made the right choice in hiring you, Mr. Frain."

"Call me Carter."

"Carter it is. I can tell you've got a good head on your shoulders. I expect that lands you plenty of clients."

"Practically none, I'm afraid," the young lawyer abashedly admitted, shaking his head.

"Why is that?"

"It's not because I'm a bad lawyer," Frain hastened to assure the bounty hunter. "But as you've seen, Low Water is a small town, with not much call for legal services. My wife and I have sincerely considered packing up and moving on. We mostly moved here to look after her ailing, widowed mother; and the poor woman passed away a few weeks ago.

"There was also already another attorney who had established himself pretty well by the time we arrived. His name is Bob Trahan, and he's a friend of both the marshal and the town's mayor, Delmar Owens. Bob handles all the town's official legal business and is its chief prosecutor.

"Mayor Owens also happens to be the only *judge* here in Low Water. He'll no doubt preside over your trial if we can't manage to get the charges dismissed before then." Frain rose up off of the stool; Jason too rose, out of respect.

"I'll head right down to the telegraph office," Frain told his client. "Hopefully, I'll have good news for you the next time we meet."

"Just one more thing, Carter," Jason said. "We haven't discussed what your *fee* will be for you legal services."

Frain smiled and nodded. "It'll be reasonable, I promise."

"But you don't know me," Mankiller persisted. "You don't know if I have a penny to my name, or would pay what I owed even if I did."

"You took my measure both as a man and as a lawyer pretty quickly, Mr. Mankiller. Rightly or wrongly, I consider myself to be equally good at judging the character of a man."

"Hold on a second," Jason said. Taking a seat on the edge of the cell's sagging cot, away from prying eyes, he removed his right boot. The marshal had stripped his pockets before locking him up, but had not thought to check his footgear.

Inside slits in the lining of each boot, Mankiller kept folding money in case of emergency. He removed the greenbacks hidden in the right one before walking over and pressing them into the surprised attorney's palm while shaking his hand.

"A retainer," he whispered, "and my personal pledge that there will be more when this is over."

Frain nodded almost imperceptibly as he closed his fist over the cash. Quickly stepping away from the cell, he pushed through the door leading back into the jail's front office.

The door nearly struck Marshal Thorpe, who doubtless had been attempting to eavesdrop on what was supposed to be a confidential conversation between attorney and client. The lawman made no apologies for his indiscretion, but simply stomped over to his desk and dropped down into his protesting chair.

"Whatever you promised to do for him, Frain," Thorpe said gruffly, pretending to be looking through paperwork so as not to look at the lawyer, "you'd best do it quick."

"Oh?" Frain's curiosity was piqued. "Why's that, Marshal?"

"'Cause Judge Owens has scheduled the trial for nine o'clock—tomorrow morning."

"What?" Frain, clearly appalled, stepped close to the marshal's desk, forcing the lawman to at last meet his eyes. "That's outrageous! I've got to be allowed time enough to prepare my case!"

"You can take it up with the judge," Thorpe replied sharply, "tomorrow morning."

"You can be damn sure I will," Frain snapped, not flinching in the menacing glare of the marshal.

"And another thing," the lawyer posed to Thorpe. "Have you done anything to try to verify the story my client told about the two men he's accused of murdering?"

"Like what?" Thorpe sneered. "Ain't provin' him innocent *yer* job, mister attorney?"

"You might at least check through your wanted posters, see if anyone with their names or fitting their descriptions does indeed have paper out on him."

"Don't you think I've already done that? First thing. Didn't find a single bill on either one of 'em."

"All right," Frain said, making no effort to hide his disbelief. "Then I guess I'd better send out a few more wires; say, to every marshal within a fifty mile radius of here."

"Spend yer client's money any way you want, shyster," Thorpe replied. "Me, I got other work to do." He turned and left the jail, after first pausing to whisper some instructions to Deputy Green.

Frain watched the lawman leave, then stepped back into the cellblock. Mankiller still stood there grasping the bars of his cage.

"I forgot to ask," Frain said. "Is there anything I can bring you: some tobacco, a deck of playing cards?"

"Nah. I'm good, long as I don't have to stay cooped up for too long. I appreciate the offer, though. Actually –" he amended, causing Frain to stop and turn back toward his cell.

"A little reading material might help pass the time. A newspaper, maybe?"

Frain chuckled slightly. "A well-read murderer, eh? I'm afraid we're too small a burg to rate a newspaper of our own." The lawyer stuck his head out of the doorway leading into the front office.

"Deputy Green? Might you have a book of some sort my client could avail himself of?" He ducked back into the cellblock. "Would a bible be all right?"

"Long as its words on paper," Mankiller replied, "I'll make do with it."

"This is all we got," the deputy said, leaning into the doorway and tossing a battered and dog-eared tabloid to his prisoner.

Jason laughed lightly, shaking his head as he glanced down at the cover of the softback book.

"What's so funny?" lawyer Frain asked.

"See for yourself," the bounty hunter replied, holding the tabloid up to the front bars of his cell. Frain bent at the waist to take a closer look. Illustrating the cover was a pen-and-ink image of a man in buckskins blazing away with a pistol in each hand as savage Indians raced toward him with murderous intent. The title of the book was of special interest:

Jason Mankiller vs. The Apache Horde
-or-
Redskins' Revenge

Smiling, the attorney looked back up at his client. "However did you manage to overpower an entire *horde*, Jason?"

"They were accommodating enough to come at me one at a time," Mankiller replied, jovially.

"Well, I will leave you to it," Frain said, once again turning away. "I have several wires to get off before tomorrow."

Still chuckling, seemingly forgetting the hazardous position in which he found himself, Mankiller took a seat on the edge of the cell's rickety cot and again examined the cover of the dime novel.

As expected, and much to his delight, he saw that the name attributed to the writer of this fantastical yarn was that of "Jay Starr."

Mankiller was one of the few people who knew that this particular literary "Mister" was in actuality a "Miss."

Though he had known *Jane* Starr for only slightly more than a year, Jason considered her to be a kindred spirit and a treasured friend. When first he met her, she was primarily engaged in the occupation of being a faro dealer in a saloon's gambling parlor: still was when last he'd seen her.

As did many in her profession, she followed the gambling circuit from town to town. When, as inevitably happened, the pool of luck in a particular site began to dry up, she and her constant companion—a Southern card sharp with the unlikely but genuine name of Cash Carpenter—would pull up stakes and journey to the next likely locale.

When she had confessed of a secret desire to become an author, it was Mankiller who most encouraged her and who suggested she try selling her writings under a male pseudonym to bypass any prejudice that might be held against her gender by either editors or readers. He had also gladly granted her permission to use his name as that of the lead character in her fanciful stories that were almost invented entirely from wholecloth. They also contained just enough truth about his real history and character to lend them at least an air of verisimilitude. And to occasionally made him slightly uncomfortable at being so exposed.

No man, after all, wants any woman to know him *too* well.

Pounding and plumping the limp sack of chicken feathers that passed for a pillow, Mankiller lay back on his cot and opened the dime novel.

He would have freely admitted to being curious about just how Jane would manage to get "him" out of what on the surface would appear to be a struggle against impossible odds!

As he lay back to make the best of a bad situation, his attorney was already going about his job, hurrying down the street toward the town's tiny telegraph office; after having first stopped in at his Spartan office to compose the messages he intended to send by wire.

He pulled up short for a moment when he spied Marshal Blue Thorpe stepping out of that very telegraph office.

The lawman did not seem to be pursuing any legal matter. He stood calmly on the sidewalk while rolling a cigarette. After lighting the quirly and tossing away the match, he stepped off the sidewalk and sauntered off in the general direction of Mayor Owens' office.

Dismissing the marshal from his thoughts, Carter Frain continued on his own mission. When he entered the telegraph office, he saw telegrapher Jack Simpson leaned back in his chair and perusing a dog-eared copy of the *Police Gazette*.

"Afternoon, Mr. Frain," Simpson said in a slow, lazy voice as he set aside his magazine. "How can I help you?"

"I've got plenty of work for you Jack," the lawyer replied energetically. "Several messages that I need to send out right away."

"'Fraid I won't be able to do that, sir," the telegrapher replied.

"Why not?"

Simpson shrugged both shoulders. "The wire's dead; has been for nearly an hour now."

"Do you know what the problem is?"

"Not for sure, no. Doesn't seem to be anything wrong on this end, near as I can tell. Most likely we've got a line down somewhere."

Frain sighed impotently. "Any idea how long it'll be before its back up and running?"

"Couldn't say for sure. Depends on how long it takes to find and repair the break. Could be an hour—could be a week."

"I don't have a week!"

"Sorry, Mr. Frain. Nothin' I can do about it."

"I know, Jack. I know." Giving the matter some quick thought, Frain extracted a silver dollar from his vest pocket and slid it across the top of the telegrapher's desk.

"Listen. If the line opens up any time before nine o'clock tomorrow morning, send word to me, will you? It's really urgent that I get these messages out."

"Sure thing, Mr. Frain," Simpson replied, scooping the proffered coin the rest of the way across his desktop before depositing it in a pants' pocket.

Less than five minutes after the frazzled lawyer departed, Simpson's telegraph key began tapping. Scribbling down the routine incoming message, the telegrapher quickly tapped back an acknowledgment.

Rubbing the leg of his trousers to feel the comforting bulge of the silver dollar sitting there, Simpson smiled as he thought of how easy it had been to earn the money: simply do what the marshal told him and lie to Frain about the line being down. That dollar would buy him the best supper in town later, washed down with a few drinks at the saloon.

The telegrapher was whistling softly as he leaned back in his chaired and resumed reading his copy of the *Gazette*.

Chapter 4

Carter Frain looked his finest when he stepped into Marshal Thorpe's office at 8:30 the following morning. While he had worked on his legal strategy the night before, his loving wife had diligently brushed and pressed his suit and polished his shoes to a high gloss.

After feeding him the hearty breakfast she had insisted upon, she had made sure his tie was straight and every inch of his woolen suit hung properly. She wanted everyone who attended the upcoming trial to be as proud of her husband as was she. There was no need to voice the hope they both had that the lawyer's performance might also serve to bring him new clients whose fees would help replenish cupboards grown disturbingly bare.

Her last actions before sending Carter into the legal fray were to kiss him lightly on the lips, then lick her fingertips and use them to press down a few errant strands of hair on the side of his head.

Frain was feeling downright feisty when he breezed through the front door of the jail, even had a slight smile on his face. That smile dismounted when he found himself apparently alone in the office.

"Hello?" he called. "Anyone here?" Silence was his only reply.

Growing concerned, he crossed the office and pushed through the unlocked door leading back into the cellblock. As he expected and found, it too was empty.

He stood outside Jason Mankiller's cell, pondering for a moment. While a fairly rare occurrence, it was not unknown in the West for an angry mob to decide to take the law into its own hands by forming a lynch party.

But surely, he surmised, he would have been aware had any such thing happened here: most tended to be loud and raucous. Nor did the marshal's office or cellblock show any signs of the mess such vigilante action would have left in its wake. Nothing was out of place, nor had the front door shown any sign of having been forced open in the night.

"Hello? Anyone here?

A more likely probability sprang to mind, and he wheeled and dashed from the office. Only now did he notice what his focus on his client and his case had kept him from seeing before; that the town's main street was unusually empty.

The answer became apparent as he raced down the sidewalk toward Low Water's combination City Hall and Courthouse. He saw several of the town's inhabitants clustered around the building's front door and window, clearly straining to see what was transpiring inside.

"Let me through!" Frain shouted as he began to elbow his way through the mass blocking the doorway, ignoring angry growls of complaint.

The rather small and cramped chamber within was filled to capacity. Breaking through the ranks of the civilians, Frain had his worst fear confirmed.

Jason Mankiller was seated alone at the defendant's table. His hands were cuffed and a length of chain connected them to a pair of shackles that bound his feet.

A short distance away, at a similar table, sat the town's prosecuting attorney, Bob Trahan. Sitting beside him and conferring with him in whispered tones was Marshal Blue Thorpe.

"It's about time you got here, Counselor," a raspy voice said sternly.

It came from the black-robed figure seated behind the elevated bench at the head of the chamber. Mayor—and Judge—Delmar Owens glared down at the dumbfounded Carter Frain. A man of nearly fifty years, Owens sported short hair that stuck up and out like graying spikes. Spectacles rested at the end of a slightly bulbous nose. A bushy moustache bobbed up and down with the movement of his jaws as he worked away at a plug of chewing tobacco lodged in his left cheek. When he chose to spit, the floor served as his cuspidor.

"I was told the proceedings would not commence until nine o'clock, Your Honor," Frain said with no sense of apology in his tone.

"Things change, Counselor," Judge Owens snapped. "You need to keep up with them."

"As you say," Frain replied, standing next to his table and placing a hand on Jason Mankiller's shoulder.

"Your Honor," he continued seamlessly, "is it really necessary for my client to be so heavily shackled? It makes him look like a wild animal; it is highly prejudicial."

"I'd rather be prejudiced than dead at the hands of a crazed *killer!*" prosecuting attorney Trahan declared, jumping to his feet.

"Your Honor!" Frain objected, motioning toward his opposing counsel.

Judge Owens banged his gavel three times atop his bench. He then sprayed tobacco juice to one side, causing the acting bailiff—Deputy Dan Green—to skip to one side to avoid it.

"The chains stay on," Judge Owens ruled. "But less theatrics, Bob," he admonished, gazing over his spectacles at the prosecutor. "Anything else, Mr. Frain?"

"Yes, Your Honor, there is. I wish to request a continuance."

"Oh? On what grounds?"

"Your Honor, none of the surviving witnesses to the matter at hand is available at the moment to testify.

"Due to the fact that the telegraph appears to be inoperative at the moment, I cannot contact them regarding depositions; nor can I reach out to any other agencies of the law that might provide vital information regarding the alleged victims of this crime."

"*Alleged* victims?" Judge Owens repeated. He swiveled his head toward the marshal seated at the prosecutor's table.

"Blue? Do we or do we not have two *bodies* lyin' over to the undertaker's parlor?"

"Actually—*three*, Mayor."

"Sounds to me like they're pretty damn *dead*, Mr. Frain!" Owens bellowed, to accompanying laughter from the gallery of spectators.

"Yes, sir. But they are not truly *victims* if they were shot in pursuance of a legal act."

"Are you admitting that they died at the hands of your client?" Bob Trahan demanded cannily.

"I'm admitting nothing, sir," Frain replied crisply, "as you well know. I am merely arguing that in the interest of fairness I should be given more time to prepare an adequate defense."

"Well, ya ain't a-gonna get it!" Judge Owens barked. "Justice delayed is justice denied. Putting things off would simply serve to infringe upon your client's right to a speedy trial."

"He's also entitled to a *fair* one, Your Honor."

"That's just what he's gettin'!" the judged snapped, again pounding his gavel on the tabletop. "Yer skatin' mighty close to bein' held in *contempt*, young man."

"My apologies, Your Honor."

"That's more like it. Anything else before we get on with this shootin' match?"

"There *is* one potential eyewitness closer to hand, Your Honor," Frain said. "That's the man who was driving the stage at the time the incident occurred. Surely no harm would be incurred by anyone if we simply wait until his route carries him back to Low Water."

"Yeah?" The judge cast his gaze over Carter Frain's head and out into the assemblage gathered behind him.

"Homer?" Owens said. "I *see* ya out there. Get on yer feet."

Amidst a low murmuring from the other onlookers, Homer Pertwee—the manager of the stage line's express office in Low Water—rose to his feet. He looked rather intimidated, practically crushing the brim of the hat he held in both hands.

"When's the *jehu* who was drivin' that stage due back in town?"

"Mebbe *never*, Delmar. I mean, Your Honor. Sir."

"What do you mean?" Carter Frain demanded, turning and fixing Pertwee with a withering glare. "Why not?"

"'Cause the home office has assigned him to a different route, that's why." Pertwee replied with a hint of defiance in his voice, though he seemed loath to meet Frain's eyes. "He's been moved to the Denver to Laramie route."

"We should still be able to get a sworn deposition from him, Your Honor," Frain pleaded, turning back toward the bench.

"Your Honor," attorney Bob Trahan injected. "Defense Counsel himself has told us the telegraph is down. He's simply stalling for more time."

Frain opened his mouth to object, but was cut short by the banging of Judge Owens' gavel.

"He's right, Counsel," Owens growled. "I don't intend to keep justice—or the jury—waiting any longer."

"The jury?" As if seeing them for the first time, Carter Frain cast his eyes over the twelve men who were assembled and seated together to one side of the courtroom.

He knew about half of them by name: townspeople with whom he shared at least a passing acquaintance. The other half he vaguely recognized by sight: mostly men of dubious character who drifted in and out of town between pursuit of professions left unspoken. A couple he thought he'd seen backing up Marshal Thorpe on a few occasions, acting as temporary "deputies."

"This is most irregular, Your Honor," Frain objected. "I was given no opportunity to question any of these men before they were impaneled!"

"They're all good, decent town folk," Judge Owens asserted harshly.

"Surely you're not questioning their fitness—their honesty?"

Frain intended to do just that, but was given pause by the looks of evil intent directed his way by members of the jury he noted had been allowed to wear their guns into the courtroom. A menacing, grumbling sound also issued from some of the bystanders sitting behind him. Still, he was prepared to voice his strenuous objection, until a hand tugging at his coat stopped him.

He looked down at Jason Mankiller, who slowly shook his head. Closing his mouth, Frain resumed his seat next to the bounty hunter.

"I don't understand this," Frain whispered, the exasperation evident in his voice and facial expression.

"I knew the court here was sort of loose about following the letter of the law—but here they seem to be intent on trampling it underfoot and leaving it lying in their dust."

Even while closely listening to his attorney, Mankiller was staring intently at the presiding judge. A note of recognition wailed inside his head, but he still couldn't place the tune.

Judge Owens' left hand slid up to his face. With thumb cupping his chin and one finger stroking his moustache, only the upper half of his face was clearly visible.

Mankiller's eyes widened with a sudden, revelatory jolt. He swiveled his head to the right, studying the features of the nearby Marshal Thorpe. Jason now knew why the man had seemed naggingly familiar to him earlier. Kicking his chair back away from him, he leaped to his feet as quickly as his shackles would allow.

"*Now* I know why I'm being railroaded!" he shouted loudly, extending his cuffed hands and pointing an accusing finger at the dumbfounded Judge Owens.

"And the people of this town need to know the *truth!*"

Amidst the uproar this declaration unleashed in the crowded courtroom, the sound of the judge's gavel repeatedly banging against his bench was as nothing.

Chapter 5

"**O**rder in the court!" Judge Owens bawled. "Order, goddammit!"

"Don't pay him no mind," Mankiller shouted. "He ain't a *real* judge at all!"

"Shut yer filthy mouth!" Marshal Thorpe demanded, leaping up from behind the prosecutor's table.

"And *he* ain't no lawman, either!" Mankiller accused, swinging his gaze toward Thorpe, then swiveling to face the townspeople at the back of the courtroom.

"They're both *outlaws* their *own* selves! *Both* of them's wanted by the *real* law!"

That was as far as the bounty hunter got with his declaration. Dan Green, the deputy standing guard nearest to the prisoner, swung his rifle. The butt of the gun cracked against the side of Mankiller's head, dropping him in his tracks.

"Get that crazy sunovabitch outta here!" Judge Owens ordered, his voice rising to a nearly hysterical pitch. "Take 'im back to the jail!"

Dan Green and a fellow deputy grabbed the unconscious bounty hunter under each arm and began to drag him toward the rear of the chamber. Stunned by everything that he had just heard and seen, Carter Frain could do nothing but stand impotently by as his client was hauled away. He was only dimly aware of Judge Owens once more gaveling for order.

"Settle down, dammit!" he ordered, "or I'll have this courtroom cleared." Not wanting to miss what might come next, the bystanders did as they were told, taking their seats and lowering their voices to little more than a hum.

"Are you ready to proceed, Mr. Trahan?" Judge Owens asked of the prosecuting attorney, who rose to his feet as casually as if nothing at all untoward had happened.

"Whoa-whoa-whoa!" Carter Frain exclaimed, coming to his senses. "Proceed with *what*?" he demanded.

"Where have you *been*?" Judge Owens chided. "With the *trial*, of course."

"You can't be serious, Judge. Especially not in light of the very serious allegations my client has made!"

"Your client—the accused *murderer*?" Judge Owens snorted. Several of the jurymen laughed aloud.

"Surely you don't *believe* his cock-and-bull story about me and the marshal being a pair of *desperadoes*?"

"Whether I believe it or not is beside the point, Your Honor," Frain replied, growing bolder. "At the very least, it calls into question your impartiality and would require you to recuse yourself from sitting in judgment of this case."

"And hand the gavel over to *who*, young man?" Owens huffed. "*I'm* the only judge this town *has!*"

"Then I move for a change of venue, Your Honor. We'll simply hold the trial in *another* town."

"The *hell* we will!" This outburst came not from the judge, but from Marshal Thorpe.

"Now, now, Marshal," Judge Owens chided mildly, shaking his gavel. "The bench appreciates your enthusiastic support, but in this case it's not necessary." He accentuated this pronouncement by gracing Thorpe with a surreptitious wink.

"Sorry, Your Honor," Thorpe replied, taking a seat.

"Motion denied!" Owens snapped, again pounding his gavel. He eyed the young defense attorney with a jaundice glare.

"You got any *other* objections, Counselor?"

"As a matter of fact," Carter Frain came back unfazed, "I *do.*"

Judge Owens heaved a heavy sigh. "And what might this one be?"

"I move that the proceedings be delayed until such time as my client has a chance to regain his senses and be returned to the courtroom."

"Why is that?"

"Because the law guarantees every man the right to confront his accusers. Mr. Mankiller can't very well do that while he's unconscious and lying in a jail cell."

"That's why he's got *you*, Counselor," the judge declared, flashing brown teeth in a grin bearing more malice than mirth. "You can do it *for* him!" He again banged the top of his bench with his gavel.

"Motion denied! Proceed, Mr. Trahan!"

Jason Mankiller was slumped on the edge of his cot two hours later when Carter Frain was escorted into the cellblock.

The bounty hunter stared down at the floor, holding a moistened bandana against the abrasion from the blow that still had his head throbbing like a Comanche drum; but he lifted his gaze at the sound of Frain approaching.

The clouded expression on the attorney's face told him all he needed to know; his trial in absentia had not gone well.

"It was a mockery from beginning to end, Jason," Frain sighed. "I hope you'll believe me when I say I tried my best."

"I do."

"There was nothing I could do. Every hand but mine was against you."

"I saw that for myself." Mankiller motioned toward the stool that stood outside his cell. "Pull up a seat and tell me all about it."

Frain did as directed, gathering his thoughts and taking a deep breath before speaking.

"The first nail in the coffin was Doctor Potter. He swore under oath—hell, they *all* swore under oath—that both *victims* had been shot in the back.

"I couldn't get him to recant under cross-examination. And when I requested the opportunity to examine the bodies myself—I was practically laughed out of the courtroom."

"Of course you were," Mankiller interjected. "That would have been the easiest of their lies to refute."

"Then the manager of the livery stable testified that you sold him the two men's horses and gear."

"I told you about that," Jason said. "I told him to give the money to the undertaker to pay for their funerals."

"I know. But when I questioned him, he denied any such thing. Since no one else witnessed the transaction, there was no one I could call to contradict his testimony."

"Even if there had been," Mankiller said bitterly, "they'd have just lied on the stand too."

"Probably," Frain concurred. "And then the express office manager claimed you'd *bragged* to him about what you'd done. He looked me right in the eye, Jason, and denied he'd ever spoken to me about what really happened.

"After that," Frain neared his conclusion, "it was all over but the shouting. My shouting.

"There was really no defense I could mount. Even if I'd been allowed to put you on the stand—which I wasn't—it would have just been the word of a bounty hunter against that of their *good* neighbors who'd testified otherwise. We never had a prayer, Jason."

"No."

"I did my best to give them a stem-winder of a closing argument, though. Hammered away at the fact that no one who actually *saw* the shooting, other than you, was available to back up the prosecution's claim of cold-blooded murder."

"Did their hand-picked 'jury' even bother to leave the room to deliberate after that?" Jason asked sarcastically.

"Just about long enough to enjoy a couple of free drinks, courtesy of the prosecuting attorney."

Mankiller nodded. "So, I know what the verdict was." His expression was stoic as he looked at his counsel. "I 'spect the judge was equally quick to pass *sentence?*"

"That's the closest to good news I have for you, Jason," Frain admitted.

"The foreman of the jury said that my arguments had given them at least slight pause. Enough that they were permitted to convict you of manslaughter rather than murder."

"What's the difference?" the bounty hunter huffed.

"The difference is...this saves you from the *rope*, Jason."

"Well, that's something, I reckon. What do I get instead?"

Carter Frain hesitated for a long moment before responding.

"Ten years hard labor...at the Pima Territorial Prison."

Mankiller slowly rose from his seat, walked on slightly unsteady legs toward the front bars of his cell.

"Tell me one thing, Carter, if you can. Just how in hell did it come to pass that two *outlaws* came to own this little piece of heaven lock, stock and barrel?"

"From what I've picked up in loose conversation since I got here," Frain began to explain, "Owens was the first to arrive here, about two years ago. He brought a bucketload of money with him."

"Mostly acquired by robbing gold shipments," Mankiller said, "if I remember what was on the wanted poster for him that I saw."

"I'll take your word for it. He told the townsfolk he was a judge, had come from a good family in California. They had no reason to doubt him—especially when he used part of his money to open Low Water's first bank.

"He was generous in his loan practices. So much so that he now holds the mortgages on half the town and all the nearby farms and ranches."

"Which make 'em all beholden enough to do whatever he says," Mankiller surmised.

"And grateful enough to elect him mayor within six months of his arrival."

"Did anyone run against 'im?"

"No. And the previous mayor had somehow mysteriously disappeared, prompting the special election that put Owens in the seat.

"One of his first official acts was to bring in Blue Thorpe—"

"His partner in most of his crimes."

"He appointed Thorpe marshal; Thorpe brought a handful of 'deputies' with him. Some of them sat on the jury today."

"And this whole town just rolled over and let 'em take over?" Jason asked with a harsh edge of contempt in his voice.

"Way I hear it, everything seemed fine at the start. Thorpe did bring a sort of order with him. Since he and Owens came to power, the town's business has been better, thanks in part to an increase in the number of men who drift in, spend their money freely, then drift on."

"I take it these aren't drovers?"

"I've seen nary a one bring any cattle with him," Frain replied bitterly. "And there's seldom more than four or five of them at a time."

"So Low Water's essentially become a safe hideout for outlaws."

"Seems that way, though none of the law-abiding citizens would use those words. The drifters keep their mayhem to a minimum, mostly."

"For fear of losing their safe haven otherwise."

"And for fear, period. Thorpe keeps a tight lid on things; a couple of our *guests* who got out of hand are still here, on Boot Hill."

"And I walked right into the middle of things," Mankiller sighed. "Big as you please.

"Thorpe probably saw me when I got off the stage, recognized me." Jason's hand went up to the distinctive facial tattoo that, along with his bloody exploits, was making him more and more familiar to inhabitants of the West.

"He was afraid I'd recognize him, too. So him and Owens cooked up this scheme to get me outta the way—more or less *legally*.

"And for fear of them—and fear of losing *money*—the whole town was willing to send a stranger who never did 'em no harm right down the river. Ever' last one of 'em—save for you, Carter—is as much to blame as Thorpe and Owens are."

"This isn't over yet, Jason," Frain said earnestly. "Now that I know the full truth about Owens and Thorpe, there's more I may be able to do. Possibly even get a federal marshal to come here and look into things."

At those words, a somewhat disturbed look came over Mankiller's face. He turned his head away from the lawyer for a moment, giving the matter thought.

"When do they plan to ship me out to Pima?" he asked at last.

"Day after tomorrow."

"Good. Good." Mankiller again paused thoughtfully. "If we're lucky, that should give you just enough time."

"Time for what?" Frain asked quizzically.

"Time enough for you and your missus to get out of town."

"Why would we do that?" The lawyer was now even more puzzled.

"Because by defending me so vigorously, you may have made *yourself* a target. If he knows you're still digging around—Thorpe'll kill you for *sure*."

"My God!" Frain gasped.

"I thank you for what you done for me, Carter," Mankiller told him. "And I'm sorry for the trouble it's brought you. Get out before it gets worse."

"But...I can't just abandon you," Frain said, struggling to make sense of it all.

"If you won't do it for me or for yourself, old son," Jason asserted, "then do it for your *wife*. If anything happens to *you*—what do you think will become of *her*?"

"Dear Lord..." Frain moaned softly.

"Pack up just what you absolutely have to have," Mankiller instructed, "but don't load it into a buggy till after sundown. Wait till it's full dark to pull out, then ride through the night. Chances are, they won't bother to follow you."

"But what about *you*?"

"Let me worry about that. You can still try to spring me, if you're of a mind to—*after* you're safely somewheres else."

"That's true," Frain mumbled, his mind racing. "I'm just not sure where we should go."

"That's up to you, o' course," Jason advised. "But if you can't think of anyplace better, I can recommend a town in north Texas by the name o' Fort Rogers."

"I think I've heard of it," Frain said.

"It's a good place, with good people. And it's growing: be a good spot for an enterprising fella to hang his shingle. A good place to raise a family.

"The law there's good and honest, too. You can trust 'em with your life."

"I take it this Fort Rogers is your *home*, Jason?"

"Close as I got to one. Don't spend as much time there as I'd like.

"I got *friends* there, too. Two in particular you'd do well to contact, whether you end up going there or not.

"One is Sam Dobbins. He's my business partner, and more. The other fella works at the bank, handles my money. Name o' Byron Longfellow."

"Sounds colorful," Frain replied, smiling slightly even as he scribbled both names down in his notebook.

"Let me see that, wouldja?" Mankiller asked. Without question, the lawyer handed him the notebook and pencil. When the bounty hunter returned it a minute later, Frain saw that he had printed a message in slightly awkward but very legible hand:

This man is Carter Frain. He is my legal representative. Help him in any way you can. Make sure he is paid fittingly for his services.

Jason Mankiller.

Frain smiled sadly. "Somehow, I feel like I haven't done a sufficiently good job to warrant *any* pay," he confessed.

"That's not true," Mankiller replied quickly and firmly. "I know you've done your best. Given the situation, no man could have done better. Now get on outta here. And do like I told you."

"But what about *you*?" Frain persisted.

"For now, you just forget about me; do whatever you have to to get yourself and your little lady outta harm's way.

"There'll be plenty of time, after you've gotten settled elsewhere, to work on getting me outta this mess I'm in." He extended his right hand through the bars of his cell.

"Till then—I'll make out all right."

Carter Frain accepted the proffered hand, gripping it firmly and shaking it vigorously. Not another word was spoken as Frain turned away and hurried out of the cellblock.

A fair sized crowd of townfolk was gathered outside the marshal's office on the morning of the second day following. A murmur rippled through it as Blue Thorpe, flanked by four deputies carrying rifles, escorted Jason Mankiller out onto the sidewalk.

Such a show of force seemed wise to all that witnessed it, even though the prisoner's hands and feet were shackled and connected with a length of chain.

Such was the deadly reputation of the Man Who Cries Blood that some feared even this might not be enough to sufficiently restrain Mankiller.

Marshal Thorpe paused at the edge of the sidewalk, holding a hand up to shield his eyes from the rising sun.

"Quite a crowd here to send you off," he said to his prisoner. "Pert near ever'body in town—'cept for your lawyer. Ain't nobody seen him since the trial." His lips curled up into a wolfish sneer.

"Prob'ly hiding under his bed."

Mankiller made no response, but inwardly and well hidden he felt a sense of relief in the hope that this meant the young attorney had managed to flee from Low Water without being detected.

The bounty hunger took one step off the sidewalk into the dirt street— and was struck in the face by a rotten head of cabbage.

This touched off a concerted barrage of vegetables, garbage and horse apples as the crowd pressed closer, hooting and jeering at a man unable to defend himself.

One bravely anonymous soul chucked a rock at the shackled Mankiller, laying open a cut in his forehead.

The small mob continued to mock him as Marshal Thorpe roughly pushed him toward a waiting wagon. It was not much more than an ordinary buckboard, but a man-sized cage of steel bands had been bolted down to the floor of its bed. Four horses were hitched to it to pull the anticipated load.

As best his chains would allow, Jason ascended the wooden steps that led up to the cage. Reaching the open door of the cage, he suddenly spun back around.

With a fearful cry, the crowding townspeople pulled back. The jeers died in their throats as Mankiller fixed them with a baleful glare. The streaming blood flowing from the cut in his forehead seemed to follow directly the path of the tattooed teardrop on his left cheek. The effect was to make him look even more frightening.

One of the deputies anxiously cocked his rifle and raised it, but Blue Thorpe reached out a hand and pushed down the barrel. Still, his free hand rested on the butt of his own pistol.

"You gutless bastards should have hung me when you had the chance," Mankiller said ominously. So quiet had the mob become that there was no need for him to raise his voice to be heard clearly by all.

"'Cause someday I'll get outta prison," he declared, "and I'll come back *here*. And when I *do*..." His eyes swept with deadly intent over all of them.

"...I'll burn ever*ything* and every*one* still here to the ground!"

Chapter 6

Having so spoken, Jason Mankiller stepped into the wagon cage and took a seat on the narrow wooden bench running along one side of it. The crowd that moments before had loudly taunted him now began to break up into small clusters. The fear in their barely audible voices was palpable.

Marshal Thorpe had taken hold of Judge Owens' arm and rather roughly pulled him to one side.

"I *told* you this was a mistake, Delmar!" Thorpe hissed even while keeping his own voice down.

"You shoulda let me string him up from the livery stable hayloft ten minutes after that sham of a trial ended!"

Owens demurred. "Now, Blue, you know it's in our best interest to let the sheep in this town believe they still have *some* control of what goes on here.

"You saw it. They were well on their way to working themselves up into becoming a lynch mob—which would have left us with clean hands."

"Yeah? Well, that ain't gonna happen *now!*"

"No. No, it's not. Mankiller put the fear of God in 'em, that's for sure. Cowed 'em good." Owens managed a wan smile.

"But what difference does it make? You know what a hellhole Pima is, Blue. He'll never come out of there *alive!*"

"I s'pose," Thorpe conceded. "I just hope the end comes quick."

"Well, now," Owens said conspiratorially, "if you're that worried—I suppose you could make sure the bounty hunter never *gets* to Pima!"

"You mean that?" Thorpe asked, brightening.

"Sure. Just make sure you tell your deputies to hide the body well and not come back here for a few days.

"None of the good people of Low Water need ever be the wiser!"

Settling down on the bench inside the wagon cage, Jason Mankiller's eyes spotted Marshal Thorpe taking one of his deputies aside, presumably to give him final instructions.

Mankiller couldn't hear any of the whispered words that passed between the two men, but could clearly see that Thorpe was quite animated, at one point poking his finger into the deputy's chest for emphasis.

Mankiller saw the deputy cast a furtive eye in his direction, the trace of an evil grin turning up the corners of his mouth. He nodded to the marshal, then hurried to take his place beside a second deputy who was already seated in the wagon's front boot, holding the reins of the team of horses harnessed to pull it.

"Hyah!" the deputy whooped, slapping the reins against the rumps of the lead horses.

Marshal Thorpe closely watched the wagon as it began to roll, and his eyes widened slightly in amazement. Jason Mankiller was leaned back against the bars of his cage, eyes closed as if preparing to take a nap! Thorpe wasn't sure, but he thought he even detected a relaxed smile on the bounty hunter's lips.

Mankiller was indeed as relaxed as a man in his position could be. He had already surmised, correctly, that the deputies escorting him would wait till they were far from preying eyes before—per Marshal Thorpe's orders—Mankiller would be shot "while attempting to escape."

Once Low Water was left well out of sight to the east, the deputy who had received direct instructions from Thorpe reached under his seat and produced a full bottle of whiskey.

"You plan ta *share* that?" his partner growled.

"Yeah, yeah. Don't worry; there's plenty. This bad boy's got a twin brother waitin' under the seat!"

As the bottle of cheap snakehead booze began to pass back and forth, Jason watched from under eyelids so nearly closed as to make him appear to be asleep. The rattling of the wagon's wooden wheels masked the slight chuckle that issued from his throat.

He knew that, in the heat of the day and with no food in their stomachs to absorb it, the hooch would have an even faster and stronger effect on the two deputies.

Still, the sun was low on the western horizon when, nearly thirty miles into their journey, the crooked lawmen pulled the wagon to a halt. It had just reached the high point of a trail that passed between two small but rugged peaks.

The deputies climbed down from the wagon seat, one of them nearly falling in the process. Mankiller noted their gaits were slightly askew as they walked toward the back of the wagon; they were clearly still under the influence of the liquid courage they had consumed during the day.

"C'mon out and stretch yer legs for a spell, bounty killer," one of them ordered, unlocking the door of the wagon cage and allowing it to swing open.

As Jason slowly stood, he saw that the second deputy, standing just a few feet behind the first, already had a hand resting on the butt of his holstered pistol. This was clearly the time and place they had chosen to carry out the dirty deed.

Mankiller almost smiled at the two potentially fatal mistakes the deputies made, either through stupidity or the dulling effects of alcohol.

It would have been far wiser, easier and safer simply to have stood outside the cage and shot him through the bars before dragging his body out. And, placed where they were, the deputy with his hand on his gun would find his own partner standing between him and his intended target.

Both lawmen were caught flat-footed when, instead of slowly climbing down the steps leading from the cage, Mankiller leaped toward the deputy standing closest to him.

The stunned deputy had no time to react before Jason grabbed him by the front of his shirt and spun him around, intent on using him as a human shield. As he expected, the second deputy lacked the fortitude to hold his fire—quickly pumping three slugs into his own partner.

Realizing too late what he had done, the murderous deputy stopped firing. His mortally wounded comrade began to sag in Mankiller's grip, but before he became literal dead weight the bounty hunter gave him a hard shove forward.

The drunken second deputy shrieked as the bloody body flew toward him. It slammed into him, causing him to spin, lose his footing and fall face down on the ground.

Before he could rise, a heavy weight fell full atop him. As the deputy tried to push up, Mankiller looped the short length of chain connecting his wrist shackles over the deputy's head and down to his throat.

He pulled back on the chain with the strength of both arms, hearing the deputy make harsh choking noises as the iron links bit into the soft flesh of his neck.

Even after the lawman's arms and legs ceased flopping and his body went lax, Mankiller continued to apply pressure on the chain until he was certain the man was dead.

Rolling off the dead man, Jason sat for a few minutes, resting as his breathing and heart rate slowed to normal.

He then dug through the pockets of the slain deputies until he found the keys that would remove the shackles from his wrists and ankles. He groaned with relief as, for the first time in the better part of a day, he was able to stand to his full height and stretch his arms above his head.

Next, being ever the pragmatist, he conducted a more thorough search of the bodies. He relieved them of all their money, slipping the coins into his pants pocket and hiding the bills inside his boot.

He then armed himself, his keen eye discerning which purloined pistol and rifle were the best. He also planted the hat that best fit him atop his head.

Only one grisly chore remained.

In the fading light of the day, Mankiller scouted along each side to the steep trail. Finding a spot where its side dropped off most deeply and precipitously, he dragged the two corpses over and flung them into an abyss where there was little chance the bodies would ever be found.

He stared after them for a long moment even after they had disappeared from sight. He had never in his life raised a hand against an officer of the law; only the certainty that these two, like their boss Marshal Thorpe, were as law*less* as any outlaw he had brought in slung over the back of a horse allowed him to be of an easy conscience.

The last thing he threw into the concealing chasm was the chains and shackles that had bound him.

The next course of action he should take was less clear to him.

Chapter 7

I t was said in certain circles that Satan himself feared the day when God's wrath might prove so enraged that He would pluck Old Scratch from his throne in Hell—and drop him into the confines of the *Pima Territorial Prison*.

Though it had been open barely five years, it already had a deserved reputation as "the prison of no return." Once inside its walls, the hardest of felons was soon reduced to a mere shell of a man. Since no inmates had yet survived to serve a full sentence, it was much speculated that none ever would.

The outer walls of the prison stood nearly 30 feet high, built from granite blocks ten feet thick. The only way in or out of the enclosure was through a pair of heavy oak gates that were reinforced with iron bands.

Atop the wall, on the west side of the gate, stood a solitary guard tower. It was manned at all times by two guards armed with repeating rifles. Also inside the tower was emplaced a Gatling gun, its revolving barrels pointing down at the middle of the prison's inner yard.

Individual guards marched continuously along the parapet of the wall, keeping a sharp eye not only on what unfolded inside the prison but outside as well.

There was little chance of anything outside the walls escaping detection. The only foliage for miles around was the few puny shrubs that had found purchase along the tiny, sluggish San Deimos River that ran slowly along to the east of the prison. The terrain was mostly flat and featureless as far as the eye could see on all sides.

One of the guards currently on duty in the watchtower set his rifle down long enough to take the fixings from his tunic pocket and roll a cigarette. When he offered it to his fellow guard it was accepted; he then expertly rolled another for himself.

"Someone's comin'," he announced as he blew out a puff of smoke.

"Noticed," the second guard acknowledged. So flat and barren was most

It was manned at all times by two guards.

of the land around the prison that even a solitary man afoot would kick up enough dust to be seen for quite a distance.

The two guards continued to smoke leisurely as the object grew slowly closer. By the time they could make out that it was a single wagon throwing up the dust cloud, they had flipped the butts of their cigarettes away.

By the time the wagon was close enough to see only a lone man was driving it, the guards again had their rifles in hand, fingers on the triggers.

By the time they called down for the wagon to halt, they could see that the driver was truly alone; the cage bolted onto the bed of the wagon was empty.

It was not so close, though, that they could make out the distinctive tear shaped red tattoo on the left cheek of the wagon's driver.

"Would you be so kind as to open the gates, boys?" Jason Mankiller called up to them. He had risen up to his feet; reins still gripped tightly in his hands.

"And just who might you be, mister?" one of the guards inquired in a testy voice.

"Me? Why…I'm a *prisoner*, old son." Mankiller shifted both sets of reins to his left hand. With his right, he swept off his hat while bowing grandly at the waist.

"I've come to turn myself in!"

Chapter 8

Jason Mankiller was again in handcuffs, but at least his ankles were unshackled. Given that he was about to have to climb a flight of stairs, he was doubly grateful for this.

It had taken several minutes for him to convince the guards to open the gates and allow him to enter the compound. As soon as he cleared the entryway, the gates were quickly slammed shut and the wagon was swarmed by guards who dragged him off the seat before thoroughly searching both him and the conveyance. He was then cuffed and two of the guards escorted him into what seemed likely to be the prison's administrative building.

With one guard ahead of him and the second coming up a few steps behind him, Mankiller managed to scale the stairway with little difficulty.

A persistent tapping sound caught his ear as he reached the second floor landing. To his immediate left was a small room, its opened door allowing him an unimpeded view of its interior.

It was clearly a telegraph room. The guard sitting at the desk there was a small man with large, muttonchop sideburns. He tapped the telegraph key adroitly a few times to acknowledge receipt of a routine message.

The two guards escorting Mankiller shifted position to place themselves on either side of the prisoner, leading him down a dimly lit hallway to a solid oak door that bore a metal placard that read: *Superintendent*. One of the guards knocked loudly on the door three times, then stood at ease as he awaited a response.

"Come," a deep voice said, carrying easily through the sturdy door.

Opening the door, one of the guards ushered Mankiller into a spacious office. Heavy file cabinets stood against the wall on either side of the doorway. Farther into the room, several feet away and facing the door, stood a large and well-constructed desk.

On the other side of the desk, a big, squarely built man stood with his back to Mankiller, hands clasped behind him. He was standing before and staring out of a large window. From this vantage point, he could visually survey the entire prison yard spread out below him.

He slowly turned to face his new inmate. Mankiller saw that what had once doubtless been solid muscle had begun to soften under the affects of age and inactivity. Crowding fifty, the man's cheeks bulged slightly over the confines of his stiff, tightly buttoned collar. Cold eyes glared from under brows that looked almost like small, gray, bushy wings. His brown woolen suit was barely large enough to hold his bulk, and Jason sensed there was still enough muscle under the thin layer of flab to make the man physically formidable.

"Wait outside," he told the guard in a voice that spoke the language of tobacco, whiskey and authority. "I'll call you when I need you."

He then took a seat at the desk, slowly lowering himself into an overstuffed chair, which let out a slight groan. Mankiller cautiously moved closer to the opposite side of the desk.

"I'm Warden Holden Mayhew," the big man said. He didn't deign to look at the prisoner, instead focusing his attention on a paper now clutched in both beefy hands. "I run this place."

"Warden. I'm Jason Mankiller."

"I know who you are," Mayhew snapped with icy malice. "What's up with this stunt you've pulled? Where are the guards that should have been with you?"

The bounty hunter shrugged. "They just sorta dropped outta sight."

"Did you have anything to do with that?"

Mankiller made no response.

Mayhew glared at him, tapping the desktop with one finger for several seconds before speaking again.

"So your guards conveniently disappeared, leaving you free and clear. But instead of taking off for the tall uncut, you continued on here alone and graciously turned yourself in. Is that right?"

"That's about the size of it."

"And just why would you do such a thing?"

"You said you know who I am," Jason replied. "I assume that's because you were wired to expect me."

Mayhew glanced down at the paper he still held in one hand. "That's right. The authorities in Low Water informed me of the particulars."

"And what would have happened if I hadn't shown up here?"

Mayhew mostly suppressed a wolfish grin. "I'd have had paper printed on you from here to hell and back."

"Exactly. And how long do you think I'd have lasted with a bounty on my head?"

"How long do you think you'll last *here*?" Mayhew said.

"As long as I need to," came the reply.

Still skeptical of Jason's story, Mayhew sighed and leaned back heavily in his chair.

"All right. Now, suppose you tell me your story."

"What story's that, Mr. Mayhew?"

"Just about every new hardcase who comes here feels compelled to tell me that they're innocent as a newborn lamb; how they never committed the crime that got them sent here."

"And do you ever believe any of those stories?"

"Never."

"They why waste your time with one?"

"Why, indeed. Let me ask you this, then. How do you intend to spend your time while incarcerated here at Pima?"

Jason gave that some thought before responding. "As much as I'm able, I mean to do as I'm told and stay out of trouble."

"That makes you far wiser than most of our inmates," Mayhew declared. "That's the best attitude to have, given that every day you'll be watched like a hawk by the toughest guards in the territory. They're armed and not afraid to use their weapons.

"In addition, there's an Army garrison posted just twenty miles from here. They have standing orders to provide any assistance I might require." He leaned forward, resting his elbows atop his desk and clasping his fingers together.

"At about this point in my standard welcoming speech, I usually warn newcomers about even contemplating any attempt at escape. Given that you willingly brought *yourself* here, I assume that won't be a problem we have with you."

"No, sir. I expect not."

"And I'll tell you now; we tend to work the inmates so hard they have little strength, energy or desire to cause us too much trouble.

"But staying out of trouble may prove harder for you than most others, Mankiller. By now, half the prison population probably knows that the famous 'Man Who Cries Blood' will soon be in their midst. By tomorrow, all of them will know.

"And some of the meanest are bound to want a piece of your hide."

"As will some of the guards?" Jason asked.

"The guards are *my* concern, mister, not yours," Mayhew growled. "Guard!"

The door opened and the summoned guard escorted Mankiller out. As he turned to leave he noted that the superintendent was eyeing him as if he too wanted a crack at the bounty hunter.

In another building, Mankiller was stripped naked and deloused. During this procedure, he saw the guard delivering the delousing powder flinch slightly as his eyes fell upon the numerous scars and old wounds that pocked and lanced Jason's battle-hardened body.

He was told that his personal clothing and belongings would be held for him until such time as he might be released. He hoped that was true, for the hidden pockets inside his boots held a considerable amount of cash.

He was dressed in standard prison garb: gray cotton trousers, long-sleeved shirt and thick-soled shoes. He was also given one thin, moth-eaten blanket.

The prison life of Jason Mankiller was about to begin.

Chapter 9

Mankiller entered the cell that would be his new home as he would any other place with which he was unfamiliar, halting just inside it to quickly familiarize himself with its layout and its occupants. He barely took note of the barred metal door slamming closed behind him.

The cell was small and dank, with only one, small, barred window set high up in the far wall allowing in the light. Below the window sat the communal slop bucket, alongside which sat a water bucket with a dipper. Most of the space in the cramped cell was taken up by twin sets of bunk beds.

There were also three other men awaiting him inside: his new cellmates.

One was an old man of about sixty. Jason pegged him as being an "institutional man," and it was true. While in a drunken haze, he had murdered his wife and a man he falsely believed to be her lover. His diminished capacity was probably what spared him from the hangman's tender touch, but he had now spent more than half his life behind bars.

A second inmate was barely more than a kid. A soft and handsome boy, he was sent here for having attempted to rob a saloon.

"Howdy!" the boy said almost eagerly, a wide smile revealing white, even teeth. He motioned toward Jason's face.

"You're Jason Mankiller, ain'tcha?" he practically bubbled. "I recognize you from pictures I seen."

"I am," the bounty hunter replied.

"My name's Trey Parker," the youth said, excited at having met an idol.

"This yere's Doak Conifer." He pointed at the old man, who was seated on one of the lower bunks. He looked even more aged than his years, long hair and unkempt beard gray, his face lined and worn, his eyes nearly lifeless.

"And that's Ira Morgan." Trey finished the introductions by rather deferentially motioning toward a man leaning against the back wall of the cell.

This was the cellmate Jason knew he would have to remain most wary of.

He looked to be a man of about thirty-five; his broad nose sat atop a broad chin that appeared not to have known the touch of a razor for at least a week. His gray eyes had the darkness and coldness of a deep lake to them.

Mankiller strode directly toward Morgan and the convict straightened, pulling away from the stone wall. Ignoring him, Jason lifted the water bucket and moved it to the opposite side of the cell, away from the slop bucket.

"What'd ya do *that* for?" Morgan challenged.

Mankiller gave him an easy, crooked smile. "I don't know about you other gents," he drawled, "but I'd just as soon not swallow another man's piss when I get a drink of water."

Conifer, the old con, chuckled. Morgan merely glared.

"What did they put you in here for, Mr. Mankiller?" young Trey asked respectfully.

"I guess you could say it was for doing my job too well," the bounty hunter replied.

"Well, here's what *I* say," Ira Morgan snarled, stepping up close to Mankiller. "In this cell—*I'm* the top dog!"

Jason casually cast his gaze around the ten feet by ten feet enclosure before responding.

"You're welcome to it, partner."

"And just what the hell does that mean?" Morgan demanded.

"It means that the top dog in a cage is still just a dog in a cage."

"I don't like yer attitude, bounty man," Morgan retorted, stepping even closer toward Mankiller.

Jason simply sighed heavily and tried to turn away, but Morgan would have none of it. With his left hand he grabbed Mankiller by the shoulder and spun him back around; his right hand was already balled and cocked to throw a punch.

He never got the chance.

As he spun around, Mankiller brought his right hand up in a sideways, chopping motion that caught Morgan right on his Adam's apple. The convict began to choke and both hands flew to his throat.

Pressing his advantage, Mankiller took a step to one side and grabbed Morgan by the back of his neck. With one fierce shove, Jason slammed his recalcitrant cellmate's face into the iron support post of one of the bunk beds.

The convict's legs buckled and he fell senselessly to the floor. A slight twitching of his legs was the only indication that he was still alive.

Having not even broken a sweat, his breathing calm and even, Mankiller turned his gaze toward his other two cellmates. Young Parker was simply staring at him in wide-eyed amazement. Old man Conifer, having enjoyed the show, was stroking his beard and chuckling.

"Anybody mind it I take this bunk?" Jason said, easily swinging up into one of the higher beds.

"Take what you like," Conifer replied. "Looks like *yer* top dog around here now."

"Sounds like too much work to me," Jason replied laconically. "I just wanna get some sleep," he said, laying his head back on a lumpy pillow.

"Why don't *you* take the job, Pops?"

The older convict began to cackle like a hen.

None of them made an effort to lift the unconscious Ira Morgan off the floor.

Chapter 10

The inmates were all rousted out at dawn, lined up for a head count before being marched into the prison's mess hall.

"What the hell happened to *you*?" one of the guards asked of Ira Morgan, spotting the mottled and swollen bruise marring his facial features.

"I fell outta bed," was the surly response.

"Yeah? Well, next time, do us all a favor; fall harder."

For a few minutes after entering the mess hall, it seemed as if all eyes were upon Jason Mankiller; those of the inmates as well as of the guards positioned throughout the hall. A catwalk ran along two sides of the hall, twelve feet above floor level, and guards were stationed in position there as well, where they could look down on the convicts. Mankiller ignored them all.

"We always eat this well?" he asked no one in particular. Breakfast consisted of a meager serving of runny grits (no salt, no butter), a hard slice of break and a tin cup of water.

"Yeah," old man Conifer replied, shoveling in a mouthful. "The closest thing ta bacon you'll get is if yer lucky enough to get a boll weevil in yer grits!"

The convicts were allotted fifteen minutes for their meal, then marched back outside. While they had been eating, several flatbed wagons had been pulled up and parked in the main yard.

As they were herded toward the conveyances, Jason spied something out of the corner of his eye that surprised him enough to warrant a second look.

Women.

His vision had not betrayed him. Off to one side of the compound, he saw a small, ramshackle hut, in front of which stood three women. The hut, in turn, sat in the middle of a high, square, fenced enclosure. Rolled strands of barbed wire topped the fence on all sides.

"What are women doing here?" he asked his youngest cellmate.

"They're prisoners here, too, just like us," Trey replied. "There ain't ever more than a few of 'em, but this joint houses men and women both."

"Sounds like a surefire invitation to *trouble*, if you ask me," Mankiller commented.

"It is," old man Conifer agreed. "Fer *them!*"

"What do you mean, Pops?"

"Well, like you see, the womenfolk is kept well away from us goats. Unfortunately for them—they ain't so safe from the *guards.*"

"And Warden Mayhew allows this?"

"Hell, rumor has it he *participates*, when the urge hits and he's been too long away from his missus. Which ain't often; I think he gets most o' his pleasure from watchin' us suffer."

"Us cons do our own laundry," Trey added, "but the women wash for Mayhew and the guards. They take care of the administration building: sweeping, mopping, cleaning up. They cook for the guards."

"But not for Mayhew?"

"Nah," Conifer said. "He don't trust 'em not ta *pizen* him. He's got his own cook."

"And I imagine him and the guards eat a sight better than we do," Mankiller drawled.

"Hell's belles," Conifer said, spitting. "Reservation *Injuns* eat better than we do!"

After hopping up onto the edge of the bed of one of the wagons, Mankiller glanced back at the small compound housing the women, to find one of them staring at him intently.

She looked brazen and bold: tall, blonde and very buxom. She stood with her legs spread, hands resting on flared hips, openly appraising the renowned bounty hunter.

Jason smiled and raised one finger to the side of his head in a slight salute to the woman—and was rewarded for his audacity by receiving a sharp poke in the ribs by the rifle barrel of a nearby guard.

"Keep yer eyes and yer mind off the whores!" the guard barked.

As if any normal man in such circumstances could, Jason thought, idly rubbing the spot where he had been prodded.

The front gates of the prison were opened and the wagons slowly rolled forward. The trip they made was a short one, barely more than two miles. Their destination was beside a high, stony hogback that was one of the rare features that rose to any height above the otherwise flat and featureless terrain.

"This is gonna be yer job from now on, Sonny," Doak Conifer told Jason, nudging him lightly with one elbow.

"Turnin' big rocks inta little rocks."

The old con went on to explain briefly that work done at this makeshift quarry constituted the principal punishment doled out to the prisoners. As he had said, they literally picked, shoveled and hammered hard rock until it was the size of small gravel.

Word was that the gravel was then bagged up and sold: primarily to the railroads, to be used as the bed for their tracks, but also to businesses and wealthy individuals as driveway material.

"And where does the money from the sale of this gravel go?" Jason asked.

"It sure as hell don't go to buy *food* for *us*!" Trey Parker groused.

"Most of it ends up in Warden Mayhew's pockets," Ira Morgan explained. One corner of his mouth curled up. "Turnin' little rocks into big bucks!"

"And we do this every day?" Jason asked.

"All day," Conifer replied. "'Cept Sunday. Then they only work us *half* a day!"

"That way, we can spend the rest of the Lord's Day praying to get out of this pit!" Trey added.

"Shut yer gobs!" a big, brutish looking guard yelled at them. Without needing to be told, the inmates slid off the beds of the wagons and lined up for work assignments.

"You look like a pick man to me, new meat," the brutish guard growled, handing Mankiller the tool he would be using.

"It's the shovel for you, pretty boy," he then told Trey Parker, who accepted the tool with slumped shoulders and a fearful look of submission in his eyes.

"You'll start out over here," the guard said, taking hold of Trey's right arm. He led the young convict off to one side until the two of them were lost to sight around a curve in the slope of the hogback.

"Poor kid," Doak Conifer said softly, stepping up beside Mankiller. "His life's become even *more* of a livin' hell since Baxter there took a likin' to him."

"Does the warden know what's going on?" Jason inquired.

"Wouldn't make him no never mind if he did," Conifer replied, spitting contemptuously. "We'd best get to work, Sonny, else they'll be layin' the wood to us."

"Make room, boys," an ugly mountain of a man in prison gray sang out as Mankiller approached a cluster of convicts already starting to work on the hard face of the hogback.

"We got us a real, live *hero* amongst us!" the man mountain crowed.

"Stay clear o' him," Ira Morgan whispered, leaning in close to Mankiller. "That there's Bear Givens, and he more than lives up to the name."

"Sounds familiar," Jason allowed, "but I don't remember the particulars."

Morgan proceeded to fill in the blanks. Originally hailing from the mountains of Tennessee, Givens had been equally at home among the peaks of the Rockies. He'd trapped some, hunted buffalo. He found his true calling when he began selling for bounty the scalps of Indians he killed—and of Mexicans and black-haired Americans, it was darkly rumored.

It was only when he gutted an unarmed white man in a drunken brawl witnessed by several other saloon patrons that Givens was finally brought to heel and shipped to Pima.

Jason thought it odd that this man had managed to maintain such muscle and bulk in this environment, given that nearly all the other cons, while wiry, were noticeably thin due to the work load and lack of adequate nutritious food. He would later learn that this was in part due to the fact that Givens made a habit of terrorizing other cons and taking portions of their meager rations for himself and in part to forcing others to do some of the heavier work for him.

"He really *is* the top dog," Morgan concluded. By his warning he seemed to indicate that he had accepted his beat-down at the hands of Mankiller and now bore no grudge against him.

"Like I said," he repeated for emphasis, "you'd do well to give him a wide berth."

"That I'll gladly do," Jason replied, with no fear to be heard in his voice. "I hope he'll do the same for me."

By the end of the day, Ira Morgan had circulated among most of the other cons. He quickly and quietly started a gambling pool, whereby bets could be placed on which of the two men would eventually kill the other.

The smart money was placed on Bear Givens to be the only one left standing.

Chapter 11

That first day's work on the rock line proved to be a long and hard one for Jason Mankiller.

From just after sun-up to just before sundown the convicts worked at their assigned jobs. They were given only occasional, very brief rest periods, during which they were given a cup of tepid water but no food.

There was no breeze to speak of, save a hot one, and the sun bore down on them mercilessly. As the day dragged on, more than one convict passed out from dehydration and exhaustion. When that happened, they were carried over to the nearest wagon by other inmates and unceremoniously slung under it for the sparse shade it provided. Upon regaining consciousness, they were expected to resume working.

But Mankiller never faltered, never complained. Nor did he react in any way to the verbal jabs of other inmates or guards.

Somewhat surprisingly, perhaps, most of the other inmates treated him no differently than they would any other con in their midst. Mankiller suspected this was because none of them (including Bear Givens) had a personal grudge against him or score to settle. None of them were in Pima because of him.

The only outlaws he ever brought in were *dead* ones.

That fact brought him more respect and fear among the convicts than it did hatred. But the cons could not be expected to hold any love for this man who was a hunter of their kind, or to care if any harm was to come to him.

Doak Conifer watched Mankiller as he worked and marveled. The bounty hunter seemed more like machine than man, maintaining a constant, steady, rhythmic and efficient stroke with his pick.

Still, he was as ready and relieved as any other when the guards at last called a halt to their labors and they were transported back inside the prison's towering walls.

The supper the exhausted inmates were fed was only a little more wholesome and substantial than had been their breakfast. It consisted of brown beans, a small slab of fatty salt pork and a piece of crusty bread, from which Jason plucked two weevils.

By the time they were herded back to their cells, every convict was dragging from weariness.

Warden Mayhew firmly believed that exhausted men were broken men and much less likely to seriously contemplate any escape attempts.

Jason had seen no sign of young Trey Parker in the mess hall during supper, and was slightly surprised to see him already lying in bed when his three comrades returned to their shared cell.

The young convict was lying on his side, face toward the wall, his knees pulled up slightly. Mankiller took a seat on the edge of his bunk.

"You all right, Trey?"

A faint mumble was his only response. Jason took hold of Trey's shoulder and gently but firmly turned him onto his back.

One of the boy's eyes was black and swollen nearly shut; the other refused to look directly at Jason. His lips were cracked and puffy, and it seemed like he had been crying.

"Did that guard do this to you, boy?" Mankiller hissed. "Baxter?"

"It's nothin'!" Trey exclaimed, turning back toward the wall. Jason felt a hand on his own shoulder and looked up to see Doak Conifer staring down at him grimly.

"Let the boy be," the old con advised. "Ain't nothin' any of us can do for 'im—and he knows it."

The rest of the week passed uneventfully, and every inmate was visibly relieved when the guards blew the whistles ending the short day on Sunday. After returning to the prison compound, each con was allowed five minutes to indulge in their weekly shower before donning the fresh suit of gray garb that would have to serve them for the entire coming week. Those who wished, like Jason, to shave were able to do so under close scrutiny.

They were then allowed to enjoy the relative freedom of the main yard. Many broke off into small groups, smoking and engaging in what passed for gossip in such a closed community. A few pulled out packs of worn and faded playing cards and played poker for penny ante stakes.

Mankiller spied Trey Parker standing alone, head tilted back as he simply stared longingly up at the open sky. Jason sidled over next to him.

"Something could be done about that guard Baxter," he said softly.

"Huh?" Trey appeared slightly startled as he was roused from his reverie.

"Accidents happen," Jason said with a shrug. To his surprise, the young inmate's response to this suggestion was more fearful than hopeful.

"No!" Trey hissed in a low voice, casting his eyes back and forth in alarm. "You might just make it worse! Just let it go—please!"

Mankiller shrugged again. "Whatever you say, kid. Just remember you don't have to face him alone." The bounty hunter then began to saunter away from the terrified con.

"Mr. Mankiller?" Trey called after him.

"Yeah?"

"You think any of us are gonna get outta this place alive?"

Mankiller smiled coldly. "I sure as hell intend to, Trey."

He then wandered off alone to the back side of the small fenced compound that housed the female inmates, taking a seat on the ground and resting his back against the wire.

Lost as he was within his own mind, he was still alert enough to feel a weight press against him from the opposite side of the fence a few minutes later. Turning his head just enough to glance over his shoulder, he was not surprised to see that the buxom blonde woman with whom he had exchanged flirtatious looks had similarly seated herself with her back pressed against the fence and him.

"Howdy," he said softly.

"Howdy," she replied, in a voice that was an odd blend of sweetness and hard living.

"Are you really Jason Mankiller?" she asked.

"None other."

"My name's Stella Freeman. I'd heard quite a bit about you even before you ended up in this fine hotel."

"Nothin' too good, I hope," he replied dryly.

She chuckled softly, and he suspected it was the first time she'd had cause to in a long while.

"Enough for me to suspect you don't deserve to be here."

"Thanks. How 'bout you, Stella? Do *you* deserve to be here?"

The woman sighed. "Oh…I suppose," she confessed.

"How's that?"

"I was running a cathouse in Pueblo. A real nice one, too. You'da liked it."

"I'm sure I would."

"I had the usual problems with it," she continued, "but mostly it ran smooth as silk. Till the night one of the johns decided his two dollars bought him the right to bat one of my girls around.

"Me and my derringer disabused him of that notion by planting a .25 caliber slug in his bony ass."

"Sounds to me like he got no worse than he deserved," Jason said.

"I thought so," Stella replied. "Unfortunately for me, the little bastard's daddy was a state senator. He saw to it that my house was shut down and that I was convicted of attempted murder."

"How long'd they put you away for?"

"Two years. I got six months to go."

"So you haven't done long time," Jason observed, "but it's been *hard* time, hasn't it?"

"You know it, lover," the woman replied. "We cook for 'em, but are fed the same slop as the male inmates. We do manage to sneak a few bites of their leavings, sometimes.

"We clean their clothes and wear rags ourselves; ones that only get washed once a week."

"But that's not the worst of it, is it?" Jason asked.

"Hell, no. The nights are the worst. We have to put up with every vice, every perversion the guards and the warden care to visit on us. And the occasional beating, of course." Stella let out a long, slow breath.

"Like I said, though; maybe it's no worse than I deserve."

"No," Mankiller growled. "Sounds to me like you're paying a lot higher price than you ever charged of a man. Nothin' right about it."

"Thank you, Jason. But I'll be all right. You'd best watch out for yourself, though. Word is that Bear Givens has it in for you; don't ever turn your back on him. Or on any of the others.

"And all but a couple of the guards are just as dog mean as the cons are. Especially Karl Baxter. He'd beat his own mother to death if the urge struck him."

"Then I guess I'd best stay on his good side," Jason jested darkly.

"He ain't *got* a good side, lover. Believe me—I know."

"It's me *they* should be afraid of," Mankiller replied, and the woman thought he spoke truly.

"I wish there was something I could do to help you, though, Stella. You seem like a good woman, down deep, and I wish I could make things a little easier and a little safer for you in the time you got left in here."

"I believe you mean that, Jason. And I thank you." Stella said no more, but she did slide the fingers of one hand through the links in the fence surrounding her. She felt them make contact with the bounty hunter's hand, and he laid his fingers atop hers, gently squeezing them.

He barely registered the shadow falling over him before a heavily booted foot kicked his upper leg.

Without thinking, he leaped to his feet, fists balled. The sight of a rifle barrel pointed straight at his belly caused him pause. On the other end of the rifle, Karl Baxter grinned in anticipation, hoping the bounty hunter would give him even the slightest excuse to pull the trigger.

Denying him this pleasure, Mankiller relaxed his stance and let his arms fall slowly down to his sides.

"You know you ain't allowed near the women, tough nut," the guard sneered. "Get back where you belong."

As Mankiller walked away, Baxter leaned against the fence, staring down at the woman still seated on the other side.

"It it's a man's company yer wantin', Stella," he grunted, "I'll be glad to oblige. I'll be back to see you tonight."

The woman shuddered but said nothing, merely lowering her head to stare down at the dirt.

The next two weeks passed as quietly as one could expect in such a sink of pestilence. During the course of one of the workdays, during a brief break for water, Mankiller drifted a short distance away from his fellow inmates.

Lowering himself down on one knee, he used his fingers to dig a short distance down below the top layer of dust coating the ground. Scooping up a small clod of darker dirt, he brought it up to his nose, inhaling deeply before crumbling it in his hand.

Rising back to his feet, his gaze drifted toward the nearby San Diemos River. Actually, it had taken a good measure of false pride and exaggeration for anyone to dub it a "river." It was actually nothing more than a shallow creek; the average man could easily jump from one of its low banks to the other.

The water those banks contained was clean at least; he knew this because the prison drinking water was drawn from it.

A rustling in the thin brush along the creek's near bank caught his eye and he saw a large, rangy jackrabbit stick its nose out to sniff at the wind.

So lost in thought was the bounty hunter that he did not hear the sound of footsteps coming up behind him.

His brain exploded with pain as a sharp blow delivered to the base of his lower spine caused him to drop heavily to both knees.

Gasping and clutching at his back, he looked up into the menacing gaze of Karl Baxter. Another guard, standing to one side, giggle sadistically.

Eyes on Baxter, Jason never saw the second guard raise his rifle and bring its butt slamming down on the side of the convict's head, causing his world to go black and unfeeling.

Chapter 12

Mankiller stood in the now too-familiar arm and leg shackles inside Superintendent Mayhew's office. The warden had kept him standing there for several minutes while Mayhew himself stood with his back to the bound bounty hunter, staring out through his precious large window. The throbbing pain in Jason's skull was still so great that he found it somewhat difficult to remain on his feet, though he showed no sign of his discomfort.

"So you were plotting an *escape*," Mayhew said at last.

Jason made no attempt at a reply.

Mayhew swiveled his bulk slowly to face the prisoner. "You don't deny it?"

No reply.

"Let me tell you the facts of life as they apply to Pima, Mankiller," the administrator said in a condescending tone.

"For miles around, the land is mostly open: devoid of all but the sparsest vegetation or hiding places.

"As I've told you before, the Army can be called upon to help track down any man foolish enough to attempt a getaway.

"And don't even think of our pitiful little stream as a course of escape, either. Wet or dry, it's never more than two feet deep year round. You can't swim in it or raft on it.

"Then there's *this*; for even *thinking* about trying to escape—a man can be sent to the *Hole*."

His fellow inmates had already educated Jason as to this particular form of punishment. It was essentially what the name implied: a solid metal box set down in the ground. It was neither tall enough for an average man to stand nor wide enough for him to fully recline.

Its roof was exposed to the sun, making it a virtual Dutch oven. The only light that was admitted was when a slot in the door was opened twice a day to give the prisoner a slice of bread and a cup of water.

Three days was the usual time allotted to those deemed worthy of this form of punishment. One spell in the box was usually all that was needed to bring a convict around to the "right" way of thinking.

In the face of this threat, Jason Mankiller still did not deign to speak. Warden Mayhew's eyes narrowed and his teeth ground together in exasperation.

"All right, then," he growled. "What *were* you doing when the guards put you down?"

"Have you ever done any *farming*, Mr. Mayhew?" Jason replied.

Mayhew blinked in surprise. "Farming? Yes, I did some when I was a boy back in Indiana."

"Me, too. In Ohio. And would you agree that it's *hard* work?"

Mayhew scoffed. "Hard? It can be backbreaking. And sometimes to no good end." He eyed Mankiller suspiciously. "What's your point?"

"I did a little digging in the dirt, out near the stream," Jason explained. "Once you get down into it, it's good soil, even fertile. Or at least it could be—if it received enough *water.*

"It wouldn't take much time or work to build a little sluice on the edge of the stream. Open the box a little from time to time; divert some water into a few irrigation ditches. With moisture, that land could be coaxed into bringing forth a crop: corn, onions, carrots. And still leave plenty of water for the needs of the prison.

"The vegetation would attract the jackrabbits I've seen about, and it'd be easy to set snares for them. Tough as they can be, a stew made by boiling them with vegetables can be right tasty and a welcome change from the usual fare around here." Mayhew made no effort to interrupt or cut off Jason, so he continued on.

"All the work of building the sluice, digging the ditches, preparing the ground, planting the seeds and tending the crops can be done by inmates— especially those who are less suited than others to break rocks."

"Are *you* one of those privileged few who would be released from the rock pile?" Mayhew asked suspiciously.

"I doubt it," Mankiller said tersely before resuming. "We already have shovels; the only additional expense might be the wood for the sluice, a few hoes and the necessary seeds.

"I have no idea what you and the guards eat, Warden, but I expect you wouldn't turn down a few extra fresh vegetables. I know us inmates sure wouldn't."

A slightly oily smile stretched across Mayhew's fleshy jowls. "What makes you think we would share this hypothetical bounty with you cons?"

Mankiller shrugged. "We can't control that. But the better fed we are, the healthier we are. The stronger we are, the more work you can get out of us. Could save you money on your food budget, too." Savings Jason was positive would make their way back into Warden Mayhew's own coffers.

"If the time comes that we have a *surplus*," Jason pressed, seeing that greed was the way to the superintendent's heart, "that Army garrison you've mentioned might be willing to buy it from you at a nice profit."

More unreported income Mayhew could add to his personal wealth. Jason could see the portly man's eyes light up like those of a four-year-old bounding downstairs on Christmas morning.

"Very well," Mayhew said, trying with vastly limited success to sound magnanimous. "We'll give it a try." He then called for a guard to unshackle Jason and escort him back to his cell.

"Just one thing, Mankiller," Mayhew said before the inmate could leave the room.

"You *won't* be working in the fields. It's still the rock pile for you."

Jason smiled crookedly, rubbing at his chafed wrists.

"I didn't expect anything else, Mr. Mayhew."

Chapter 13

The following day being Sunday, the convicts enjoyed their half-day of rest. Jason Mankiller sought his own relaxation by sitting in an area of partial shade against one wall of the prison compound. Leaning back against the hard stone, he closed his eyes and allowed his nostrils to drink in droughts of dry air greatly fresher than would have been the odorous ether inside his shared cell.

Not so tightly were his eyes close, though, that he did not see the inmate Bear Givens approaching him even before the massive and murderous convict stepped up and kicked Mankiller's foot.

"Get up," Givens ordered. "You and me need ta talk."

Sighing wearily, Jason pushed up to his feet. Givens walked away a few feet as if fearful of being overheard, motioning with a jerk of his blocky hand for Mankiller to follow.

"You and the warden appear ta be gettin' mighty cozy," Givens said in an accusatory tone.

"What makes you say that?"

"You and him was pow-wowin' fer quite a spell yesterday."

"We had a lot to say."

"Like what?"

"That's none of your damned business, Bear." Jason was quickly growing tired of this conversation; it seemed to have no real point to it.

"Behind you, Mankiller!"

Jason recognized the voice calling out the warning as belonging to his cellmate Ira Morgan. Though he had no good reason to trust the former top dog he had dethroned, he still heeded the call and spun on his heels.

The move saved his life.

A cohort of Bear Givens had sneaked up behind the bounty hunter and was lunging at him with a crude but deadly shiv he had most likely constructed by removing and sharpening a piece of metal from a bunk.

The pointed blade missed Mankiller's back by no more than an inch. If not for the warning, it probably would have sunk into one of his kidneys.

Jason grabbed the attacker's wrist with both hands, twisting so hard

"You and me need ta talk."

that the bone snapped. The con screamed in pain as his handmade knife dropped from nerveless fingers and fell to the ground.

Still, the sneak attack had given Bear Givens an opening, and he did not hesitate to press his advantage. He swung his ham-sized fist, catching Mankiller on the jaw and sending him staggering.

Jason managed to regain his balance and shake some of the cobwebs from his brain before Givens threw his next punch. Mankiller ducked beneath it and delivered a left uppercut into Bear's groin.

Givens grunted and both hands instinctively dropped to cup his battered testicles. Mankiller used this lack of defense to deliver a pounding left and right combination to his opponent's face.

With an animalistic roar, Givens launched himself forward, succeeding in wrapping Mankiller in both his huge arms. Jason let out a yelp as Bear's teeth sank into the soft flesh of his left ear lobe.

He was unable to keep the larger man from pushing him backwards. He then felt his heels strike something behind him; it was the first con that had attacked him, now lying curled on the ground moaning and holding his broken arm.

Jason tripped over him, allowing Bear to lift him off his feet and throw him to the ground. Breath whooshed from his lungs as Givens landed atop him.

A couple of other convicts grabbed hold of the inmate who had helped trip Mankiller, roughly lifting him and tossing him out of the way.

Bear's teeth released his grip on Jason's ear and he raised his head slightly. Mankiller took that moment to snap his own head forward, slamming its crown into Givens' nose.

Bear's grip on him loosened and Jason was able to toss his attacker off. The bounty hunter struggled to his feet and staggered back against the prison wall, using its sturdiness to keep him upright as his chest heaved in an effort to regain his breath.

He squinted at a rather unexpected sight. His cellmate Ira, who had called out the warning to him, was passing amongst the convicts who had gathered as spectators to the much-anticipated fight now in full progress. Money was changing hands and it was clear Ira was taking *bets* on the outcome.

The jailhouse bookie smiled and winked at Mankiller.

Jason pushed away from the way, only to run into a straight jab that laid open a cut along his right cheek. He struck back fiercely; within minutes it was impossible to tell which blood splattering him was his own and which was Bear's.

Ducking a punch, Mankiller rammed Given's in the belly with his head. The blocky con grunted but barely moved. Linking both hands together, he clubbed Jason to his knees.

Again on the ground, Mankiller swept one arm hard enough to take Bear's left leg out from under him. As the con landed heavily on his back, Jason jumped up and fell back down, using the momentum to drive an elbow into Givens' stomach. The blow to the middle caused his upper body to rise, and as it did Jason's elbow flew up to greet it, sending a tooth flying from Bear's bloody mouth.

Pushing himself erect, Mankiller grabbed the stunned Givens by the back of his collar and dragged him through the dirt to the compound wall. Dropping back to his knees, and with his hands under the semi-conscious convict's armpits, he lifted Bear to a sitting position.

He then took hold of Givens' head in both hands and began to bang the back of it against the unyielding stone again and again and again. When a bloody smear began to stain the wall, Mankiller stopped.

Scurrying crab-like, he found and retrieved the fallen shiv that had been intended to be the instrument of his own demise. Hurrying back to Givens, he slapped the beaten man repeatedly; not to inflict further injury upon him but to make sure he was awakened enough to understand what followed.

Straddling Bear's lap, Mankiller used the fingers of his left hand to hold the brutish con's right eye open. With his right hand, he held the shiv as if meaning to plunge it into the orb. Givens' lips began to quiver in silent supplication.

"You ever cause trouble for me again, Bear," Mankiller warned in an ice cold voice that proved there was no bluff in him, "or any of the other men in my cell, and I won't kill you." He waved the point of the improvised knife in tight circles.

"I'll cut out both of your God-damned eyes!" Givens tensed as if he expected this to happen regardless.

"Do you understand me?" Jason hissed.

"I said—do you understand me?"

Bear Givens slowly nodded.

Pulling the knife back, Mankiller rose up on rubbery legs. Several other inmates swarmed around him, a couple roughly slapping him on the back.

"Guards are comin'!" someone sounded in alarm.

Hearing this, Mankiller took a few steps away from the benumbed Bear Givens and heaved the crude knife he was holding as far from him as he could.

"What'd ya do *that* fer?" Doak Conifer asked.

"Because it would be quicker and easier to make or take another one if I needed it than it would be to do three days in the hole if they caught me with that one now," Jason explained tersely.

Doak chuckled and nodded.

The cluster of convicts that had witnessed the fight now began to break up and drift away. Before the guards got too close, a couple had lifted Bear Givens to his feet and began to drag him away. No one deigned to assist the little weasel who had tried to stab Mankiller from behind. Holding his broken arm, he staggered off alone.

Several other cons gathered around Mankiller so as to shield him from the guards' eyes; hiding his injuries and the fact that he had just participated in a nearly fatal fight.

They knew that the following day the guards would probably neither greatly note nor overmuch care about whatever bruises, welts or scabbed over cuts either Mankiller or Givens had sustained. After all, these were fairly common sights in Pima.

For the moment, all the guards did was curtail the remaining free time in the yard the inmates would normally be allowed, instead ordering them back to their respective cells.

Moments after their own cell door slammed shut, Ira Morgan approached Mankiller. Glancing back over a shoulder to see if anyone outside the cell was watching, Ira then reached out and slipped a wad of paper money into Jason's hand.

"What's this for?" Mankiller asked.

"It's yer split from the fight," Morgan explained cheerfully. "I bet every cent I had on you, bounty man. With the odds bein' three to one *against* you—I made a killin'! One I don't mind sharin'!"

Mankiller stared down at his winnings before shoving the money into the front pocket of his prison trousers.

"I'm kinda surprised," he said. "I wouldn't think the warden and the guards would even allow prisoners to *have* money."

"Oh, sure," Morgan replied. "It was Mayhew's idea; it's another one o' his schemes to line his own pockets.

"Yer bound to have seen the little commissary that's built on to the back end of the administration building. Well, sir, it's run by Mayhew's *brother-in-law*!

"He sells us candy, tobacco and the fixin's, toiletries—hell, even a little flask of bootleg whiskey from time to time. All at prices higher'n a cat's back, o' course.

"Him and the warden split 70% of the profits. The rest is divided among the guards, to buy their silence. It's an easier way to get our money than stealing would be, and it ain't nearly as illegal. And we got no place else to spend it."

"Where'd the money come from to start with?" Jason asked. "And where do fresh funds come from?"

"Family, mostly. And a few other ways."

"Like selling sexual favors to the guards?" Mankiller inquired disdainfully.

"Naw," Doak Conifer now interjected. "That's about the only thing money *ain't* used fer in this corner o' hell." He glared at the bunk Trey Parker would normally have occupied but which was now empty.

"A few give it willingly...more often, it's *taken*."

An awkward moment of silence was broken by a grinning Ira Morgan playfully slapping Jason on the shoulder.

"Hell, Top Dog," he crowed, "if you keep doin' what yer doin' long enough...and if I live long enough to reach the end of my sentence and keep bettin' on you...

"I'm liable ta leave here with enough money ta go *straight!*"

The light moment quickly evaporated as their cell door grated open. The animalistic guard Karl Baxter roughly shoved Trey Parker into the cell before slamming the door shut.

The brutalized young convict stood on weaving legs; silent as his cellmates stared at him. His lips were again swollen and cut and a gash high on his left cheek was still oozing blood. Without a word, he threw himself on his bunk and rolled over so his back was to them.

Mankiller took a step toward him, but old man Conifer grabbed him by the arm.

"Son, there ain't—" he began, before Jason jerked away from his grasp.

"Don't tell me there's nothing anybody can do, old man," he snarled.

"Because there damn well is!"

Chapter 14

It was three days later that it all came to a head.

Jason Mankiller was pounding away at a section of the rock face of the prison quarry. His pick rose and fell with almost machine-like efficacy.

Yet even as focused on his work as he appeared to be and was, he maintained a sharp defensive awareness of everything around him.

For now at least, he felt like he was safe from any retaliatory act on the part of fellow inmate Bear Givens; the strutting con was still moving gingerly from the beating he had suffered at Mankiller's hands. Given the number of potential other dangers, though, Jason felt compelled to keep his defenses up.

His constant alertness was what signaled him that something was amiss at the periphery of his vision. He turned his head only slightly, but it was enough for him to catch plain sight of the sadistic Karl Baxter. The perverted guard was holding young Trey Parker's upper right arm, dragging him along. The two of them continued walking till they reached a spot where a large boulder had slid to the bottom of the sharply inclined hogback; they were then lost to his view as they circled it.

"Getting some water, boss!" Mankiller called out to the guard standing nearest to him.

"Get that water," the guard replied, otherwise paying little heed.

The bounty hunter strolled over to the communal bucket and took a dipper of tepid water. He didn't return to his original spot on the rock pile after draining the dipper, however. Rather, as inconspicuously as possible, he sauntered along the way Baxter had led Trey.

Mankiller's breath hissed through clenched teeth as he turned the corner of the concealing boulder. From behind, Baxter's left forearm was against the back of Trey's neck, pushing his face against the unyielding boulder. With his right hand, the guard was holding and twisting the young con's right arm behind him and upward at a painfully unnatural angle.

Trey was whimpering softly, like a beaten puppy. His pain and helplessness fueled his captor's twisted delight and desire. Giggles were interspersed with sickening moans of pleasure.

"Baxter!"

Startled, the guard turned at the calling of his name. Jason Mankiller faced him. He had turned his pick upside down, now wielding it like an ax handle. Before Baxter could react further, Mankiller struck him a heavy blow across the bridge of his nose.

With a cry of pain, Baxter released his hold on Trey Parker and staggered back, blood already gushing from his shattered nose. Mankiller dropped his pick and stepped closer.

Grabbing Baxter by the hair atop his head, Jason smashed a fist into the guard's gaping mouth. After the third such blow, he released Baxter, who promptly collapsed in a limp heap.

Instantly losing interest in him, Mankiller turned toward Baxter's victim. Sobbing softly, Trey Parker had slumped to his knees and Jason dropped down beside him.

"You all right, kid?" he asked softly.

Before a response could be made, Mankiller was driven to the ground by a heavy weight. Three more guards, having been drawn to the site by the sounds of the struggle, began to punch and kick him. In no real position to defend himself, Jason curled into a ball to protect his internal organs as much as possible.

His instinct was to try to find an opening to fight back, but he suppressed the urge when he spied a fourth guard standing a short distance away, with his rifle aimed at the fallen bounty hunter.

So Mankiller took the physical punishment instead, not knowing how long it continued or how many blows had found their target. Once they had beaten him nearly senseless, two of the guards grabbed him by the arms and dragged him over the rock strewn ground to one of the nearby wagons, where they chained him to a wheel.

"It's the hole for you for sure, Mankiller," one of the guards grimly gasped, wheezing from the exertion of having taken part in the beating.

"Ta *hell* with the hole!"

The exclamation came from Karl Baxter as he roughly pulled other guards aside to get to Mankiller. His nose was flattened against his face, courtesy of the pick handle, and blood still flowed freely from it.

The injury altered the timbre of his voice so the words almost whistled out of his mouth. Both eyes had already begun to blacken, giving him the appearance of a masked bandit. So thoroughly had Jason worked him over that it would be at least a week before he would be able to comfortably eat solid food. Going down to one knee, he grabbed Mankiller by the hair and jerked his head up.

"Layin' hands on a guard gets you ten *lashes*, bounty killer!" he snapped with malevolent glee.

"Spread-eagle him to the back of the wagon!" Baxter ordered his fellow guards, who moved quickly and unquestioningly to obey.

Face down, Jason's arms were spread wide, his wrists tied down. Two of the guards took delight in tearing his shirt away to expose the bare flesh of his muscled back.

Karl Baxter walked to the front of the wagon, where he retrieved a coiled *bullwhip* from under the seat. Moving up behind Mankiller, he leaned in close and caressed Jason's cheek with the leather whip.

"You have the pretty boy to thank for this," Baxter whispered, so softly that none but Jason could hear him.

"And after I enjoy this—I'm still gonna enjoy *him*!"

The other convicts had been rounded up and herded over to stand in a semicircle, in hope that witnessing what was about to transpire would serve as a deterrent and a warning to them to obey the rules. Baxter let the whip uncoil naturally, gave it a few light flicks as though warming up, letting Mankiller wait in awful anticipation.

When the guard snapped the whip for real, it cracked like thunder. Mankiller jerked hard as the lash laid itself across his back. A groan escaped his lips, but nothing more. He had once at least briefly endured torture at the hands of Comanche Indians without giving them the satisfaction of hearing him scream, and he meant to do the same today.

Such was the measure of this man that he was able to keep that resolve through the first four lashes, though he could feel his skin being split asunder. Blood and his own urine stained his gray trousers.

By the fifth blow, however, he was pushed beyond human endurance. He screamed with lung-bursting intensity.

Baxter paused at that. He bent at the knees, hands on his knees, fighting to draw air in through the pulpy mess that was his nose. Thinking this might signal the end of the punishment, one of the other guards moved to untie Mankiller.

"No!" Baxter roared as best he could, furiously waving his fellow guard away.

With renewed vigor he again laid the lash to Jason, again and again. The screams stopped, but only because looming unconsciousness was dulling the pain slightly. Jason felt his legs, as if they were detached from the rest of him, begin to sag beneath him.

"That's ten!" he faintly heard his cellmate Ira Morgan shout.

Mankiller must have heard wrong, though—for yet another strike tore at his flesh, making him jerk spasmodically. Then another. Still more.

"That's *enough*, Baxter!" This time it was one of his fellow guards shouting at the crazed Baxter.

But it wasn't enough for him. His arm, though it now felt like it was holding a ten-pound weight, rose and fell again.

When the lashing paused next, Mankiller managed to weakly look back over his shoulder. The guard who had shouted for Baxter to stop had now come up behind Baxter, pinning his arms to his side. Using all his strength, he was managing to pull Baxter away.

Jason saw nothing more but the utter darkness that then descended upon him.

Chapter 15

Consciousness for Mankiller returned in a cascading series of tiny, flashing lights: each bringing with it a lance of pain.

He tried to move, and the lances paled to insignificance against the sheer agony that racked his entire body and elicited a keening moan.

"Just lie still," a gravelly voice said from above him. "You ain't goin' anywhere for a while nohow."

Jason was lying facedown on a sparsely padded table. He endured the pain of turning his head to the side; the better to pull his nose away from the surface that smelled rankly of sweat, blood and liniment.

His eyes managed to focus sufficiently to realize that the only slightly clean and antiseptic place in which he found himself had to be the room that served as what passed for the prison's infirmary, located at the rear of the administration building's first floor.

That brought a troubling realization. He had heard that the man assigned to be the compound's doctor—Sam Fix—had mostly worked his charms on cattle, pigs and horses before finding himself here.

Gripping the sides of the table, Jason tried to push himself up and off. His reward was stabbing pain from gullet to groin. He again cried out and fell back down on his belly.

"Did that bullwhip scramble yer brains, too, son?" Dr. Fix growled. "What part of 'lie still' did you not understand?"

"I can put sheep dip on myself," Mankiller moaned.

"Ah. I see my reputation precedes me. Well, for your information, ya damned idjit, there ain't much difference between a man and a pig." Mankiller hissed as the physician laid a wide cloth soaked in something that smelled vaguely like vinegar across his lacerated back.

"'Cept that hogs tend ta be a mite *smarter!*" Fix concluded. His raspy voice then softened slightly. "Now try to get some rest, son. You were near done in."

The night that followed was spent mostly sleepless, but by the next day Mankiller's extraordinary recuperative powers had brought the level of pain down to just below the level of constant agony.

In mid-afternoon, Warden Mayhew dropped in to pay his respects, accompanied by two armed guards.

"How is he, Doc?" Mayhew asked. He spoke as if Jason himself was not even in the room.

"Sliced ta ribbons, that's how he is!" Dr. Fix snapped. "You need ta teach them damned guards o' yers how ta *count*, Warden."

"What do you mean?"

"I mean maximum punishment allowed is ten lashes. This poor devil took at least half again that many.

"In more than one place, the lash cut clear to the bone. It took half the sutures I've got on hand to sew him back up. His back looks like the last place entry in a quilting bee!"

"Yes, well…I'll be sure to issue the proper reprimand," Mayhew replied in a cold and detached voice.

"How long before he's fit to go back to work on the rock pile?"

"Work?" The exasperated physician ran a hand over his stubbled chin. "You might wanna wait till the man can *walk*!"

"How long, Doctor?"

Fix let out a long sigh. "Even given that the boy seems to have the constitution as well as the brains of a *mule*—I'd say it would be at least a week."

"Perfect," Mayhew declared, not the slightest inflection in his voice, "given that's how long he'll be in the *hole* for striking a guard."

Dr. Fix's mouth fell open in disbelief. "The *hole*? The man's already been beaten half to death! Isn't that punishment enough? Without constant treatment, those wounds could fester and become infected. He could die!"

"Then he'll die!" Mayhew shot back. "One of my guards was also beaten half to death, by the prisoner. Discipline has to be maintained. An example has to be made."

"Yeah," Dr. Fix chuffed. "I suppose draggin' his dead carcass outta the ground will send just the sorta message you want."

"Watch your tongue, you washed-up old horse doctor!" Mayhew barked. "I'd have a harder time replacing my pocket watch than I would finding someone to take your place."

The aged vet muttered something under his breath. "At least give him a coupla days in here before you bury him alive."

Mayhew glared angrily at him, then threw up his hands. "Tonight. He has tonight to be pampered by you. But come first light tomorrow—he goes in the hole!"

"Sorry I couldn't be of more help to ya, son," Dr. Fix apologized to Jason after Mayhew stormed out of the infirmary. "I guess maybe I *am* pretty useless."

"You did the best you could, Doc," Mankiller replied. "I never ask more than that from any man."

Given that the slightest movement brought splinters of pain with it, the bounty hunter slept but little more that night. As the first gray fingers of dawn presaged the coming of the sun, Dr. Fix entered the infirmary.

He gave Jason no greeting but instead went to his small and inadequately stocked medicine cabinet.

"Mornin'," he said at last, bending slightly at the waist to look Mankiller in the eye. He held up a small glass vial that contained a dark liquid.

"Whilst I was tryin' ta go ta sleep last night," he said. From the smell on his breath, Jason surmised he had used some sort of spirits as his sleep aid.

"An idea come ta me. This vial contains *laudanum*. I can't give you much: Mayhew watches over my medical supplies like a hawk, and would notice a missing bottle.

"I'm gonna slip this in yer pocket, before the guards come. I hope it'll get you through the worst of what's about to come yer way."

"I thank you for your kindness, Doctor," Mankiller replied, attempting a smile. "It won't be forgotten."

He managed not to cry out when two guards entered a short time later and roughly dragged him off the table and out of the infirmary. He became even more determined to make no sound when he saw that all the other inmates had been assembled in the yard to witness his ignominy. Only when the iron door leading into the hole was slammed shut and blackness had fully descended upon him did he allow a low groan of agony to issue forth.

He vowed that he would endure the constant pain without benefit of the liquid opiate the doctor had slipped him. He kept that vow for most of the first day before succumbing and taking the tiniest of sips of the palliative.

It was a testament to his fortitude that he was able to make the few precious ounces in the vial suffice for three days. By then, the pain was manageable through sheer force of will.

Time was one of the greatest enemies in the hole. Though there was no way to mark its passage in the continual darkness of this solid cage, it seemed to drag interminably. This was especially intense given Mankiller's inability to sleep fully for any extended periods.

So he devised methods to help the time pass. One way was by singing. Jason couldn't carry a tune in a bucket, but that wasn't important in this setting.

Over and over he sang away time in his admittedly limited repertoire: from the sacred—hymns such as *Amazing Grace*—to the profane: bawdy dance hall songs.

In his mind, he also "re-read" books he had read as best he could remember them, often assuming the role of actor as he spoke the most memorable lines of dialogue aloud.

Thoughts of the plots of books recounting highly fictionalized tellings of his own life and supposed deeds brought a smile to his face—as did thoughts of their author. He and Jane Starr had forged a bond he lacked the vocabulary to accurately or fully define, but which he deeply cherished.

From his pants pocket he would withdraw a small stone he had managed to palm while toiling on the rock pile. It was a small, flat, round stone approximately the size of a silver dollar.

As had been his habit for the past few years, he would hold out first one hand and then the other, palm down. He then used the fingers to flip the rock from one side of his hand to the other, end over end across his knuckles; repeating the process until his hands were nearly numb.

Facile and limber fingers were a tool of survival in his trade, as was the cultivating of equal dexterity in both hands. Being able to fire a gun with equal accuracy and lethality with either hands had proven to be a life-saving skill. In the nearly total darkness of the hole, he engaged in this exercise by the hour.

The rough walls of the box constantly rubbed and chaffed the wounds left on his back by the bullwhip; Jason often felt rivulets of blood flowing down his itching flesh.

Near the end of his fourth day in solitary, Mankiller was surprised when the door slot opened and he saw that his evening "meal" was being served by the guard named Clem Butler.

Butler was the mutton-chopped telegrapher Jason had spied on his first day at Pima. He was also the one who had first stood up to Karl Baxter to prevent him from whipping Jason to death.

"Since when did you start serving the meals around here?" Jason asked.

"I'm bringing more than bread and water," Butler replied in a loud whisper. "I brought news I figured you would want to hear now rather than after the warden finally lets you out of the box."

"What news?"

The guard looked shame-faced as he responded. "This morning, that kid from your cell—Trey Parker—he didn't show up for breakfast.

"When his bunk was checked...he was found to be dead."

Mankiller's voice took on a cold and menacing edge. "How'd it happen?"

"Near as we could tell...looks like he hanged himself with a bedsheet." Butler cleared his throat.

"I reckon life in here just prove to be more than the kid could handle... so he ended it."

"Yeah," Jason said grimly. "And maybe he had a little *help* to that end."

"Now, I—I don't know nothin' about that," Butler fearfully stammered. "I just thought you'd wanna know."

"I thank you for that consideration at least, Clem."

With that, the guard closed the small portal in the door and Mankiller was again plunged into darkness.

Chapter 16

Jason Mankiller had to be dragged out of the hole three days later. A solid week in the iron box had left the muscles of his legs too painfully cramped to support his weight, to even allow him to stand unassisted, let alone walk. The burning pain of blood rushing into wooden limbs alone would have been sufficient to bring tears to the eyes of a lesser man.

By the time they had him halfway across the yard on the way back to the main cellblock, though, he shook himself free from the helping grasp of the two guards escorting him. His steps were initially as halting and unsteady as those of a toddler, but he by God would not allow the other inmates to see him in any state other than astride his own two feet.

So intently focused was he on simply remaining erect and continuing to place one heavy foot in front of the other that he did not think to look up and about, else he would surely have spied Warden Mayhew standing at his beloved window glaring down at the stumbling bounty hunter.

The pane of glass and even the stone walls of the cellblock were not enough to fully muffle the cheering and stomping of feet from the inmates who greeted Mankiller. The warden scowled; instead of breaking the bounty man, he'd made him a damned hero to the other inmates.

Mankiller stood just within the confines of his cell until he heard the door slam ominously closed behind him; then, with a soft moan, he allowed himself to sink down to a sitting position on the edge of one of the lower bunks.

His eyes fell sadly on the adjacent bunk, where Trey Parker would doubtless have been reclining had he still been alive. On the bunk above the empty one, old man Doak Conifer sat, staring down solicitously at Jason but saying nothing.

A movement caught his eye and he turned his head to see Ira Morgan, a big grin on his face, dancing a clumsy jig.

"Yer provin' ta be quite the cash cow, bounty hunter!" Morgan howled, stepping forward to thrust a roll of money into Jason's hand.

"And what's this for?" he asked.

"Hot damn, boy," Morgan gushed, "ain't never been a soul before took the kinda lashin' you did, nor been put in the box for a solid week!

"Every yahoo with a buck ta spare bet me you'd be nothin' but a stone cold *corpse* by the time they finally pulled you outta that hole. But I had faith in ya!

"By the time I collect from all of 'em, only the free men in this pen will be richer'n *me*!"

Mankiller smiled wanly and thrust the bills into his pocket. He then turned his gaze upward toward Doak Conifer.

"What really happened to the kid?" he asked.

"Aw, hell," the old con wheezed. "You know what happened to him."

"I know he's dead. I wanna know how and why."

"Neither of us was in here when it actually happened," Ira Morgan said, his demeanor turning serious. "Baxter made sure o' that. So we don't know for certain sure. Mebbe Trey finally decided to stand up to Baxter. Or mebbe Baxter just got tired of him."

"Or mebbe he just felt like killin' somebody that mornin'," Doak added.

"Yeah," Mankiller said softly. "And maybe someday someone'll feel like killing *him*."

Chapter 17

On the first Sunday afternoon following his release from the hole, Jason Mankiller was relaxing in the prison yard with his cellmates. All of them tensed slightly when they saw a swaggering guard approaching them.

"On your feet, Mankiller," the guard said, a slight sneer on his lips. "You got some *visitors*."

Jason glanced at Doak and Ira; the surprised looks on their faces were equal to that on his own. Inmates in Pima were allowed visitors on occasion, but few ever came: these were the first during Mankiller's time here.

The visitation room occupied a small, freestanding wooden building located not far from the front gates. It was a narrow, low-ceilinged affair: its only furnishings three tables with chairs set on either side.

Before being led into the chamber, Mankiller again had to have his wrists and ankles shackled together and submit to being searched, lest he get any wild notions in his head. (As if the armed guards who would never be more than a few feet away would not be deterrent enough!)

As expected, there were no other prisoners inside; few of those caged in Pima had anyone who cared enough to make the trip. Those who did have loved ones who might wish to provide occasional succor usually urged them not to come to this place of hopelessness.

Jason smiled, though, as he was motioned toward the nearest chair, for standing across the table from him was a welcome sight.

Sam Dobbins was not impressive to the eye, being a fairly nondescript, middle-aged man. But he was a sweet sight to Mankiller.

When Jason had drifted into the north Texas town of Fort Rogers nearly two years earlier, broke and without prospects, Dobbins had been the first to befriend him and lend a helping hand.

He was more than just a friend. He'd made Jason part owner of his saloon; the two men now co-owned several businesses, making them an economic force in the growing town.

Standing beside Sam Dobbins was Carter Frain, Mankiller's lawyer during the travesty of a trial held in Low Water.

The two men separated, revealing a third visitor whose presence had been concealed by their greater size and height had accompanied them. The smile froze on Jason's face, then melted away.

It was Jane Starr.

Upon seeing him, she started to step forward, but Frain took hold of her arm to hold her back. Sam Dobbins fervently whispered to her. Her brow furrowed in displeasure and she looked slightly annoyed as she folded her arms in front of her, but she took a step back and allowed the two men to approach the table first.

"Sam!" Jason welcomed, reaching across the short span of the table to take his friend's hands. "I wasn't sure you got my message; wasn't sure you'd come."

"I got it right enough," Dobbins replied. "And weren't nothin' would keep me from comin'!"

Only now did Mankiller know his strategy had succeeded. After he had slain the two crooked deputies who had been escorting him, but before he had driven himself on to Pima—he had made a brief stop in a town along the way.

Besides using some of the money he had purloined off the deputies to pay for a final good meal, Jason had also sent off telegraphs to Sam Dobbins and his money manager Byron Longfellow, succinctly apprising them of the basic facts of his legal predicament.

He'd also sent one to Carter Frain, in care of Dobbins, in the hope that the attorney would follow his advise and relocate to Fort Rogers. Clearly he had. Jason released Sam's hands and extended his own toward the smiling lawyer.

"We'd have come even sooner," Frain said as soon as he and Dobbins took seats and Jason did likewise, "but we wanted to wait until we had some actual news to give you."

"Then I take it you have," Jason said eagerly.

"Some," Frain said cautiously, not wanting to raise Jason's expectations to too high a level.

"The minute he contacted me, we set ta work," Sam interposed.

"First, we went to Fort Rogers' marshal, Clayton Russell," Frain resumed the telling. "He helped us find wanted posters on the two men you killed while they were trying to hold up the stage.

"Thank God, that old lawman seems never to throw anything away. We even found old papers on Marshal Thorpe and Mayor Owens from back when they were more honestly crooked."

"That's how I finally remembered who they were," Jason explained. "Russell let me go through his posters whenever I was in town. I'd seen their dodger then, but never encountered them till I had the misfortune of riding into Low Water.

"That's why it took me a while to remember who they really were."

"At the moment," Frain said, "they're not our main concern. I've mostly been using *my* time—and *your* money—" He saw Jason chuckle softly and nod his head approvingly.

"Anyway," the lawyer continued, "I've finally managed to contact all the other passengers who were with you that day, and the driver as well. I have sworn statements, duly witnessed, from all of them attesting to what really happened.

"We'd have come even sooner..."

"Then you can use that to get me out of here," Mankiller said hopefully.

Frain held up a restraining hand. "Not so fast, Jason. I don't want to give you false hope or raise your expectations too high, too soon."

"Why? What more should it take?"

"Well, ordinarily, I'd take this sort of new evidence to present to the presiding judge; use it to at least get you a new trial."

Mankiller grimaced and nodded. "But in this case, the 'presiding judge' would be Delmar Owens—the man who sent me here in the first place."

"Exactly. So I'm trying a different tack. I'm doing everything I can to get an appointment to meet with the territorial governor himself; get these sworn depositions and other evidence directly in front of him. I'll be heading back to the capital as soon as I leave here, and I won't stop pestering the bureaucrats until I get that meeting.

"I also have statements from several character witnesses I took at Fort Rogers. At Sam's suggestion, I even contacted an old friend of yours in the Army."

Jason raised an eyebrow quizzically.

"In response," Frain explained, I got a positively glowing telegram from a Lt. Colonel named *Custer*. Seems the man has great affection for you."

"The feeling's mutual," was all Mankiller said in reply, smiling gratefully. In addition to serving faithfully under him during the final year-and-a-half of the *Recent Unpleasantness*, Jason had also done some scouting for George Armstrong Custer and his 7th Cavalry up in Kansas.

"What about Owens and his marshal, Thorpe?" he asked of his attorney. "Can't any pressure be brought to bear on them?"

"I don't think that's likely, Jason," Frain admitted grudgingly. "The authorities I've spoken with show no inclination to take action against them. The alleged crimes that got them on wanted posters are now old news, and both were legally elected and appointed to their respective current positions.

"You know how it is out here on the frontier. More than one lawman rode on the owlhoot trail before he took to wearing a badge."

"Yeah," the bounty hunter acknowledged.

One corner of Carter Frain's mouth turned upward. "I have heard some interesting news about my former home town of Low Water, though."

"Oh?"

"Yes. It seems you made a certain, rather forceful...*promise* when you bid it and its citizens farewell?"

Mankiller shrugged sheepishly.

"It seems that pledge—along with the fact that the two deputies who left town with you never came *back*—has put the fear of God into the good folks of Low Water.

"So much so that apparently a goodly number of them have packed up and left town for good!"

"They're the smart ones," was Jason's only muted comment.

Sam Dobbins placed a hand on Frain's arm. "Is that about all the legal stuff we need to discuss, Carter?"

"For now, yes, I think so. Why?"

"'Cause we got us a woman back there who's faunchin' at the bit like a mule with a bee up its butt!"

Frain looked over his shoulder to see that Jane Star had begun to pace nervously back and forth. She shot the lawyer a glare that would have curdled milk while it was still in the udder.

"Yes, Frain said, rising to his feet. He reached out and took Mankiller's hand. "Try to stay strong, Jason. And know that we're doing everything we can, as quickly as we can, to get you out of here."

"I know you are, Carter. I have faith in you."

"And just as soon as he succeeds," Sam Dobbins said, also offering his hand, "I want you to come straight *home!*"

"I'll do it, Sam. Count on it."

The moment the two male visitors stood up and stepped back, Jane Starr rushed forward. Smiling, Mankiller stretched his shackled hands out to her across the table. She clutched at them both, lifting them to her lips and kissing them tenderly. When she lifted her face, the bounty hunger was troubled to see her beautiful eyes moistened by tears.

"Why did they have to *chain* you?" she asked, taking a seat but never releasing her hold on his hands.

"It's just the rules, Jane," he said softly. "They don't hurt."

"They hurt *me!*" she exclaimed, her voice choking. He could tell from the way her eyes darted back and forth that she was also taking note of the other signs of physical hardship that were evident on his face and hands. She was far too intelligent for him to lie to her about their origins, so he made no attempt to do so.

Instead, he simply took a moment to drink in the welcomed sight of her. Her raven black hair was neatly coifed, framing a face that spoke of strength as well as charm and beauty. She had worn what was probably her best dress to see him.

"I'm happier to see you than I can say," he told her with total candor.

"But you shouldn't have come here, Jane. Not to a place like this; not to see me like this."

"Don't be foolish, Jason. I'm just glad Cash and I happened to be back in Fort Rogers when the news came of what had happened to you. If Sam and Mr. Frain hadn't agreed to let me accompany them—I'd have just come on my own."

Mankiller knew this to be true. Just as he knew that the "Cash" to whom she referred was Cash Carpenter, the professional gambler who was her nearly constant companion and much more. He was good folk, too, and had proven to be a trusted friend.

"Tell me something happy, Jane," he urged his visitor.

She lowered her head for a moment, then looked up at him with a smile revealing white, even teeth.

"I finally did it, Jason," she said excitedly. "I finally got to travel to New York City!

"It was so big, with buildings so tall it almost took my breath away just looking up at them!

"Cash and I went to the theater and to a different restaurant every night; I ate food I'd never even heard of!

"Of course, Cash being Cash, he managed to find himself a few poker games, too. But while he did that, I just wandered the streets and the parks like a lost urchin. Just watching the people: more people than you could count.

"I finally met my publisher fact-to-face, too. He took me out to lunch and told me how happy they were with the sales of my books." She gave Jason another smile.

"You might like to know there will be a new "Mankiller Thriller" as he likes to call them, coming out soon!"

"And what dastardly menace will I be facing this time?" the bounty hunter asked her with true, unvarnished enthusiasm.

"You're going to single-handedly take down a white slave ring in San Francisco!" she gushed.

"Ah, yes," he replied. "I remember it well."

Both of them actually laughed aloud then, sharing the knowledge that of course any such yarn would be a total fabrication, the product of nothing but Jane Starr's fertile imagination.

"And don't forget I'll expect a signed copy," he reminded her. "Ahh. Sounds like you and Cash had a high old time."

"Oh, we did, Jason. It was wonderful." She affected a rather smug look.

"Not bad for a poor little orphan girl from St. Louis, is it?"

"No. Not bad at all," Jason said, flashing a proud smile.

He didn't tell the woman that it was *he* who had urged Cash Carpenter to take Jane on the trip he knew she so greatly desired; nor that he had given Cash most of the money required to make the journey a reality.

"Your time's up, Mankiller," a guard said, stepping closer. Jason noted that it was Clem Butler, the only guard in the prison who had shown him any trace of humanity.

"Just one more minute!" Jane pleaded.

"I'm sorry, ma'am," Butler said, and Jason could detect genuine regret in his voice. "But I've already given him more time than the regulations allow. C'mon, boy."

As the bounty hunter rose from his chain, so did the woman seated across the table from him. Tears again welled in her eyes and she again clutched his hands and kissed them.

"It'll be all right, Jane," he said soothingly; but he was as reluctant to let go as was she. He finally stepped back and waved his shackled hands at her and her two male companions, who had stepped up closer behind her.

Mankiller turned his back on them and began to walk away—till a loud gasp caused him to stop and turn back in their direction.

Jane, a look of utter horror on her face, was pointing at him with a hand that strongly trembled.

"Oh, my God!"

Too late, Jason realized that the back of his shirt was moist and clinging to his skin. Some of the deeper abrasions from his recent lashing had again begun to ooze, soaking through the flimsy material of his shirt in bloody, crisscrossing lines.

"What have you done to him?" Jane moaned. Her look of horror gave way to one of agitation. Then her normally lovely face became almost ugly as it contorted with an overwhelming rage.

"You dirty...stinking...vicious...*animals!*" she screamed. "What in bloody *Hell* have you done to him?"

Emotion and anger replaced reason, and the woman began literally to crawl across the table separating them, intent on plucking Jason from the clutches of the guards.

Sam Dobbins and Carter Frain leaped forward, grabbing the hysterical woman and pulling her back before the guards could raise hands against her.

"Let me go, dammit!" she shrieked, bucking and kicking. "Let me go!"

"Don't bring her back here again, Sam!" Mankiller shouted as the guards hurriedly dragged him out of the room.

"You hear me? Don't ever bring her back here!"

Chapter 18

Shortly after dawn of the following day, Jason Mankiller was lined up with the other prisoners in the main yard, preparing to be taken to the rock pile for another day's work.

Before they could depart, a buckboard wagon came rolling through the open front gates. As it passed the prisoners, Jason caught a glimpse of the load it was carrying: farm implements and bags that surely contained seeds. He smiled grimly.

"No work for you today, Mankiller," a guard said, taking Jason's arm and pulling him out of line.

"Huh? Why not?"

"The superintendent wants to see you."

Looking up, Jason saw Warden Mayhew at his usual spot in front of his big office window, looking down on the yard. Jason shrugged and offered no resistance to being led away from the work detail.

He was mildly surprised when he was ushered in to Mayhew's office to discover that the guard Karl Baxter was also there, but gave it no second thought.

"You wanted to see me, Warden?" Jason asked.

"Yes," Mayhew acknowledged, lowering his bulk into the chair behind his desk.

"I heard about your visitation yesterday." From the smug sneer on Baxter's face, Mankiller had no doubt who had reported it to the warden.

"What about it?" he asked Mayhew, ignoring the guard.

"Oh…it's just that experience has taught me that visits such as that often have one of two effects on a prisoner's state of mind.

"They can give him false hope…or they can put thoughts of escape into his head."

Knowing it would be pointless to argue, Jason said nothing.

"I think three days back in the hole would suffice to kill either."

This did evoke a response. "You got no right to do that," Jason protested. "I've done nothing wrong."

Without thinking, he had taken a step toward the warden's desk. He stopped dead in his tracks when he saw Karl Baxter's hand drop to the butt of the pistol he wore on his right hip; Jason also heard the guard who had escorted him in cock his rifle.

"Don't ever talk to me about rights, Mankiller," Mayhew said coldly. "The only right you have here at Pima is the right to die if you step too far out of line."

Jason didn't say another word. Nor did he offer the slightest resistance as he was led away, nor as he again descended into the pit of darkness.

During his seventy-two hours without light, he drew cold comfort by replaying over and over in his mind the brief but heartening visit he had enjoyed with Jane and the others. Unable to see with his eyes, with his mind he was able to paint a vivid recreation of her smiling face.

At least Warden Mayhew was true to his word, and Mankiller was released on the evening of the third day and taken back to his shared cell.

After the door was closed, Doak Conifer remained at its bars keeping watch to make sure the guard had walked away. The old convict then shambled over to where Mankiller had seated himself on the lower bunk previously occupied by Trey Parker.

Reaching inside his tunic, Doak withdrew a small piece of tough salt pork. He had smuggled it from the mess hall earlier, anticipating Jason's release from the hole and knowing he would have received nothing more filling than bread for the past three days. Holding it in both hands, Doak presented it to Mankiller as if it was a religious offering.

"Thanks, Pops." Jason began to gnaw on the pork as if it was the finest and most tender of steaks.

"I stole ya a little somethin', too," Ira Morgan said, handing Mankiller a smaller piece of pork. He then smiled. "No money for ya, though. Dumb as they are, I couldn't find a single con stupid enough to lay bets on your odds of makin' it out of the hole this time."

"That's all right, Ira," Jason said, returning his smile. "I'm sure you'll find something else to bet against my life sooner or later."

Morgan chuckled softly.

Forcing himself to slow down in eating the pork lest he make himself sick at his stomach, Mankiller looked more closely at his cellmates. Ira sat across from him with his head down, staring sullenly at the floor. Doak's face looked even more worn and tired than usual.

"So," Jason said between bites, "what's been happening?"

"If it's possible," Doak replied bitterly, "things have gotten even *worse* since they threw ya in the hole.

"Day before yesterday, Karl Baxter put the whip to another man." The old con winced at the recent memory.

"This one wasn't as lucky or as strong as you. He was dead by the time they could haul him back to the infirmary."

"The other prisoners have started grumbling," Ira added.

"That's what prisoners do," Jason replied.

"Yeah, but this is worse," Doak told him. "Bear Givens has been eggin' 'em on. He's talking about starting a mass *riot* and tryin' for a breakout."

"That would be pure-dee crazy," Mankiller said sternly. "Sure, we got the *numbers*—but the guards have the *guns*. And that's even without counting the Gatling over the front gates

"Oh, a few might make it over the walls—but most would soon be caught or die in the wilderness.

"A lot more would die right here, mowed down in the yard." He shook his head slowly.

"Here's my advice, boys, and you can take it or leave it. If anything like that happens—the second you hear a gun go off, you find yourself a hole and crawl into it. And you stay there till it's all over."

"Oh, it's gonna happen, all right," Ira said. "I'd bet on it." He flashed a brief smile. "*If* I was a bettin' man, that is."

The next morning, Mankiller thought he could palpably feel an aura of danger in the air as the prisoners were marched out of the mess hall and herded toward the wagons waiting to take them to the rock pile.

The first sign that his instincts were correct came when the big convict Bear Givens seemed to trip over his own feet and fall to his hands and knees. When he made no effort to rise back to his feet, a guard stepped closer to him.

"This is it!" Mankiller urgently whispered to Doak Conifer and Ira Morgan. "Get ready to move!"

"Get up, Bear!" the guard ordered, poking the convict in the back with the barrel of his rifle. Givens seemed to be complying, though slowly and rather clumsily.

He then sprang upright, roaring like his namesake. Caught totally by surprise, the guard had no time to react before Bear clubbed him to the ground with clasped hands.

In a single move, the convict snatched the rifle from the guard's hands and turned it on him. He took delight in putting a bullet in the man's belly.

This was the signal for which the other cons had been waiting. En masse, they rushed to attempt to overpower the other guards.

Bear Givens stood proudly over the guard he had shot, knowing the wound he had inflicted was surely fatal but that the man would be a long time in dying. The con laughed with delight at the thought.

He then bent down to grab the pistol the guard had been wearing in a waist holster. Keeping the rifle for himself, Bear handed the pistol to the nearest other con.

The riot Givens wanted had commenced. Amidst the chaos of convicts wrestling with guards, shots rang out sporadically.

Then came a steadier stream of flying lead as the guards in the tower turned their deadly Gatling gun down toward the main yard and opened fire.

Nor were they discriminate in their aiming or firing. The staccato bursts of slugs sprayed from side to side blindly. At least a few of the guards who would die that day would take cold comfort in having known they had fallen gunned down by their own compatriots.

"Take cover!" Jason Mankiller shouted to his two cellmates. He followed his own advice, diving under the nearest wagon. Crawling to the opposite side, away from the tower, he yelled at some of the cons cowering there to help him flip the wagon onto its side so as to provide them with more cover. To facilitate this, Jason scurried to the front end of the wagon and released its team of horses.

It still required several collective heaves before the heavy flatbed wagon's near wheels left the ground and the whole conveyance ponderously tipped, crashing onto its side.

As bullets slapped into it, Mankiller's eyes lit upon a pickax lying in the dirt a few feet away from his position. Any weapon was better than no weapon, so he made a dive for it.

Another inmate had the same idea and both men laid hands on the pick handle at the same time.

To the other con's surprise, Jason instantly let go. But this was simply to free his hands. He smashed a right fist into the other man's mouth, followed by a left-right combination to the jaw. The other inmate fell away and Mankiller was in sole possession of the pick.

His intent was still only to stay hunkered down behind the wagon until the struggle around him reached its end—but his eyes fell upon a sight that changed his plans.

Two of the convicts had something other than escape on their minds. They had raced over to the small, fenced compound that housed the three female prisoners. One of them was futilely clawing at its locked front gate, while the other had begun to climb in an attempt to simply scale his way over the fence; ignoring in his lust the coils of barbed wire that topped it.

Taking a deep breath and tightening his grip on the pickax, Mankiller bolted from the relative safety of the overturned wagon. As he ran in a weaving manner, slugs aimed in his direction kicked up small clouds of dust. One bullet sailed close enough by his head for the bounty hunter to hear the distinctive whine of its passing.

Reaching the women's compound intact, Mankiller swung the pick, hitting the con attempting to tear down the gate with his bare hands on the back of his thick skull with the flat side of the tool's head. The impact caused the con's forehead to bang off the gatepost and he fell heavily to the ground.

The wide toes of the prison-issued shoes were not made for finding purchase in the links of a wire fence, thus the con attempting to climb up and over it had made but little progress.

By jumping up, Mankiller was able to grab hold of the cuff of the con's trousers. Jason's added weight caused the man's hands to be ripped away from the fencing and he fell hard on his back to the dirt below.

The con barely managed, in a fog, to rise up onto his elbows when Mankiller reared back and kicked him in the head. The con felt no more.

Hefting the pickax in its intended fashion, Mankiller began to bang at the lock holding the women's compound gate closed. Three powerful blows were sufficient to shatter it.

Two of the women inside the small compound fell to the ground alongside the wall of their communal hut, expecting that Mankiller had in store for them the same fate as had the other two male convicts.

But the blonde and buxom Stella Freeman rushed forward, throwing her arms around Jason's neck. His free arm circled her waist and pulled her closer, but then he pulled back away from her.

"This hut's too flimsy to provide any real shelter," he told her. "Our best bet is to hole up somewhere inside the main administration building."

He and Stella pulled the other two women to their feet, Stella assuring them that Mankiller was there to help them.

Jason first led them to the nearest of the main compound's outer walls, as far from the ongoing riot as possible and outside the horizontal range of the Gatling gun in the front tower.

Gunfire mingled with shouts of rage and screams of pain. It seemed to Jason at a glance that at least three inmates were falling for every guard that succumbed. But having been pushed to the breaking point, the prisoners were beyond caring about the threat to their lives. And each guard that fell meant another rifle and pistol was now in the hands of the rioting convicts.

When some guards were overwhelmed they weren't afforded the mercy of a quick death by gunshot. They were stomped and pummeled; at least one was virtually torn to shreds by the cons' bare hands.

It became necessary for Mankiller to lead his little band of women away from the relative safety of the wall to make their way across an open expanse leading to the prison's main building.

This also involved weaving their way around the scattered bodies of convicts who had been gunned down, probably by the merciless Gatling gun. Mankiller abruptly stopped beside one of those bodies, dropping to his knees.

He bent over the lifeless form of his aged cellmate Doak Conifer, a bullet had taken out the back of the old con's head. Though they no longer saw anything, the eyes of the convict were still open, as if searching the sky above for some sign of heaven.

"I told you to stay under cover, Pops," Jason whispered, reaching down and gently closing the Conifer's eyes. "You shoulda listened to me, old-timer."

As Mankiller slowly came to his feet, the sight of another struggle caught his attention. Some twenty feet away, the brutal convict Bear Givens was locked in a fight, trying to wrest away the rifle of a guard who probably spotted Givens a least fifty pounds in weight.

Givens had apparently either lost his own rifle or simply discarded it when it ran out of ammunition. He clearly meant to take another.

Even amidst the swirling dust and dark gun smoke, Mankiller could see that the endangered guard was Clem Butler, the guard he had first seen in the compound's telegraph office. He was also the guard who had saved Jason from an even worse beating at the hands of Karl Baxter and who had been kind enough to bring word of Trey Parker's death.

With a twisting jerk, Bear pulled the rifle out of Butler's hands, then backhanded the guard and sent him sprawling on the ground.

"Stay here!" Jason told the women, then raced toward the fallen guard. Already, Bear Givens had turned the rifle on the downed Butler and was preparing to shoot him.

In an act of desperation, Mankiller raised the pickax he was carrying with both hands and flung it through the air like an Indian tomahawk.

The pick spun end over end three times as it whistled through the air—

then struck Givens in the back with such force that the point of its head burst out through his chest. The murderous con's body arched and blood bubbled up from his lungs and through his lips.

His lifeless body had barely hit the dust when Mankiller reached the spot. He snatched up the fallen rifle with one hand while offering the other to help Clem Butler rise up from the ground. Once back on his feet, he made a move to take the rifle away from Jason, who pulled it away from his grasp.

"If you don't mind," Jason told the guard, "I'll keep this for now. You still got your pistol."

Butler hesitated for only a few seconds before nodding his acquiescence.

Keeping their eyes on the ongoing chaos, Mankiller and Butler backed toward the spot where Jason had momentarily left the three female inmates.

"We need to get to the administration building," Jason told the guard. "You lead the way; I'll cover our rear."

Their passage was fraught with danger; bullets flew wildly around the yard as guards and convicts exchanged fire. Equally threatening were the slugs that still rained down from the Gatling gun above.

As they drew within sight of the front doors of the main building, Mankiller stopped and turned at the sound of a familiar voice bellowing in pain and fear.

Halfway across the yard, he saw the sadistic guard who had so viciously whipped him and had murdered young Trey Parker. Karl Baxter had himself now fallen into the hands of a group of rioting convicts.

Baxter was thrashing about wildly as the cons raised him over their heads. Jason saw that he was already bleeding from multiple wounds; could hear the pitiful screams for mercy and aid gushing from his lungs.

Without thought, Mankiller snapped his rifle to his shoulder and sighted in on Baxter's head, meaning to at least put him out of his misery quickly rather than leave him to the slow, excruciating torture the convicts no doubt had in store for the guard who had so tormented them.

The movement of raising the rifle caused a twinge of pain to tighten Jason's back and the only partially healed wounds placed there by Baxter and his bullwhip. In the steaming hot air, Baxter's contorted features seemingly metamorphosed into the face of the young Parker as it must have looked when he was found hanged in his own cell.

Mankiller lowered the rifle without having fired a shot.

Nor would he ever lose a single minute of sleep over this decision to leave the murderous Karl Baxter to his richly deserved fate at the hands of the crazed inmates of Pima.

Jason turned his back on the impending execution, hurrying Clem Butler and the three women ahead of him into the administration building. As soon as they entered, Jason slammed the doors shut and threw the bolt locking them.

"Help me pile stuff in front of 'em," he told Butler. "We'll block it off as best we can."

Butler hesitated. "What if there are other guards out there with the same idea we had? They won't be able to get in."

Mankiller impatiently grabbed the guard by the front of his tunic and pulled him close to one of the doors so he could look through the small pane of glass set into it out at the continuing battle going on in the yard.

"Take a good look," Jason snapped, "but make it quick. Any other guards still out there have either found shelter of their own—or they're dead!"

Butler licked lips gone dry as sand, then nodded. He quickly assisted Mankiller in piling up chairs, hat racks and anything else with any bulk in front of the bolted doors. Both men knew that this and the wire mesh screens covering every window would not deter the rampaging convicts forever, but every minute gained was an additional minute of life.

"Take the ladies to the top of the stairs," Jason then told Butler, pointing to the steps that led to the upper floor of the building. "Wait for me there."

"Where are *you* goin'?" Butler demanded.

"To keep someone else from getting killed, I hope," Mankiller drawled, then set off at a run toward the back of the building's first floor.

He felt a slight smile tug at his lips as he burst through the door of the compound's infirmary. Doctor Sam Fix had tipped over his examination table and was crouched fearfully behind it. He held a small scalpel in his hand.

"You planning to go down *fighting*, Doc?" Jason asked.

The former vet looked rather sheepishly at his ineffectual weapon and shrugged his shoulders.

Spying a black medical bag sitting atop another nearby table, Mankiller grabbed it and tossed it to the slightly befuddled physician. The bounty hunter then quickly stepped over to the medicine cabinet. Finding it locked, he didn't bother to ask Dr. Fix for the key. He simply used the butt of his rifle to shatter the glass.

"Fill that bag, your coat pockets and anything else you can think of," he directed Fix, "with any kind of medicines and supplies you think might be useful once this has all played out.

"Those crazed convicts *will* get in here sooner or later. And when they do, they'll swallow anything they think might get them drunk or dull whatever physical and emotional pains ail 'em.

"When they're done, the only things left to help the truly needy will be whatever you and me carry away now."

With trembling hands, the aging physician began to scoop up vials and bottles, instruments and bandages, dumping them unceremoniously into his medical bag. Passing the bag to Mankiller, he then filled the pockets of his wrinkled white coat before filling both arms.

When he stopped but still stood looking frantically about him, Mankiller stepped behind him and pushed him out of the infirmary.

"That's gonna have to do, Doc," he told Fix, shoving him toward the stairwell.

He himself paused for a moment at the foot of the steps. He could hear pounding at the building's barricaded front doors. At least a few of the rioting convicts had already begun the assault on the place.

"You and the womenfolk stay here for just a minute, Doc," he said after racing up the stairs to the second floor. "You come with me," he told Clem Butler, taking him by the arm and pulling him aside.

The two of them entered the small telegraph room set off to one side to find the current guard manning the station was cowering in one corner of the room; seated on the floor with his legs drawn up to his chest.

The man offered no resistance as Mankiller grabbed him by the collar, lifted him off the floor, pulled him across the room and slammed him into the chair in front of the idle telegraph key.

"Start using that key, man," he ordered the nearly paralyzed guard. "Send a message to that Army garrison Mayhew likes to brag about.

"Apprise them of the dire nature and urgency of the situation here and request their immediate assistance. Make it sound even worse than it is and sign it with the warden's name.

"Then send the word out to every town with a telegraph office within thirty miles of here. Even if they can't send help, they can be alerted to any prisoners who might manage to scale the walls and escape."

Mankiller stopped talking then, but the quivering guard made no effort to start tapping the key. Hesitant to take orders from a man who was himself one of the prison's inmates, the guard instead looked over at Clem Butler for guidance.

"Do what he says, dammit!" Butler snapped.

"And keep on doing it," Jason added. "Until help arrives or some of the cons think to tear down the wires outta here."

He reached down and took the telegrapher's pistol from its holster; the guard offered no resistance, already intently tapping out the necessary messages. Jason handed the pistol to Butler.

"It'll be of more use in your hands than his," he said.

"Lock the door behind me when I leave and block it with anything you can pull in front of it. Conserve your ammunition. Don't shoot unless you have to—and make every shot count."

Mankiller turned to go, but Butler stepped in his path, offering his hand.

"Thanks for savin' my life, mister," the grateful guard said.

"Just returning the favor," Jason replied, accepting the offered hand. He smiled crookedly.

"If I ever get outta this place alive, Clem—I'll buy you a drink."

As he closed the door of the room behind him, Mankiller could hear the telegrapher frantically tapping away at the key of his transmitter. He also heard the bolt being thrown to lock the door.

Chapter 19

"**N**ow it's time to look out for ourselves," Mankiller said as he rejoined Dr. Fix and the three female convicts who were awaiting his return.

Leading the way, he quickly walked to the door leading into Warden Mayhew's spacious office. He didn't bother to knock, but breezed right in.

The portly Mayhew was standing with his back to them, poised before his precious big window and looking down on the ongoing insurrection below.

At the sound of the door being slammed shut, he spun toward them. Fear made his eyes fairly glow and he was holding a small pistol in his right hand.

"We're not here to hurt you," Mankiller said, holding both arms up and out. His words seemed to register, for Mayhew's tense stance relaxed ever so slightly. He still pointed his pistol at Jason and the others.

"Lower your gun," Mankiller said forcefully but not threateningly. Mayhew looked down at the pistol as if only now noticing he was holding it. He tipped its barrel downward.

"And for God's sake—get away from that damned window!"

As if on cue, a bullet plowed through the glass, slanting upward and burrowing into the ceiling. Small shards of glass peppered Mayhew and he appeared to be in shock as he skittered into the nearest corner of the office.

"Give me a hand, Doc," Mankiller said as he bolted the office's thick door. Stepping to one of the file cabinets flanking the portal, he tipped it over so it would further block the door.

With Dr. Fix's assistance, he pushed two other cabinets over and atop the first, creating a heavy and formidable barricade.

Mankiller then walked over to where Warden Mayhew cowered, taking him by one hand and lifting him up. The stunned administrator gave no resistance as Jason led him to the opposite corner of the wide office. Already sitting in that corner was a five-gallon, clay water cistern on a porcelain pedestal.

"Stella," Jason said, turning toward the women, "would you lovely ladies be so kind as to join the warden over here?"

Stella let out a laugh that ended in a lilting snort, then led the others in following Jason's direction.

"Help me move this desk," the bounty hunter then told Dr. Fix.

"Damn!" the physician declared as they slid the oak desk across the floor. "I've treated *horses* that didn't weigh this much!"

"Nothin' but the finest for the warden and his guests," Mankiller drawled. "And the better protection for us it'll be."

The two men pushed, pulled and turned the desk diagonally, in essence turning the corner of the office into a three-sided enclosure. Jason and Dr. Fix climbed over it to join Mayhew and the women.

"Don't just sit there," he said to the warden. "Come here and put your back into it!"

With much straining, the three men succeeded in tipping the desk over so that its thick, solid top now faced outward toward the doorway.

Jason slumped to the floor, breathing heavily and mopping sweat from his brow. Just a few weeks earlier, he probably could have moved the desk and tipped it over without any assistance at all.

But undernourishment and physical abuse had already taken their toll. He had lost weight he couldn't spare, much of it muscle mass; and while he was still probably stronger than most men were, those muscles had noticeably weakened.

"What do we do now?" Warden Mayhew asked, finally gaining a voice.

"Now we wait," Jason replied with a philosophical shrug.

What do we do now?"

Time had been swirling around and past them like a raging flood in the aftermath of the start of the riot. But now that they were mainly safe and away from the center of the conflict, the minutes crawled with agonizing slowness.

A few more bullets crashed through the office window, letting in sounds from the outside. Those sounds included continuing gunfire and screaming—some of it in the form of cries of rage or exaltation and some of it cries of fear and pain.

"Can I get a drink of water?" one of the women asked at last.

"Sure," Jason replied. "Stella, why don't you handle the dispensing of water? Be stingy with it; I hope we'll only be here for a few hours, but we need to treat it like we're in for a long siege. Can you do that?"

"Anything you want, sugar," she said with a smile.

"Ahh," Dr. Fix sighed. "If only we had something a little *stronger* with which to quench the thirst!"

"What about it, Mayhew?" Mankiller asked wickedly. "You keep a little wet sunshine in a desk drawer?"

"Go to hell, gun trash!"

"I'll take that as a '*yes*'!" Dr. Fix exclaimed. Rising to his knees, he began to pillage through the exposed drawers of the overturned desk.

"Ah!" he chuckled, smacking his lips loudly in anticipation as he extracted a nearly full bottle of bonded bourbon from one of the drawers.

"Like the man said—nothin' but the finest for you, eh, Warden Mayhew?" he heckled before tilting the bottle up to his mouth and taking a long, healthy swallow. He then tried to pass it over to Jason, who halted him with an upraised hand.

The fact was that the bounty hunter seldom partook of any spirits other than the occasional beer. In part this was because a man in his line of work and with his reputation could not afford to let his senses be diminished.

And in part it was because the one and only time he had allowed himself to get falling down drunk was as an eighteen-year-old boy in the aftermath of the days-long slaughter at Gettysburg. He had awakened the next morning to discover that his fellow soldiers and drinking buddies had taken advantage of his stuporous condition to have the tell-tale red teardrop tattoo inked onto his cheek while he was passed out.

"Ladies first," was all he told Dr. Fix, motioning toward the three women crouched nearby. Stella Freeman snatched it gratefully and lifted it slightly in Jason's direction.

"To Jason Mankiller," she toasted, "who knows how to treat a girl right!"

The other two female inmates let out a whoop and a holler in response. After each of the women imbibed in a healthy, stinging swallow, they passed the bottle back to Dr. Fix.

No effort was made to include Warden Mayhew in the celebration and he sat off to one side sulking like a petulant child.

"Why are we just sitting here?" he snapped at last. "We should be out there doing something!"

Mayhew may have actually cared a little about the danger to his personal little fiefdom, though far less about the fate of the guards who served him in it. Mostly, he just hated the fact that, here and now at least, it was Mankiller and not he who was in charge.

"How much good do you think you and that little popgun could do?" Jason said disdainfully.

"Think you could rally the troops? Hell," he scoffed, "most of 'em are probably *dead*—which is exactly what you'd be in about a minute if you was to show yourself out there.

"Our best hope is if the guards in the tower can keep it from falling into the hands of the cons—and that the cons are more interested in getting over the wall than they are about getting in *here!*"

For the next couple of hours, they sat in their corner. Dr. Fix had found a pack of confiscated playing cards while he had searched for the bottle of liquor (now long since drained dry) and he and the three women passed the time playing poker for matchsticks.

The sounds of battle continued to wax and wane. At length, a loud noise from downstairs told them the convicts had finally gotten serious about breaking into the administration building.

It took them awhile to get past the bolt and the makeshift barricade Jason and the guard Clem Butler had thrown in front of the doors, but at last the noise of heavy shoes clopping up the stairs carried through the door leading into the warden's office.

At the sound of the first shoulder slamming against the blocked door, Warden Mayhew rose up on his haunches, poking his head above the desk and cocking his pistol. Mankiller grabbed the barrel of the gun and pulled it down.

"Why did you do that?" Mayhew demanded angrily.

"No bigger than that gun is," Mankiller explained in exasperation, "its slugs would probably never penetrate the door—nor hit anybody if they did.

"And do you have any spare *ammunition* in this office of yours?"

"Of course not," Mayhew huffed. "Why would I?"

"You wouldn't," Mankiller replied. "And you can be sure those fellas on the other side of the door know it, too.

"That means all we've got is what's loaded in my rifle and that pistol right now—whereas you can bet the farm that one of the first thing them ol' boys did when they were able was to break into the prison armory.

"That means they're loaded for bear, with every rifle and pistol, every bullet they could lay their hands on." He jerked his head in the direction of the locked portal.

"We've got to hope that the door and the barricade will be enough to keep them out of here. But if they don't, we've got to cling to every last slug we've got—and make sure every shot we take does some damage."

"But like you said," Mayhew declared, the slight quiver in his voice betraying his fearful nervousness, "we've still got the guards in the tower and on the ramparts. I'm confident they can hold these miserable wretches at bay."

"It might be better for us if they *can't*," Mankiller observed.

"What do you mean by that?" the warden demanded shrilly.

"Well, look at it this way," Jason explained calmly. "If they can breach the tower, kill the guards and quiet that Gatling gun—there won't be a blasted thing standing between them and escape.

"If that happens, I have to think most if not all of them will be a sight more interested in leaving this place in their dust than they will be in getting their hands on these women...or on *you*."

Warden Mayhew gulped loudly and dropped back down below the cover of his desk.

Chapter 20

Moments later, the banging and pounding on the warden's office door ceased as the convicts beyond apparently reached the conclusion that it was unbreachable in this fashion. Footsteps could be heard moving away.

"They're gone!" Stella Freeman sighed in relief.

"They'll be back," Jason warned; but he reached out to squeeze the woman's hand and give her a reassuring smile.

Exactly as Mankiller had anticipated, a short time later they heard a new, sharper sound. The convicts had found an *ax*, and were using it on the thick door.

It took nearly a quarter of an hour, with occasional breaks as one inmate spelled another in wielding the heavy ax, but eventually splinters of wood could be seen flying from one spot in the door.

"Stay down," Mankiller ordered. Rising to his knees with his elbows supported by the desk, he sighted his rifle on the spot where the ax was chipping away.

When the blade of the ax finally fully penetrated the door, Jason still held his fire. After a hole bigger around than a man's fist was finally achieved, the ax blows momentarily stopped—and one of the inmates beyond was foolish enough to place his face against the hole to spy inside the office.

That's when Mankiller pulled the trigger.

There was no scream of pain—his target, struck right between the eyes as the slug burrowed its way deeply into his brain, was dead before his vocal chords could make a sound. The body was flung back against his cohorts, who scrambled out of the way. The jumble of their voices as they conferred on their next course of action carried through the hole in the door.

"The *Army's* on its way here, boys!" Mankiller shouted out to them, and they all instantly went silent.

"You'd be better served trying to find a way *out* of this prison than *in* to this room. The only thing you'll find in here is your own death! And living's always better than dying!"

The muttering of voices in conflict flowed clearly to the bounty hunter's ears. A hand holding a pistol suddenly thrust through the hole in the door; a shot blindly fired whined harmlessly across the room.

At first sight of the hand holding the revolver, Mankiller had smartly snapped the butt of his rifle up against his shoulder. His own subsequent shot flew true, penetrating the hand and causing it to drop the pistol. The accompanying cry of pain was nearly lost in the sound of footsteps as the convicts fled back away from the barricaded door.

Mankiller seized that moment of their confusion to jump up and leap over the desk behind which he had been crouched. He raced across the room to snatch up the fallen pistol before quickly jumping back behind the cover of the desk, rejoining the others.

"Do you know how to use a gun, Doc?" he asked Dr. Fix.

The aged physician licked his lips nervously and rubbed sweaty hands up and down his white coat. He had partaken of more of the liquor than had the others, and his wide eyes were slightly bloodshot.

"I've had to put a horse down a time or two," he said. "But I doubt I could hit anything that was more than two feet away."

"How about you, Stella?" Jason asked of the former madam.

"Can I use a gun?" she scoffed. "Did you forget what put me *in* this little slice of Heaven?"

Mankiller smiled and handed her the pistol.

"At most you've got five bullets in there," he reminded her. "You might want to save the last one."

"For myself?" she asked grimly.

"Naw. You'll be fine. It's for *him*," Jason replied, nodding toward the cowering warden. Mayhew expelled a fearful gasp, while Stella and the two other women joined in laughter.

"God help us all," Dr. Fix said in mock reverence, rolling his eyes skyward.

A long, tense wait followed. All save Mayhew remained stoic. Mankiller said little; he never expressed his concern that the convicts might eventually realize that they could gain entry into the warden's office reasonably safely by simply dousing the outer surface of the door in kerosene and setting it ablaze.

After hours more of relative silence, the sounds of heavy gunfire scorched the air, accompanied by the clopping of horses' hooves. Again risking leaving the safety of the overturned desk, Mankiller scurried over to the office window and cautiously raised his head to peer outside.

"The Army's here!" he informed the others.

He thought it best that they remain in their place of cover for now, and all agreed. The heaviest firing continued for only a short time, with sporadic shots following for half an hour thereafter.

A pounding sound rose on the inner stairway of the administration building, and to Jason's sharp ears the noise seemed to come from the heels of boots rather than shoes. Loud banging—probably against the locked door of the telegraph room—was followed by indiscernible shouts.

Seconds later, a similar knocking was heard at the door leading into Warden Mayhew's office.

"Who is it?" Mankiller called out.

"Captain Emil Jannings," a strong voice replied from the other side of the portal. "Of the U.S. 9th Cavalry."

"You know him?" Jason asked Mayhew. The warden nodded rapidly.

"Stand down," the bounty hunter called out to the soldier. "We're all friendlies in here, but it'll take us a minute to remove the barricades."

With assistance from Dr. Fix (the warden not deigning to join in), Mankiller pulled the filing cabinets from before the door and threw open the bolt.

Led by the captain, half a dozen soldiers rushed into the large room. Unmindful of Jason's assurances, their rifles were raised and ready for use. Bringing up the rear of the rescuers was the guard Clem Butler and the young telegrapher who had summoned the cavalry; neither of them appeared any the worse for wear.

"Warden Mayhew," Captain Jannings respectfully addressed the besieged superintendent, gracing him with a casual salute.

"Most of the prisoners have surrendered and my men are seeing to it that they are once again confined to their cells."

"Thank you, Captain," Mayhew said. "Fine work." Now that he was no longer in personal danger, the warden's air of arrogant confidence was quickly returning.

"A few appear to have gotten over the walls," Captain Jannings continued. "I'll send patrols after them, given that I fear these two men and those who managed to hold the front tower may be the only surviving guards you now have. We may be bolstered by posses from some of the nearest towns."

"The escapees should be fairly easy to spot, given the terrain and the distinctive gray prison garb they'll be wearing."

"You might tell your boys to keep a wary eye out for anyone in a guard's uniform, too," Mankiller suggested.

"Why's that?" the cavalry officer asked.

"Some of the inmates might have thought to strip dead guards of their clothes, figuring they'd be less apt to be spotted as prisoners that way."

"He could be right, Cap'n," a sergeant offered. "I did notice a coupla bodies down in the yard who'd been stripped down to their flannels."

"Very well. Warn our men of that possibility; tell them to take no chances. Pass the word along to any civilian posses who might show up." As the soldiers moved to comply, Warden Mayhew turned to face Mankiller.

"I think you'd better hand over that rifle now," he said sternly.

Jason shrugged. "Sure. No need for it now," he said as he complied with the order. Mayhew accepted the rifle with his left hand, then raised his right—pointing the pistol he still held in it at the bounty hunter's midsection.

"Guard," Mayhew said to Clem Butler while not taking his eyes off Mankiller, "take this man into custody. He's earned another week in the hole."

"What?" Jason exclaimed, dumbfounded.

"What do you mean, Warden?" Butler asked, equally puzzled. "This man saved all our bacon!"

"Did he?" Mayhew replied icily. "For all we know, he masterminded this whole thing. When it then got out of control, he did what he had to do to save his own skin. This was the best place to do it.

"It's undeniable that he seized control of my office at gunpoint." He smiled unctuously. "I saw him kill a fellow inmate with my own eyes. He's *lucky* I don't have the lash put to him as well."

"This just don't seem right, sir," Butler demurred.

"I didn't ask for your opinion, mister!" Mayhew snapped. "Maybe you'd like to *share* what little space there is in the hole with him."

"It's all right, Clem," Mankiller said, nodding at the guard. "It's best to do what he says."

He glanced at Captain Jannings, but it was clear the cavalry officer felt he had no authority to assert himself into a matter of punishment being meted out to a prisoner.

"Just a minute," Stella Freeman said. Stepping forward boldly, and before anyone could stop her, she threw her arms around Jason's neck and gave him a deep and passionate kiss.

"We'll be back in our birdcage long before you get out of the hole," she said, explaining her actions, "so I figured this might be my last and only chance to do that!"

"Get him out of here, God-dammit!" Warden Mayhew shrieked shrilly.

Jason smiled at Stella and gave her a wink as Clem Butler took hold of his arm and led him away.

He chuckled aloud when he and Butler reached the entrance to the hole. A wide piece of broken board was leaning against the steel door of the pit. On the board, one of the inmates (Ira Morgan, perhaps?) had decided to have a little fun in the midst of the riot by crudely painting a two-word epithet.

Mankiller's Hole.

Chapter 21

When the door leading into the pit was flung open, momentarily blinding Jason Mankiller with the swath of sunlight it allowed to enter, he honestly could not have told you how long he had been inside this time. He was fairly sure it had been more than a week, though.

When hands reached out of the light to grab him and pull him out of the shadows, he feared it might be only to stand him up before a firing squad.

Blinking and shielding his hands with one cupped hand, his vision gradually returned. When it did, he was able to see several guards. Some of their faces were new to him: doubtless replacements quickly hired to replace those killed in the recent riot.

Both they and a goodly number of his fellow inmates who were also standing close by eyed him with looks that ranged from dismay and pity to disdain and contempt. To his surprise, one of the onlookers was smiling at him.

It was his attorney, Carter Frain!

Hands outstretched, Jason took a few tentative steps before his legs buckled and he fell into the waiting arms of Frain, who held him upright. The lawyer winced at the stench emanating from the emaciated body Frain knew had been robust and healthy not long before.

"I've got good news, Jason," Frain told him.

"I could use some," Mankiller replied in a hoarse whisper.

"I finally got in to see the territorial governor a few days ago. I presented him with the sworn affidavits, the character references, records on the men you killed as well as on Mayor Owens and Marshal Thorpe.

"Realistically speaking, at most I was hoping it would be enough for him to order a new trial for you at a new venue.

"But then he received a copy of a field report from an Army field officer named Jannings, including testimony from one of the prison guards. It laid out the basic details of what happened here with the prisoner riot—and the role you played in quelling it."

"You said something about 'good news'?" Mankiller prompted; he was finding it difficult to remain fully alert or to remain standing.

"He issued you a *pardon*, Jason," Frain said, a sympathetic smile splitting his face. "A full pardon!"

Jason blinked several times. "Does that...does that mean I'm *free*?" he asked hesitantly.

"Free and clear," Frain cheerfully replied. "A copy of the pardon is sitting on the warden's desk, I've got a wagon waiting for us—and I'm taking you out of this house of pestilence right now!"

He took hold of Mankiller's arm and started to walk toward the waiting conveyance. Several of the convicts and a few of the guards were intently watching them, and when Jason saw one particular face he paused.

"Just a minute, Carter," he told his attorney. With halting steps, he turned and walked toward Ira Morgan, his sole surviving cellmate.

"Looks like you're gonna be top dog again, Ira," Mankiller said, taking the convict's hand. As he did, he pressed into its palm all the money he had accumulated during his time in Pima.

"I've got plenty of money on the outside," Jason said in response to a quizzical look from the convict. "And I'm free." He patted Morgan on the shoulder.

"You need this more than I do, Ira. You take care...and give long thought to that idea you had about going straight. So long."

"So long, Top Dog," Morgan replied, smiling tightly.

Mankiller slowly made his way to the small buckboard Carter Frain had rented for transport. The lawyer was standing beside it, patiently waiting for him.

"I've got your personal belongings in the back," the attorney told him. "I figure first chance we get we'll find a place where you can wash the stink of this place off you and change into your own clothes."

"And get a good meal?" Jason said hopefully.

"The biggest and best available," Frain assured him.

"Just another minute more, all right?" Mankiller said, leaning over the bed of the buckboard. Frain noted he appeared to be making sure all his belongings were there, going so far as to fish down into one of his boots. Still fighting to maintain his balance, the bounty hunter turned and approached one of the guards standing a little ways apart from the others.

It was Clem Butler, the only one among all the guards who had made an effort to treat Jason fairly. As he had done with Ira, Mankiller took Butler's hand and pressed a thick wad of cash into it.

"For that drink I promised you," Jason said with a smile.

Butler quickly closed his fingers around the bills, lest someone see and report him and he have it taken away by the warden.

"I can tell by the feel of it," he said softly, "that there's a lot more there than the price of a drink."

"It's all yours to keep, Clem," Jason said with conviction, "and not nearly enough to pay back what I owe you. I do have one more favor to ask of you, though."

"Name it. If it's in my power, I'll do it."

"I'd appreciate it if you'd try as best you can to keep an eye out for Stella Freeman; make the time she has left here a little easier."

"Consider it done, bounty man," Butler said firmly. "I'll make sure no one lays a hand on her."

"We need to get out of here, Jason," Carter Frain said, motioning toward the buckboard.

"Coming." Mankiller gave Clem Butler a short nod. "Thanks again." The guard returned the nod.

"I'm a little surprised the warden ain't here to see me off," Jason said as Frain offered him a steadying hand.

"He may have bigger things on his mind," the lawyer replied. "Before I left the capital, the governor had already ordered an inquiry into the events surrounding the attempted mass break-out here.

"I don't know how you survived it, Jason. It must have been a goddamned bloodbath for convicts and guards alike. One of the few surviving guards admitted to me that the size of their cemetery here has *doubled*.

"Questions about how the warden runs this place have also been raised, naturally. Rumors are circulating that Mayhew was already under investigation in the matter of certain…financial improprieties.

"If there's any justice in this world," Frain concluded, "the corrupt bastard will end up an inmate here himself!"

"I'd like to be there when they slam the cell door on his fat ass," Jason added.

He let Frain assist him in climbing up to the box of the buckboard, but before he took a seat he stole a glance up at the second floor of the prison's administration building.

Warden Mayhew was standing framed by the shattered remnants of his beloved office window, looking down at the main yard.

Mankiller caught his eyes, glared up at him coldly. This silent duel of wills lasted for a full minute before Mayhew broke off eye contact and stepped back away from the window and out of sight.

As the buckboard, with Carter Frain holding the reins, rolled through the open prison gates and out onto the flat prairie, Mankiller drew in a sharp, deep breath.

"By God," he said, chuckling softly, "outside of those walls, even the *air* feels cleaner!"

Chapter 22

Jason Mankiller felt a bit like a resident in one of those picturesque nursing homes reserved for old soldiers.

He was in fact once more in the only place he had thought of as truly being his home since he'd left the farm in Ohio shortly after his father died in the wake of the end of the War Between the States.

Fort Rogers, Texas had become quite a thriving and growing community, and he owned a good piece of it thanks to wise investing of the money that came to him by way of the outlaw bounties he regularly collected.

"Blood money" some called it; though not to his face. Word had spread far and wide that he only pursued owlhoots who were wanted *Dead or Alive*—and that he never bothered with the "alive" part.

His own belief was that the money he collected was as green as any other; and he'd yet to encounter anyone whose scruples were such that they refused to accept it from him in exchange for goods or services.

At the moment, he was content to do no more than sit and sway in the padded rocking chair parked on the sidewalk running in front of the *Bloody Eye* saloon.

He was half owner of the establishment; kept a suite of rooms upstairs there as his personal residence. But Jason still thought of it as really being Sam Dobbins' place and was content to let the middle-aged man run it in any way he saw fit.

The only time he had disagreed with Sam, and let him know it, was in the naming of the saloon. Originally known as the *Last Stand*, Sam had felt it would benefit financially from being more closely and full connected to Mankiller. The large sign above the front bore the new name and a painting of an eye crying a drop of blood.

Jason was embarrassed by it, thought it too crass and commercial. But he had acceded to Sam's wishes and had to admit, if only to himself, that the saloon's profits had increased largely because of his association with it.

Though it was not a particularly cold day for the fall, Jason sat with a thick comforter covering his lap and legs. Jane Starr had insisted upon him taking no chances of catching a chill and was at this very moment hovering over him; making sure the edges of the comforter were tucked snugly under him.

"Would you quit making such a fuss, woman?" he groused; though his seeming annoyance was pure pretense.

"I've been here for a week now; people are gonna think I'm some kind of invalid!"

"Well, you damned near *were!*" she snapped back, fists on her hips and a scowl on her face.

"If we hadn't gotten you out of that rat's nest when we did," she continued, and Jason now heard a slight catch in her voice, "you might be *dead.*"

Smiling tenderly, he reached out to her and she took his hand, fighting back tears.

"But you *did* get me out," he reminded her. "And I'm gonna be just fine."

"In time, maybe," she replied warily. "Once you've had a chance to heal and put some meat back on those bones."

"That shouldn't take long, darlin'—given the way you've been feeding me."

"Can I get you something now?"

"No; I'm good. Just sit with me." She gladly complied, pulling a nearby ladder-back chair closer to him and dropping down onto it.

"Tell me more about your New York adventures," he said.

"Oh, I'm sure they'd just bore you."

"Not in the least. Did you see the ocean? What was it like?"

"Oh, I did," she said, lightly clapping her hands together. "I spent an entire day there. It's so *big*, Jason. I didn't know there was so much water in all the world. It makes the Mississippi River look like a rain puddle by comparison. When the waves come to shore, they look like the jaws of some giant monster that's trying to eat the earth." She clapped a hand to her mouth for a moment before continuing.

"But you wouldn't believe how *indecent* some of the women at the beach look. The bathing costumes they wear leave nearly *half* their leg exposed!" She shook her head sternly.

"I don't intend to expose that much flesh on my wedding night!"

Jason burst into laughter that ended only when it descended into a coughing spell. Jane joined in the laughter, but leaned forward to make sure he hadn't loosened the comforter.

"I hope you don't intend to put *me* in one of those—what'd you call 'em?—bathing costumes in one of your stories about me," Jason said with a smile.

"Never," she replied. "You're too busy killing outlaws and red Indians to participate in such foolishness!"

"Yeah," he agreed in the spirit of her facetious remark. "It's got so I've barely got time for a Saturday night bath!"

"I know better than that," Jane said, then sniffed in an exaggerated manner. "In fact, is that *lavender* I smell on you?"

"You oughtta know, woman. *You're* the one what poured it into my bath water!"

She smiled in response, but it quickly faded. "I wanted to get the smell of that horrible place off of you as quickly as possible.

"And I still cringe at the look of your back."

"Aww, it hardly hurts at all now. Doc Crotty's been checking in on me and he says the wounds seem to be healing real good."

"What about the wounds he can't see?" Jane asked pointedly. "The ones that no tincture or ointment can heal?"

"Physician, heal thyself," the bounty hunter quoted back to her. "It's up to me to soothe those ills."

"Which means you're going to kill more people," she said, in sorrow rather than judgement.

"Which means I'm gonna do what I feel I have to do," he replied, in a voice Jane was perceptive enough to know meant this particular thread of conversation was at an end.

"Tell me more about New York," he said, drawing himself up straighter in the rocker. "About your writing." Jane knew that even though his education consisted entirely of what he had received at the hands of his sainted mother before her death, Jason had a true love of reading and held high regard and pride in Jane's literary talents.

"It's funny," she observed. "I really loved it all: the lights, the music, the theater. The hustle and bustle.

"But after a few days, I noticed that in the moments before I drifted off to sleep, I was thinking more and more about being back here in the West. I love it, too. The open spaces, the mountains, the fresh air." She reached out and squeezed his left hand.

"The people."

"Maybe you can kill two birds with one stone," Jason suggested. He slowly waved a hand in the air before his eyes.

"Write a book called 'Jason Mankiller in New York'." He winked at her. "'Or—a fish out of water'."

"You joke," she said, wagging a finger at him. "But my publisher already suggested the very same thing for real!"

"Then it must be a good idea," Jason joked. "Just remember…no bathing costumes."

"Cross my heart," she replied. She then gasped slightly as a new thought popped into her head.

"I almost forgot. I may be doing even *more* writing as a result of my trip to New York!"

"Oh? How's come?"

Jane tilted her head slightly upward, affecting a feigned air of snobbishness. "I'll have you know that I am now the client of a literary agent there!"

"Well, la-dee-da," he joshed. "Pardon my ignorance, but what does that mean, exactly?"

"It means he represents me and my work in front of publishers. In the time I was there, he took me around to several newspapers and the offices of nearly half a dozen magazine publishers.

"Come to find out, the folks back East can't get enough of stories about the wild frontier. True stories or otherwise. The papers and periodicals go through new material like a steamboat goes through kindling.

"And not just stories about gunfighters. All kinds of adventures: even travelogues, too. And just about anything having to do with the 'savages'."

"Red ones or white ones?" Jason asked.

She laughed. "Both!"

"Sounds like you're gonna be as busy with pen and paper as you want to be," Jason observed.

"It does, doesn't it? I even have an offer to write something for *Harper's Weekly*!"

"It doesn't get much bigger than that. You've done yourself proud, girl," he said sincerely. "If it keeps up, you might even be able to give up dealing faro."

"I mostly already have," she told him. "I'm still traveling the circuit with Cash, but I leave most of the gambling to him."

"Is he all right with that?"

"He seems to be. A fresh deck of cards and an inviting seat at a poker table seem to be all it takes to keep him happy."

"I'm sure having you along makes him even happier."

"I suppose. He certainly needs *someone* along, to keep him out of the worst of trouble."

"I'd say he's got a good partner, then."

Both of them looked to one side at the sound of approaching footsteps on the wooden sidewalk. Jane didn't notice that in the same instant Jason's right hand dipped under the comforter on his lap—instinctively reaching for a pistol that at Jane's insistence was still up in his rooms.

His body relaxed instantly as he recognized his attorney, Carter Frain. The lawyer smiled and tipped his hat to Jane by way of greeting.

"May I have a few minutes of your time, Jason?" he asked politely.

"Just not *too* much," Jane spoke before Mankiller could open his mouth. She rose from her chair, offering it to Frain.

"He doesn't want to admit it—or for anyone else to even know," she said, "but he still tires rather easily."

"Anything else you care to tell the man, Mother?" Jason drawled.

"Yes," she replied, sticking her tongue out at him before turning toward Frain. "Make sure he stays covered up. I don't want him catching a chill."

"Yes, ma'am," Frain replied meekly.

"Supper tonight?" she asked Jason, resting a hand on his shoulder.

"Yes, ma'am," he returned, mimicking Carter.

"From the little I've seen of that woman," Frain said after Jane had entered the saloon and was safely out of earshot, "she reminds me of a *cat*. I suspect she could curl up in your lap and purr one minute —

"And claw your eyes out the next!"

"That's why I try my damnedest always to stay on her good side," Jason observed, smiling and shaking his head.

"And how are things with you, Carter?"

"Couldn't be better, Jason. Couldn't be better. Following your advice and bringing my wife Polly here was the smartest thing I've done since I married her."

"Does the little woman share that opinion?"

"Absolutely. We've leased a nice little cottage just a couple blocks from the courthouse, with the option of buying. Between shopping for furniture and hanging new drapes, she's been the happiest I've seen her in ages."

"Good, good."

"Once we're fully settled in, you'll have to come to supper, of course."

Mankiller smiled. "Being a man who's gone hungry a time or two in his day, I seldom turn down an invitation to free grub."

The lawyer's face suddenly grew serious. "From the way you looked the day we drove out of Pima, I'd say they'd done more than just let you go hungry. They'd damned near starved and beaten you to death." He laid a solicitous hand on Mankiller's knee.

"I'm sorry I didn't get you out of there quicker, Jason."

Mankiller dismissed the thought with a wave of his hand. "You put that idea right outta your mind, Carter. Y'hear? The deck was stacked against us from the get-go and you still managed to pull my ashes outta the fire."

"But not before your ashes got good and scorched," Frain replied with dark humor.

"I'm getting better by the day," Jason assured him, then rushed to move onward. "Tell me more about you and the missus."

"Well, let's see. Like I said, we're settling in nicely. We hadn't been here a week before ladies from the church Welcoming Committee showed up on our doorstep with pies and the like. Polly's already become friends with several of them.

"And I'm doing well professionally as well. I've had several small cases already and one of the larger local ranchers just put me on retainer."

"I had a feeling you'd do right well here," Mankiller commented. "Sooner or later, just about everybody has need of a good lawyer."

Frain raised an eyebrow. "Yes, well…I strongly suspect that a good deal of the interest in me comes because of my association with *you*, Jason."

"Pshaw!" the bounty hunter scoffed, rocking slightly faster. "If anything, being linked to an incorrigible like me would *hurt* a man in your line of work."

"I think we both know that's not true," Frain replied. "I discovered very quickly that you've got a lot of friends in this town."

"Yeah," Jason admitted. "They're good people, most of 'em."

The lawyer smiled mischievously. "One person doesn't seem to think too highly of you, though…the editor of the *Diligence*." He was referring to the town's weekly newspaper.

Mankiller barked out a laugh. "Ezra Vail! Yessir, the man would gladly have me run outta town on a rail—and provide the tar and feathers himself!"

"How come? What's he got against you?"

Jason shrugged. "Guess he just don't like my kind."

"What kind is that?"

"The kind he thinks brings trouble. The kind a town would be better off without."

"You sound almost like you think he's right."

"Maybe he is, Carter. I don't know." It was clear he meant to say no more on the subject.

"You said one of the ranchers put you on retainer?" he asked.

"That's right."

"What does that mean, exactly?"

"Basically, it means he sort of put me on his payroll. He pays me a set fee every month and in return I agree to represent his interests whenever he might have need of my services."

"Hmm." Mankiller mentally chewed on that thought for a moment. "And can a lawyer have more than one of these…retainers?"

"Certainly. Within the reasonable limits of his time and capabilities, of course."

"Uh-huh." Again the rocking increased in tempo. "Would you be willing to make such an arrangement with me?"

"Seriously?"

"Sure. Given my line of work and the number of irons I've got in the fire, I think it might be wise to have a good ash hauler on call."

"You *do* seem like someone for whom having a lawyer available day and night would be wise." Frain chuckled.

"It would be a pleasure, Jason. Just come by my office any time you feel up to it."

"I'll do that. You can bank on it."

The attorney snapped his fingers. "I almost forgot; one of the reasons I dropped in on you was to tell you that I've received fresh news about my old town of Low Water."

Mankiller stopped rocking and his ears perked up. "Yeah?"

"Yes. Naturally enough, word of your release from Pima reached the townsfolk there in no time. That sparked an even larger and rather more panicked exodus than before.

"According to my source…the place is practically a ghost town now."

"Good," Mankiller replied in a voice that was low but menacing. "Even though they all deserve to burn…I'd just as soon nobody was inside the buildings when I put the torch to 'em."

Carter Frain squirmed uncomfortably in his chair. "I have to tell you, Jason—I was hoping you'd given up on that idea."

The bounty hunter fixed him with a baleful glare that made the lawyer even more uncomfortable.

"Maybe this way, no matter where those folks finally light, they'll remember what they done to me and prob'ly others…and will do their best never to let it happen again." He saw that Frain still looked skeptical.

"Let me ask you this, Carter. Is there anybody else who'll make sure the worst elements of that blight on the face of the earth are brought to justice?

"If so…I might be willing to let it go."

Frain shook his head. "I'm afraid there isn't. I've spoken to representatives from the U.S. Marshals Office. I was again told that the mayor and marshal were lawfully appointed by the people of Low Water. And it would be hard to prove they willfully framed you.

"Even the fact that Owens and Thorpe are wanted men themselves doesn't seem to carry much weight. Not enough to get outside law to act, anyway."

"Then they'll just get away with all their crimes," Jason replied. "Unless I do something about it myself."

"You're in no shape for such an undertaking," Frain reminded him.

"I was hoping you'd given up on that idea."

"No," Mankiller agreed, looking down at his still thin arms and flexing his fingers. "Not today. Not tomorrow.

"But soon enough I will be. And when I am…I mean to wipe that town off the face of the earth."

Chapter 23

Strangely, given the ominous pronouncement he had just made, Mankiller now smiled slightly.

"I know you're not yet officially on…what was that word, Carter?"

"Retainer," the lawyer prompted.

"Yeah. That's got a nice, respectable ring to it. But I was wondering if you might take on another job for me, soon as you can."

"You know I'd be glad to. What is it?"

"Something I'd kinda like to keep just between the two of us. Man-to-man, you might say."

"Something of a…personal nature?"

"I guess you could say that." With two fingers of one hand, Mankiller motioned for his attorney to lean in closer.

He wanted no one else to hear the words that passed between them.

That night found the bounty hunter returned to his rocking chair outside the Bloody Eye saloon, sated by a most satisfying supper. With the sun now long down, there was a decided chill in the air, making him glad he had deferred to Jane Starr's instructions that he again employ his comforter. He even had it pulled up under his armpits.

The air was just cold enough to bring a bracing sting to his lungs as he breathed it in. During his convalescence, he had also discovered how entertaining it could be simply to watch and observe other people and their behavior. He'd been pleasantly surprised at the handful of citizens who had taken the time to give him greetings and wish him well.

His head swiveled as the nearby batwing doors of the saloon swung open and a familiar figure stepped out onto the board sidewalk.

It was his friend, Cash Carpenter. As was his wont, the gambler was dressed impeccably. Offsetting his pale blue suit was a bright, red, silk vest. The glow cast by the match he brought close to light a cigarette revealed handsome features. After exhaling a puff of smoke, he inhaled deeply.

Glancing over at the seated bounty hunter, Cash smiled. He noted that, even while in recovery, Mankiller held to his almost ritualistic dexterity exercise; Cash could see a single blue poker chip being passed from finger to finger atop Mankiller's left hand.

"The cards turn against you, Cash?" Jason inquired.

"Quite the contrary," the gambler replied in his soft Southern drawl.

"I've actually been on quite the winning streak. But from time to time I feel the need to stretch the legs and replace the miasma of booze, tobacco and desperation in my lungs with a draught of fresh air."

"Aren't you afraid that interrupting a streak might end it?"

"Not at all, Jason. Unlike some of my lesser compatriots who play the pasteboards, I realize that skill has as much to do with winning as does luck.

"A brief respite won't diminish my skills. And Lady Luck comes and goes on her own capricious timetable."

"Yeah," Mankiller concurred. "But sometimes it takes awhile for a fella to realize she's packed her bags and left town."

"Indeed. All the more reason to wine and dine her to the maximum when she does grace you with her presence."

"Do you ever set a little something aside during the times when you're flush?" Jason asked.

"Heavens no!" Cash replied, feigning shock. "As a wise man who was doubtless a gambler himself so aptly put it: Eat, drink and be merry—for tomorrow you may *die*."

"Is that Jane's philosophy, too?" the bounty hunter casually inquired.

"The poor child is still prone to bad habits," Cash said lightly. "I recently discovered she has actually opened a small *savings account* at the bank!"

"Shocking," Jason said dryly.

"Appalling was the word I used. Sometimes I fear she's picking up such strange habits from you. You're a bad influence on the girl, Jason. There's no question about it."

"I've had worse things said about me."

"As have I," Cash said, not bothering to conceal a broad grin. "And no doubt we both deserve it."

"No doubt." He glanced up at Cash. "Still…it might be a sign that she's looking for a little more stability in her life."

"Whatever for?" the gambler rejoined. "She gets something far better by sticking with me: *excitement!*"

Any reply Mankiller made was drowned out by the sound of raucous singing from a pair of drovers staggering arm-in-arm down the sidewalk. Though headed for the Bloody Eye, it was clear they had already made stops at some of the town's many other drinking establishments.

So deeply were they in their cups that the one on the inside tripped slightly over Mankiller's feet.

"Get yer clodhoppers outta the way!" the drover yelled, his speech greatly slurred. "I coulda broke my neck!"

"My apologies, mister," Jason said, drawing his feet in closer to the front of his rocking chair.

"I don't want no 'pologies," the trail hand snapped. "I wanna break yer damned nose!"

"There's no need for that, friend," Cash Carpenter said, holding up a placating hand. "Why don't you come inside, and I'll spot you and your partner to a drink?"

"You stay outta this, fancy boy!" the drunken drover said, pointing a threatening finger at the gambler. "Else I'll bust yer nose, too!" He then turned his rheumy eyes back toward Jason.

"How come yer all covered up like a grandma? You sick?" He leaned in closer. "You a *lunger*, mebbe?"

"No." It was just a one-word response, but had the impaired cowboy been sober, he'd have recognized the cold steel in it.

The eyes of the second drover narrowed as he took a close look at the man in the rocking chair. Some spark of recognition flared briefly in his addled brain, and he tugged at his friend's arm.

"C'mon, hoss," he pleaded. "Leave him be and let's go take t'other gent up on his offer of a free drink. I'm thirsty."

His companion roughly shook him off. "We'll drink after I put this feller in his place." His hand fell menacingly to the butt of his holstered pistol.

Jason raised his head, only now bothering actually to look the drunk in the eye. His left hand flipped the comforter off his lap, revealing the cross draw holster he now wore.

In defiance of Jane Starr's wishes, and knowing the night often brought out the worst sort of creatures, he had armed himself before taking his evening rest in the rocker. The fingers of his right hand began to lightly tap the grip of his Colt's pistol.

"Mankiller!" the less intemperate of the two drovers gasped; now fully able to see the bounty hunter's countenance and the red teardrop tattoo it sported.

The sound of the dreaded name did more to sober his belligerent comrade than would have a pot of black coffee. Wide eyes looked at the pistol protruding from the cross draw holster, then flicked to Jason's face. He, too, now saw the tear drop tattoo and he gulped so loudly it sounded as if he was trying to swallow his own Adam's apple.

"I—I guess no real harm was done," he stammered. "Might be best if we just forget all about it."

"I'd appreciate that," Mankiller said calmly.

This time the drover offered no resistance when his friend again grabbed his arm and dragged him into the beckoning arms of the Bloody Eye.

Jason's head swiveled to follow their progress. As he did, he saw that Cash Carpenter had taken a step back into the shadows. It was not so dark, though, that Mankiller could not see that the gambler's right hand was slid under the lapel of his suit coat.

Jason had no doubt that the hand rested on the butt of the short-barreled .38 Cash wore in a shoulder holster—and that Cash had intended to use it if need be in defense of his friend. The eyes of the bounty hunter and of the gambler met in silent communion.

Then both men began to laugh.

Chapter 24

Friday afternoon of that week found Jason Mankiller once again on his now familiar perch outside the front doors of the Bloody Eye.

Not that he was being lazy: far from it. Every day, at least twice a day, he engaged in longer and longer walks to restore the strength in his legs. Usually he walked alone. This bothered Jane Starr, who feared this left him as a too enticing target for anyone with evil intent. Whenever possible, she walked with him; ignoring his declaration that this would simply give any potential assassin *two* targets.

Neither he nor Jane had arisen early enough for a morning stroll on this day. They'd had rather a late night of it, beginning with attending a performance at the town's Grand Comique Theater (the establishment co-owned by Mankiller and Sam Dobbins).

The theater's current offering was a rip-roaring melodrama appropriately entitled: *Six Buckets of Blood –or– Who Stabbed the Captain?*

This was followed by a late supper at the Hansen House and a few turns around the dance floor at one of the local hurdy-gurdy parlors.

It had been well past midnight when they returned to the Bloody Eye, where Jane had decided to keep Cash Carpenter company at his usual poker game while Jason ascended to his rooms and quickly fell into a deep and restorative sleep.

A smile now creased his weathered face as one of his younger friends approached from up the street. It was the young newsboy Toby Applegate, a poor but ambitious and hard-working lad Mankiller had taken under his wing.

"Morning, Toby," he said in greeting.

"Mornin', Mr. Mankiller."

Jason frowned slightly. "We're business associates, remember, Toby? That means you can call me Jason."

"Yes, sir."

Mankiller chuckled. To help the fatherless boy and his family, the bounty hunter had devised a means of slipping him a little extra money he knew Toby would otherwise be too proud to accept. Jason paid him a little extra to insure that Toby always promptly provided him with a copy of the latest edition of the newspaper whenever Jason was in town.

He was slightly puzzled, though, when Toby pulled a copy of the paper out of the bundle under his left arm and presented it to Jason.

"What's this?" he asked the boy.

"Latest edition," Toby replied. "Hot off the presses, just like you want."

"I don't understand, son. Didn't you already sell me a copy of the *Diligence* just a few days ago?"

"Sure did," the newsboy acknowledged. "Mr. Vail says that with the town growin' the way it is, there's more news to report and more people who want to read it.

"So now he puts out a new edition *twice* a week."

"Seems to be a mite thicker, even," Jason observed as he accepted a copy from Toby.

As was his habit, he then tossed a nickel to the boy: two cents for the newspaper and three cents as a tip. This time, though, he noticed a certain hesitance as Toby stared down at the coin.

"Something wrong, son?" the bounty hunter asked.

"No, sir. A nickel's just right." Closing his hand around the coin, Toby turned to leave.

"Hold on," Jason called after him. Only now had he glimpsed at the masthead on the front page of the paper.

There, the price was marked "5 cents."

"Is this right, Toby?" he asked, holding up the paper and tapping it with one hand.

"Yeah. What with there bein' more pages, Mr. Vail figgered he oughtta raise the price."

"Hmm. Seems to me like he's just liable to run off readers by charging that much," Jason opined, then shrugged. "But it's his newspaper; I reckon he can charge as much as he likes."

"Does that mean you don't wanna buy it no more?" Toby asked.

"Not a'tall. A man's got to keep up with the latest happenings. You keep on making sure I get every edition." He then fished another nickel out of his pocket and tossed it to the smiling newsboy.

"One other thing, Toby, long as you're here. That publisher fella—your Mr. Vail—does he treat you all right?"

"Just fine," the boy assured him. "He's even started teachin' me how to set type."

"That's good. He might learn you a good profession for when you get older."

"Yeah." Toby scuffed the dirt street with the toe of one well-worn shoe. "He still don't cotton much ta *you*, though, Jason. Just take a look at his front page editorial."

Mankiller chuckled lightly and shook his head as he scanned the headline above said editorial.

The Serpent Returns to Our Garden.

Ezra Vail was in fine fettle, his fiery hyperbole soaring to new heights as he bemoaned Jason's recent return to the fair city of Fort Rogers. He again expressed his strongly held view that the bounty hunter should not be allowed within the city limits. He went so far as to warn that Mankiller's mere presence there might literally bring the wrath of God down upon the town and its citizenry.

The editorial bolstered his opinion with a skewed and highly inaccurate recounting of Jason's close encounter with the two drunken cowhands a few nights earlier. In this version of the incident, Mankiller had capriciously and violently chosen to terrorize an innocent, law-abiding gentleman who was merely out for a peaceful evening stroll!

Mankiller chuckled aloud again, but Toby failed to see the humor.

"Ain't you skeered his words might turn people agin ya?" the boy asked.

"It ain't words that are scary, Toby," the bounty hunter replied. "It's the thoughts behind them. And people are gonna think what they want." He tapped the paper lightly with the back of his hand. "There's nothing here I can't handle."

He then winked at the boy, but his expression was serious. "But if this

Vail fella ever raises a hand to *you*, son, or abuses you in any other way—then he'll have my full attention. If any such thing ever happens, you come tell me, y'hear?"

"Yes, sir," Toby gulped.

"Good. Now, then...tell me about your mama," Jason said, eager to change the topic of conversation. "How's she doing?"

"Just fine," Toby replied. "But her and Miz Mendoza been wonderin' why you ain't come ta visit 'em at the restaurant yet."

Mankiller frowned slightly. Toby's mother, Sarah Applegate, was a young widow forced to care for herself and her children alone. She'd been having a pretty rough time of it until Jason had arranged for her to be hired as a waitress by his good friend Rosario Mendoza.

But before he had last left Fort Rogers, Jason had entered into another business venture with his partners Byron Longfellow and Sam Dobbins. Under the terms of their agreement, Sarah Applegate was to have been placed in charge of a laundry the three men had purchased.

"Don't your mama work at the laundry no more, Toby?" he now asked the boy.

"Oh, sure. Doin' real well with it, too. But her and Miz Mendoza's become good friends, so Ma still helps her out at the restaurant sometimes, too. You know, when it's real busy. Brings in some extra money."

"Hmm. And what about the little girl?"

"You mean Anita?" Toby replied. His voice indicated that the welfare of Rosario Mendoza's young daughter was of little interest to him.

"Yeah. How's she?"

"Aww, about as good as a stinky ol' girl can be, I reckon."

Jason fought to suppress a laugh.

"Well, Toby, you be sure and give your mama my best—and tell her I apologize for my lapse in social graces. I'll be sure to rectify that failure at my earliest convenience."

Now it was Toby who frowned. "Gosh; I ain't sure I can remember all that."

Jason leaned forward, stretched an arm out and tousled the boy's already unkempt hair. "You just tell her I said 'Hi,' and that I'll come see her and Rosario as soon as I can."

"Okay. I can do that." Toby started to turn away, paused, then turned away fully. Two steps later, he stopped and turned back toward the bounty hunter.

"I almost forgot. I took Mr. Longfellow his paper before I came over here. He asked me to tell you he needs to see you over at the bank quick as you can."

"I'll do that, partner," Jason replied, smiling as he watched the industrious lad trot away.

He'd just been reminded of another lapse, though. Byron Longfellow had not only been a good friend to him but had proven to be an invaluable and trustworthy business associate.

Mankiller hoped nothing had happened to change that.

Chapter 25

Jason Mankiller felt self-conscious and uncomfortably vulnerable as he walked toward Fort Rogers' sole banking establishment.

Those feelings arose from the walking stick he was using. Jane Starr had purchased it and insisted he employ it until such time as his legs became fully steady again. Being a woman, she had of course rebuffed his protestations and declarations of already being fully fit to walk on his own two feet, thank you very much.

So he used the cane.

It *was* a fine bit of work, of smooth and polished mahogany. A silver eagle's head topped it. And it *had* been a gift, one with the best of intentions behind it; so he felt obliged to use it.

He strongly hoped that observers thought he was merely making a fashion statement.

He also made sure to use it in his left hand, leaving his right free to flash over to his cross-draw holster in the unlikely event that he needed to defend himself.

Upon entering the bank, it took the bounty hunter but a moment to spy Byron Longfellow seated behind his desk. Seeing Mankiller wave at him with his cane, Byron stood and motioned Jason over.

The hand Longfellow extended to Mankiller was firm but slightly clammy; the smile he flashed seemed somewhat strained, giving Jason pause.

"Sorry I haven't been by to see you sooner, Byron," he said as he took the offered seat in a chair opposite the bank clerk.

"You were in no shape for socializing when you made it back here," Byron assured him. "If anything, I should be apologizing to you for not looking in on you."

"I'm sure you've been busy."

"I have." As if to emphasize that fact, Longfellow tapped a thick sheaf of papers sitting atop the desk in front of him.

"I think you'll be happy to know that all our joint enterprises are doing very well for us. I can already tell our newest investment is going to pay off extremely well.

"Just as you told me would happen, about two months ago the railroad announced it would be running a new line right along the southern edge of town."

Mankiller smiled. It was not due to any prescient powers he possessed that he had known beforehand that this would happen. By purest chance he had been close enough at hand to save a lone traveler from a pair of heartless highwaymen who had intended to rob and murder him. The man whose life he'd saved was the lead surveyor for the railroad, and it was by way of showing gratitude that he had given Jason the confidential foreknowledge that it intended to run a spur line through Fort Rogers.

Jason had in turn passed that knowledge along to Byron Longfellow. Armed with that insider tip and knowing that land prices were still greatly deflated by the Depression of 1873, Longfellow had used some of Jason's accumulated wealth to buy a long swath of those cheap, depressed plots.

"We've already more than recouped our investment from the plots I've sold to prospective businesses," Longfellow now told him.

"I thought we might keep a few plots for ourselves. Build holding pens for cattlemen bringing in their herds to be shipped out by rail. Maybe a restaurant for those making short layovers."

"Sounds good," Jason said, nodding.

"Our other properties continue to show solid, steady profit and growth," Longfellow continued. "The Bloody Eye, the Hansen House hotel, the Grand Comique Theater; all doing just fine.

"We've also rented out other spaces near them for a billiard hall and bowling alley, a saddle shop and a women's dress shop."

"I'm damned impressed by all this, Byron," Jason said, exhaling incredulously. "As always, I thank you for managing my money so wisely and so well."

"Well, I have a financial stake in the success of these ventures as well, remember," the bank clerk said. "And I appreciate your trust and your generosity in including me."

"You've earned every penny you've made," Mankiller replied. He then leaned forward, placing his folded hands atop Longfellow's desk. His face took on a more serious mien.

"Now, why don't we cut through the horse hockey, old son?"

"Huh?"

"Why don't you tell me the *real* reason you wanted to talk to me?"

"Is it that obvious?"

"Plain enough for a blind man to see."

The bank clerk began to needlessly shuffle some of the papers stacked before him, averting his eyes.

"It's been a long time since last you were here in Fort Rogers," he finally said. "Months. Close to half a year."

"Yeah. And?"

"Things *happen*, you know?"

"What sorta things?"

"I'm engaged, Jason." The words came out in a sudden rush. "I'm going to be married."

"Well, congratulations!" Mankiller smiled warmly. "Who's the lucky girl; or can't you tell me?"

Longfellow's facial tone went from glowing red to deathly pale in seconds as he stammered out his answer.

"It's...uhh...It's Rosario Mendoza, Jason."

In response to those words, the bounty hunter simply stared at Longfellow impassively for what seemed like an incredibly long time. The nervous clerk could feel trails of sweat running down inside the cellophane collar of his starched white shirt.

Finally, as he thought the tension might literally make him explode, he saw the corners of the bounty hunter's mouth turn upward just before he began to chuckle loudly.

"Hell, Byron," Mankiller said at long last, "what'd you think I was gonna do—*shoot* you?"

Smiling sickly, Longfellow pulled a handkerchief from his coat pocket and mopped at his forehead.

"Of course not," he asserted, in a tone that was less than convincing. "It's just that I know you and Rosario...well, you have a *history* together."

"She's a good woman," Jason averred. "Mighty good. And she's been a real good friend to me. You have any objection to her continuing to be one?"

"Oh, no, no, no!" Byron hurriedly assured him. "I know she thinks the world of you, Jason. Lots of folks hereabouts do."

"I don't know if I'd go so far as to say that," Mankiller replied, absently patting the folded newspaper thrust in his coat's inside pocket.

"But tell me all about it," he urged. "You and Rosario, I mean."

Now visibly relaxed, Longfellow was happy to oblige. "I have to say, Jason, that I was taken with her the first time I laid eyes on her: when Sam and I approached her with your offer of running the restaurant.

"Once she had it up and running, I started eating there on a regular basis. Doing my part to support her efforts, you know? The more I saw of her, the more I got to know her, the more I liked her.

"It took me a couple months," he admitted rather shyly, "but I finally worked up the gumption to ask her out for a dinner she wouldn't have to cook herself."

Mankiller chuckled softly at this.

"To my surprise and delight," Byron continued, "she accepted the invitation. Things progressed real nicely from there. When I got around to asking her to marry me—she said yes without a moment's hesitation."

"Uh-huh. And what about the little one?" Jason said, referring to Rosario's daughter.

At this, Byron frowned slightly. "Anita's not taking to the idea of me marrying her mother, I'm afraid." He grimaced before going on.

"I think it's mostly because of *you*, Jason."

"Me? How so?"

"That child loves you to the moon and back, friend. So she's kind of resentful of me. She'd much rather have *you* for her new father!"

Mankiller again chuckled, somewhat wistfully. "Yeah. Me and her do have a kinda special relationship. I'll give you that.

"But she's a bright child and she'll come around," he asserted. "You've just got to give her time, that's all. Be patient with her."

Longfellow nodded his agreement.

"Meanwhile," Jason said, feeling it wise to change the subject, "there's another matter of business it might behoove us to discuss."

"Certainly. What might that be?"

Mankiller cast his eyes around the bank. "It struck me as I came in that you're at the same desk you occupied when last I was here. Do you hold the same position, as well?"

"Yes." Longfellow sounded somewhat puzzled as to the direction in which the bounty hunter was headed.

"Well, given all the additional revenue you've been bringing in, it seems to me you oughtta be in line for some kind of promotion, or at least a generous pay raise."

Longfellow sighed and shrugged philosophically. "Don't say where you heard this, but the fact is that the owner of the bank and all the officers are *family*—related either by blood or marriage."

"Ah." Jason need hear no more. Still, it didn't sit quite right with his personal sense of fair play.

"The town sure is growing," he said, seemingly apropos of nothing.

"It is," Byron replied. "Getting bigger by the day."

"So, then, let me ask you *this*; do you reckon it's big enough now to support *two* banks?"

"I suppose it is," Longfellow said somewhat hesitantly.

"Then let's cut to the chase," Jason said resolutely. "Do you, me and Sam have the resources to do just that?"

Byron blinked owlishly, taken totally by surprise. Before responding, he opened a thick ledger book and pored over several columns of figures.

"I think we could probably manage it," he said, speaking slowly, "if we wanted to chance it. But it might be a big risk to take, Jason—especially for you. Most of the money on hand for that kind of start-up is yours, after all."

"I appreciate that. But even if it was to fail, we'd still have our other businesses, right?"

"Yes. But you'd have no additional reserves, no financial cushion. You could take a big hit."

"Byron, the first day I arrived in Fort Rogers, I had nothing but a nickel in my pocket, the clothes on my back and the gun on my hip. You can't get much poorer than that."

Longfellow had an earnest, almost anguished look on his face. "But you literally put your life on the line to earn what you've got, Jason. All Sam and I invest is a little time and a little money. It doesn't seem prudent or maybe even right for you to take such a gamble."

"Tell me straight," Mankiller replied. "Do you or do you not think we could make a go of it with a second bank?"

Longfellow stared down at his clasped hands for long moments, while the bounty hunter patiently waited for his response.

"I think so," the clerk said at last. "I believe I could run an operation like this better than this bunch does." He slowly shook his head. "But I sure can't guarantee it, Jason. I just can't."

Mankiller shrugged. "Life don't come with many guarantees, Byron. Hell, some poor farmer could accidentally run me over with his wagon when I walk out of here." He leaned back slightly in his chair.

"And we don't have to decide right this minute, either. You take your time, work on the numbers in your books as long as you need to, figure out all the angles. If you honestly think it has a good chance of working—only then will we pull the trigger."

"That sounds fair," Longfellow concurred. "All right."

"One other thing you need to think on," Jason continued. "Sam's got a good head on him for running saloons and the like, but he's no banker. Neither am I.

"That means if we do this...it'll be up to *you* to be the man in charge. President of our bank. You think you're up to that?"

This time, there was no hesitation. "I know I am."

"So do I. Just one more thing, and this I insist on." Mankiller smiled slightly. "We are *not* going to call it the Bloody Eye Bank."

In response, Longfellow laughed loud enough for some of the other clerks to glance over in mild puzzlement.

"Agreed," he said, then cocked his head as a new thought occurred to him. "But you know, you have brought to mind another important asset we have at our disposal."

"What's that?"

"Speaking frankly—your *reputation* as a gunfighter. Once word gets around—and you know Sam will make sure it does—that the money in that bank belongs to the infamous *Man Who Cries Blood*..." Longfellow gestured with both hands.

"There won't be an outlaw in the country who'd be foolish enough to try to steal it!"

Jason managed a rueful smile. "I hadn't thought of that. Why, hell, old son, we're just liable to put *this* place out of business!"

"We might at that, Jason."

"This could pay off big, Byron," the bounty hunter said, again growing serious. "That'd be a good thing for a man about to start a family."

Longfellow frowned slightly. "You're not wanting to do this just for me, are you, Jason?"

"I'm doing it for all of us," came the reply. Mankiller glanced around the bank, but he was seeing far more than just its four walls.

"I know what some folks think of me and the way I make my living," he explained. "But whenever I come back here, I feel like I'm a part of something bigger than myself. If I can be a party to making it even bigger and better, that makes me feel even more like I belong."

"It's a good feeling, isn't it, Jason?"

"Mighty good."

"And you *do* belong. Please don't ever forget that."

"Thanks. I won't." With that, the bounty hunter sighed and heaved himself up and out of his chair.

"Thanks for all you do for me, Byron," he said, reaching across the desk to shake the clerk's hand.

"And congratulations on your upcoming nuptials."

"Thanks, Jason. You will try to attend the wedding, won't you? It'd mean an awful lot to me and Rosario both."

"Well, now, you know me, Byron. I'm apt to be off gallivanting after some owlhoot when the happy day comes. But if I'm not—you can be sure I'll be at the church with bells on."

"Fair enough."

"There is just one other thing," Mankiller added. There was a slight smile on his lips, but its warmth did not spread to his icy eyes.

"If you ever mistreat her or the little one—for any reason—you'll answer to me." He tipped his hat, then made his way out of the bank.

And though he knew the bounty hunter's threat was serious, Longfellow finally breathed a deep sigh of relief.

Chapter 26

Like a bird in a cage, Stella Freeman gazed longingly up at the freedom of the clear blue skies overhead.

Life inside the Pima Territorial Prison had settled back down to its own form of normalcy in the weeks since the prison riot had rocked it to its foundations.

Though the chores Stella and her fellow female inmates were forced to perform were hard and sometimes demeaning work, they at least made the time pass a bit quicker. It was the hours from dusk to dawn that often seemed to crawl by at less than a snail's pace.

Adding to the woman's sense of longing was the absence of Jason Mankiller. While she was happy he had gained his freedom, she greatly missed his mere presence. Just watching him as he walked about the main yard, a lion amidst a pack of jackals, had given her a feeling of peace and security.

Her head turned at the sound of a key being turned in the lock that held closed the gate of the women's compound. Puzzled, she watched as the guard Clem Butler swung the gate open.

She never knew why, but in the weeks since the riot, Butler had seemed almost like a guardian angel to her and the other two women, insuring they were spared the worst of the depredations at the hands of his fellow guards.

"Come on out, Stella," he said.

"Just me?" she queried, glancing over at her cellmates standing nearby. Butler nodded.

"What's up, Clem?" she asked as she passed out of the small enclosure.

"You'll see," was all he would say in reply.

Her heart sank slightly, surmising that she was being taken to the guards' quarters, where she would be expected to satisfy whatever desire—sexual or otherwise—had seized upon them.

She scowled in wonder as Butler instead led her toward the prison's front gates, which stood open at the moment.

Standing there alongside a pair of other guards was the prison physician. Doctor Fix was wearing his best suit and a fedora hat. A battered, old brown suitcase sat on the ground near his right foot; he held his medical bag in his left hand.

"What's going on, Doc?" Stella asked as she drew near. "What are you doing here?"

"I'm getting ready to *leave* this canker sore on the earth's ass, my dear," he said gruffly. "What are *you* doing here?"

She turned her eyes toward Clem Butler, hoping the guard might supply the answer.

"You're being released, Stella," he finally told her. "You're free to go."

"What?" She was too stunned to say much more. "How come? I still have time on my sentence."

"The rest of your time's been commuted. Somebody must have pulled a few strings on your behalf." Butler smiled and motioned toward the open gateway.

"Go on, woman. Get outta here!"

"May I?" Doctor Fix said, offering his left arm to Stella. Numbly, she accepted and strolled with him out into the gathering gloom.

Their path led past the last wagon bringing in prisoners from their toils at the rock quarry, one of whom was Ira Morgan. Since the death of Bear Givens in the abortive prison riot, Morgan had come to be widely regarded as the new top dog of the yard. Even though Jason Mankiller was no longer there, Ira's close association with him still carried a lot of weight with the other inmates.

Morgan smiled as he saw Stella Freeman walking away. He had still maintained his role as Pima's prime bookmaker and had bet all comers that Mankiller would find a way to get the woman released ahead of schedule.

He rubbed his hands together in eager anticipation of the payout that he felt sure would soon be coming his way.

A short distance outside the prison walls, Stella saw a man standing beside a waiting carriage. He was dressed in a fine linen suit, with a derby hat resting rakishly atop his head. Another man, clearly the driver of the carriage, sat stiffly holding the reins of its team of horses.

"Miss Freeman?" the well-dressed man said, doffing his hat as she and Doctor Fix approached.

"Yes." Stella's bewilderment was simply growing deeper.

"My name is Carter Frain. I'm an attorney—and a friend of Jason Mankiller."

"Oh!" Her face brightened.

"At his request, I managed to convince the prison board that you should have your sentence reduced to time served. You're a free woman." Frain thought it best not to mention the amount of Mankiller's money he had used to grease palms and aid in bringing to life the merciful impulses of the board members.

"Oh, my," was all Stella could gasp out, so large was the sudden lump in her throat.

Frain reached into his inside coat pocket and removed an envelope that fairly bulged with the contents within.

"This is for you," he said, handing the envelope to a stunned Stella.

"I think you'll find enough there to finance a fresh start to the next stage of your life," he told her, smiling benignly.

"But...why?" the woman asked, tears welling in her eyes as she clutched the envelope to her ample bosom.

"All Jason told me was that he felt you were a person who deserved a second chance. For him, that was all the reason he needed."

"What are you gonna do with yourself, Stella?" Doctor Fix asked.

"I—I don't know," she replied, clearly taken aback.

"The money's yours, free and clear," Carter Frain said. "No strings attached. You can go wherever you want, spend it however you like.

"However," he continued, "Jason suggested that Denver might be a good place for you to find plentiful opportunities for your particular set of skills."

In the fading light, Frain couldn't tell for sure if the woman was blushing.

"Then Denver it is," she stated firmly. She then turned toward the aging physician beside her.

"What about you, Doc? What are your plans?"

"I'm afraid I have none, my dear," he confessed. "My thoughts hadn't carried me beyond wanting to be shed of this place!"

"Well, you know," Stella told him, smiling warmly, "the type of business I operate often has use for the services of an old vet like you. Would you care to come to work for me?"

Fix barely gave the offer time for one thought, let alone two. "I would be delighted, Stella. Delighted."

"I have something for you as well, Dr. Fix," Frain said. "I thought I would have to make a separate appointment to see you, but since you're right here, right now." The attorney withdrew a second, slightly thinner envelope from his coat and passed it to the old physician.

"What's this fer?" Fix muttered.

"Jason said to tell you that your kindness had not been forgotten." Carter took a step to one side and waved one arm toward his buggy.

"If you care to avail yourselves of the hospitality of my conveyance," Frain told them, "I would be happy to transport you to the nearest town."

He offered a hand in helping Stella up into the carriage, which she gladly accepted. As she placed a foot up on the carriage steps, she paused to look back over her shoulder. The darkly sinister silhouette of the prison walls caused her to shudder involuntarily. She then shifted her gaze to Frain.

"Please tell Jason I can never thank him enough for what he's done," she said.

"I'll be glad to."

A slightly wicked smile brightened the woman's face. "And tell him I expect him to come visit me sometime.

"He'll always be welcome."

Chapter 27

Jason Mankiller fought to curb his natural nervous energy and remain still in the straightback chair in which he sat.

He made no similar effort to hide the annoyance on his face as Doctor

James Crotty fluttered around him, listening to his heartbeat and the rhythm of his breathing.

"Everything sounds fine," the physician declared at last.

"Hell, I coulda told you that, Doc."

"Yes," Crotty replied, his tone and expression showing his own annoyance, "and you *could* have come see me when you first got back to town. I understand you've once again allowed this poor body of yours to be raked over the coals."

"It isn't like I did it a'purpose," Mankiller said defensively. "Besides, I've been receiving real good care."

"So she told me," Crotty snapped. "But it was Miss Starr herself who came to me and asked me to examine you."

"That's the kind of thing she'd do, all right."

Doctor Crotty's features softened with the natural sympathy he possessed as he cast his gaze over the multiple scars and abrasions scoring Mankiller's torso. His practiced eye told him many of them were recent in origin.

"My God, man," he murmured. "What, by all that's holy, did they *do* to you in that place?"

"No worse than they did to others," the bounty hunter lied.

"Then the facility should be condemned and torn down." The physician held out two fingers. "Squeeze these as tightly as you can," he instructed his patient. Jason complied, first with his right hand, then his left. Crotty then knelt on the floor and took hold of Jason's left ankle.

"Try to straighten your leg," he said, using his hands to resist Mankiller's efforts. After doing the same to the right leg, the physician stood.

"That woman of yours is liable to put me out of business," Crotty chuckled.

"You're almost as good as new. Your arms and legs could still use a little more exercise, perhaps. But you've mostly recovered."

"Be sure to tell Jane that," Jason said dryly, starting to slip back into his shirt. He hid the relief he felt at this pronouncement. Though he'd made light with others about his slowness in getting around to see them, the harsh truth was that he had been nearly broken by the time he left the confines of Pima and the mending had come frustratingly slow for him.

"I will," Crotty told him. "And I want to take this opportunity to thank you again, Jason."

"What for?"

"For the money you put up to build my new clinic and apothecary."

"What, by all that's holy, did they do to you in that place?"

"The town needed it," Mankiller replied with a shrug. "'Sides, my partner tells me we're making a nice chunk of change from our share of it. It was just good business, Doc. No need to make more of it."

"Good business," Crotty said with a smile. "Right. We both know you make more money from your saloon on a busy Saturday night than your share of the clinic pays you in a month."

"Then maybe it wasn't such good business," Mankiller grumbled. "I'll have to talk to Longfellow about that."

"You do that. And you also stop by before you drift on again; you should see what your money has meant to the community.

"Plus, you have yet to meet my wife. Don't think she hasn't reminded me of that a time or two."

"Seems I've let *all* my social responsibilities go to seed," Jason said, continuing to hide even from his physician the true reason for his lapse. "I'll be sure to come by soon. I promise."

"I'll hold you to that. I think you'll be pleased with what we've done. We've even begun to get patients from all the other outlying areas and from several of the ranches.

"It's my hope that someday I'll be able to make it into a full-blown hospital."

"That's a noble ambition, Doc. I'll do anything I can to help you make it a reality."

"I just hope I'll be treating *you* there," Doctor Crotty said, laying a hand on Mankiller's shoulder. "When you're an old, old man."

"I hope you're right, Doc," Jason replied, smiling at him warmly.

"But maybe you'd better leave the *miracles* up to the clergy!"

Chapter 28

Mankiller stood staring at his reflection in the mirror for a full minute. He allowed as how he was not a bad looking man. His face was brown and weathered by sun and wind, but not so badly as to make him look older than his years. There was no gray in his hair as of yet, even though he was pushing thirty. His blue eyes, at moments like this when he was not engaged in confrontation, softened his looks considerably.

He touched the teardrop shaped, red tattoo on his left cheek. Others might find it frightening or off-putting, but he saw it primarily as a reminder of the fearful days of the War Between the States. Many tears and much blood had been shed both on and off its battlefields, and neither should be forgotten.

He was dressed in his finest: a dark gray suit over a white linen shirt held closed at the collar by a black string tie. He'd had his boots sent out earlier for a fresh, high gloss shine.

As he stepped through the doorway of his suite on the second floor of the Bloody Eye saloon, he nearly collided with his friends Cash Carpenter and Jane Starr. Both were also dressed nicely, but unlike his theirs was more or less standard attire for the couple.

"Jane and I were just about to retire for a nice supper," Cash told him. "Would you care to join us?"

"Another time, maybe," Jason politely declined. "I was just on my way out to take care of some overdue business of a personal nature, down to Rosario Mendoza's restaurant."

To his surprise, Jane's body seemed to stiffen slightly at this. "You *know* she's planning to marry that banker fellow, don't you?"

"Perhaps you and I should consider matrimony, darling," Cash jested before Jason could make any reply.

"Don't be ridiculous," Jane huffed mildly. "The first time you gambled away the rent money—I'd feel obliged to shoot you!"

"Is it any wonder I love her?" Cash said to Jason.

Cash and Jane both laughed heartily as he walked away arm-in-arm, leaving a bemused Mankiller standing alone, shaking his head.

Descending the staircase leading to the floor of the saloon, Jason threw a careless wave to his partner Sam Dobbins, who was doing extra duty behind the bar on this busy evening.

The bounty hunter had barely breezed through the batwing doors and out onto the boardwalk beyond when he nearly collided with his lawyer, Carter Frain.

"I'm on my way to supper," he said, motioning for Frain to follow. "Walk along with me."

"I'll only take a minute of your time, Jason. Polly's got supper waiting for me at home." Mankiller continued walking, but at a slower pace.

"I just got back from Pima," Frain said, falling into step alongside Jason. "I thought you'd like to know that everything went well."

"So you got Stella out of that cage?"

"I did. And on her way to Denver. Along with that old horse doctor you told me about."

Jason chuckled. "I 'spect the two of them will make a right lively team."

"I imagine so. Miss Freeman also asked that I extend her thanks to you—along with an open invitation to renew your acquaintance at any time you please."

Mankiller smiled. "It's good to have friends."

"It is," Frain agreed, abruptly stopping in his tracks. "Which reminds me that I should probably be thanking you as well."

"What for?"

Frain made a clicking sound with his tongue against the roof of his mouth as he shook his head. "When I went on to you about the nice little cottage me and the missus found, you never said a word, never let on."

"I'm a bit confused, counselor."

"Come on, Jason. Just before I left for Pima I found out that the cottage—and my office space—are owned by *you*."

"They *are*?" Jason replied, feigning ignorance.

"You know damned good and well they are," Frain said, pretending ire. "That's why I got such a good deal on both."

"Well," Jason said, "if you'd rather pay *more*—you can take it up with Byron Longfellow."

"Oh, that's all right," Frain said with a smirk. "I wouldn't want to insult you by refusing your generosity. I just wanted to thank you."

"You're welcome," Mankiller said gruffly. "Now, if you don't mind—I'm hungry!"

"Of course. Oh!" Frain snapped his fingers. "Just one more thing and I know you'll want to hear this. While I was in New Mexico, I received news from a colleague that I know will interest you."

"All right," Jason sighed.

"From what he told me, the authorities were all set to begin a formal investigation into the operations of the Pima Territorial Prison—when Warden Mayhew up and disappeared. Dropped plumb out of sight, he did. It was an interim superintendent I dealt with when I got Stella out."

"That's not too surprising," Mankiller said tightly. "The man's got the morals of an alley cat—and the spine of an eel. Just the kind who'd take off for the tall uncut at the first sign of trouble.

"But sooner or later, one way or another…he'll pay his dues."

"The same is true for all the folks in Low Water who railroaded you into prison," Frain said, in a not-so-subtle attempt to again dissuade Mankiller from seeking revenge on those who had so grievously wronged him.

"I appreciate all your help, Carter," the bounty hunter replied coldly. "And I value your counsel.

"In *most* matters."

Without another word, he resumed walking down the street, leaving Carter Frain to fret alone.

Chapter 29

At the moment, Sarah Applegate was not a happy woman.

It was an even busier than normal Saturday night in Rosario's restaurant; so it was that Sarah had offered to help her friend out by lending a hand waiting tables.

It was a job she took to naturally and usually rather enjoyed. But the three men she was now attempting to serve were quickly sapping the job of all its joy; making the extra money it brought into her family funds almost seem not worth it.

They were all rude and uncouth: conditions to be expected of many of the men in a typical frontier town such as Fort Rogers. Even now, a full decade after the end of the War, the West was filled with men who were little more than aimless drifters such as these were.

One of these three, a mean-spirited rogue by the name of Graham, had decided to sharpen his appetite and indulge the animalistic nature that made him more fit to walk on all fours by making life miserable for his waitress.

"What kinda slop is this?" he demanded as Sarah placed a bowl on the table in front of him.

"It's the stew you ordered, sir," Sarah replied in the most respectful tone she could manage.

"Didn't order no such of a thing!" the man roared.

"I'll take it back and bring you whatever else you'd prefer," the woman said, reaching to retrieve the bowl.

Graham grabbed hold of her wrist. "I just might like ta have me a slice o' *you*!" he said, eliciting childish giggles from his two companions.

"I'm not on the menu, mister," Sarah said coldly.

"I don't take back-sass from no woman!" the drifter snapped, tightening his grip on the woman's wrist and twisting it.

"You're hurting me," she told him through clenched teeth.

"I'm gonna do more than hurt ya," he threatened.

"Don't—" Sarah bit off her words as her eyes caught glimpse of a welcome sight.

"Jason!"

Mankiller was standing just inside the entryway of the restaurant. His face was impassive, but his eyes flared with hateful fire as he stared at the table where the three drifters sat. Even with the heat of his stare, the two who were beside Graham froze solid with their hands in plain sight resting palms down.

Sarah managed to jerk free of the startled drifter's grip and rushed toward the bounty hunter, encircling him in her arms. His arms returned the embrace, but his eyes never left the table.

He gently pushed the woman to his left side, in the same motion sweeping the tail of his coat away from the cross-draw holster riding on that hip. His left arm remained around her waist, but his right hand hung loose and free as he walked Sarah over to the table. He now ignored two of the men, but his eyes bore unwaveringly into the dark face of the man who had been abusive to Sarah.

"Is there a problem with the service you're getting here, mister?" he asked. Graham's two companions held their breaths, certain that they were about to witness a killing.

For all his bluster and bullying behavior, though, Graham had never faced a man such as this—and deep down he knew *he* was the one who would die if he dared to press things further. The tattooed man facing him was clearly willing to risk death for a woman and a bowl of stew, but the drifter wasn't.

"No problem," he finally managed to say in a voice barely above a whisper. "The service here is first rate."

"I expect that'll be reflected in the size of the *tip* you leave for the young lady," Mankiller said. It was not a question.

Licking his lips fearfully, the frightened drifter nodded his head in a jerking motion.

"Yessir. You can be sure it will."

"Then enjoy your meals, gents."

With his left arm still around Sarah's waist, Mankiller walked her past the table, heading toward the kitchen area at the back of the restaurant. The grateful woman rested her head on his shoulder.

"Thank you for coming to my rescue," she said.

"Hell, I thought it was *him* I was rescuing," Jason jested. "When I walked in, you looked like you were about to cut him down to size.

"I figured the poor fella didn't stand a chance!"

Sarah laughed and hugged him more tightly. "Toby told me you were coming, and you sure picked a good time to show up."

"I was hungry, that was all."

"Speaking of hunger," she said, clearly relaxing more with each passing step, "I hope you'll find the time to stop by and have dinner with me and the children some evening before you leave town."

"What makes you think I'm leaving?"

"Sooner or later—you'll always leave."

"Yeah, I guess that's right. But if anything would tempt me to stay an extra day, it's one of your home cooked meals."

"Then it's settled. As I recall, you like my fried chicken and blackberry cobbler."

"I expect I'll like whatever you care to serve me, Sarah."

"It's a date, then," she said, squeezing his waist before pushing away from him to leave him to enter the kitchen area alone. He smiled, thinking that the woman actually looked younger and prettier than when he first met her. Having been relieved of some of the burden bearing down upon her in trying to fend for her family had in turned allowed her to fill out a bit while simultaneously losing some of the worry lines that had previously made her look more plain that was the actual case.

The first thing he noticed upon entering the back room was that business in the restaurant was apparently now so brisk that Rosario Mendoza had hired two other women to do the actual cooking, under her watchful eyes.

Those eyes widened as they chanced upon the bounty hunter and her flushed face lit up with delight. She let out a short, high-pitched squeal before throwing herself into his arms and kissing his face repeatedly.

Just as quickly, she pushed herself away from him. Her fists rested on her flaring hips and a stern scowl distorted her lovely facial features. Thick black hair streamed down either side of her head, complimenting her soft brown skin and nestling just above full breasts.

"*Now* you come waltzing in here?" she scolded. "Why did you wait so long to come see me?"

"Well, now, Rosario," he replied somewhat haltingly, taking off his hat and compressing it between both hands, "I was a bit *peaked* when I come back to town, you know."

"You *still* look horrible," she said harshly, frowning as she eyed him up and down.

"So thin. That *woman* has not taken care of you properly!"

Jason grinned slightly. "Then maybe a good *meal* would do wonders for me. I've heard tell a man could get one here."

"Oh!" Flustered by what she felt was a lapse in manners, Rosario circled around Jason and began pushing him forward by placing her hands against his broad back. He gladly allowed himself to be directed toward a small table set against one of the back corners of the kitchen.

"You stay, you sit and I will get some *real* food into you *pronto!*" she said. "On the house, of course."

"Yes'm," he said graciously. Since he was actually the principal owner of Rosario's restaurant, free food was probably his due; he didn't deign to tell her he full intended to leave the price of the meal with the cashier out front when he departed, including a little extra for her to slip into Sarah Applegate's evening tips.

It only took a minute or two for Rosario to return with a plate of food, but she noticed Mankiller had used that time to slightly alter the position of the table.

It was now tilted at an angle away from the wall instead of being flush against it. This allowed the bounty hunter to place his chair directly in the corner; protecting his back and affording him a clear view of both the back door of the restaurant and the swinging door that led into the kitchen from the dining area.

Rosario sighed sadly. Such was the life this man she cared for deeply had chosen for himself that even among friends he must always be on the alert for potential danger.

When she placed the large, oval platter in front of him, Jason saw that half of it was piled high with hot frijoles. The other side held tamales and chicken enchiladas, swimming in a rich, spicy sauce. Beside it she set a plate of fresh, buttery corn tortillas.

She then rushed off again, only to return with a large ceramic mug and a pot of bubbling coffee. Mankiller arched an eyebrow at her.

"You trying to just feed me?" he asked, "or to fatten me up for Thanksgiving dinner?"

"Don't joke—eat!" she commanded. Knowing the quality of her cooking, he was glad to comply.

She planted herself in the chair across from him, poured herself a cup of coffee and watched expectantly as he began to work on the meal. She twisted her hands in her apron as if fearful that he might not like what she had served him.

Realizing this, Jason almost cruelly withheld any comment until he had tasted a bite of everything on the plate, then paused to take a deep sip of the rich, dark coffee; detecting a mild hint of chocolate in it.

"I 'spect there might be a place that serves a better spread," he said, fighting not to smile as he saw Rosario's shoulders slump slightly.

"But since you have to pass through the Pearly Gates to reach it—I reckon this is the best *I'll* ever taste!"

The woman's hands flew to her face as if in shock. Eyes cast upward; she then crossed herself before laughing aloud.

"Yes, sir," Jason continued, talking around a bite of tamale, "Byron won't ever have cause to complain about the cooking in his marriage."

Rosario's expression grew more sober.

"Do you not approve?" she asked in a small voice.

"You're a woman fully growed, Rosario," he replied, sipping at his coffee. "My opinion really shouldn't matter."

"But it does to me," she replied. "And to Byron."

"I can tell by the look in his eyes and the way he talks about you that he's crazy mad in love with you," Jason said. "Is the feeling mutual?"

The woman thought deeply before responding. "As you say, I am a full woman. My life has taught me there are many different kinds of love.

"I do have a love for Byron; I think it is enough to make both of us happy."

Mankiller chewed on that along with one of the feathery tortillas. "Just one more question, then."

"Yes?"

He waved the remnants of the tortilla like a flag. "Will I still get these free meals after the nuptials?"

She laughed and waved her hands as though slapping at him. The laugh ended in a deep sigh and she smiled at him warmly.

"I want you to always be in my life, Jason," she said sincerely.

"Then you have my approval," he replied with equal sincerity. "And my blessing."

"Byron is a good man," Rosario said wistfully. "A gentle man, a kind man. He will be a good husband to me and a good father to Anita."

"I don't *want* him to be my father!" a voice behind Rosario shouted harshly.

As Rosario swiveled in her chair at the strident voice behind her, Jason saw that her daughter Anita was now standing there. No more than five, the girl had grown since the bounty hunter last had seen her, as children are wont to do. But she still seemed like just a tiny little thing to him.

Nestled in her arms was the little mongrel dog she had named Hector. She deeply loved the pooch, all the more so since he had been given to her by her even more beloved "*Senor* Jason."

"Shame on you, Anita Maria!" the child's mother scolded.

"Well, I *don't!*" Anita yelled, stomping one little foot petulantly.

"That don't mean you can't come over and give *me* a hug, does it, poppet?" Jason said calmly, pushing back a little from the table and extending his arms toward the child.

With a squeal of delight, Anita dropped Hector, raced over and literally threw herself into Jason's arms. As he lifted her up onto his lap, she squeezed him with all her might. She then leaned back and fixed him with a most serious stare.

"Why can't *you* be my daddy?" she asked candidly.

Jason heard the girl's mother gasp loudly, saw her blush fiercely; but he merely smiled indulgently at the question.

"Why, I get to be something even better than your daddy," he told the confused child. "I get to be your *pal*."

Anita frowned. "What does that mean?"

"That means I don't have to do all those tough daddy things; like making you eat your veg'tables and telling you when you have to go to bed.

"Byron and your mother's got to do all that—and all the other tough things, to make sure you're safe and that you grow up good and proper.

"It's hard work, being a mama and a papa, but they're both willing to do it 'cause they love you so much." He chucked her under the chin with one callused finger.

"And because they do that—*I* get to do all the *fun* stuff with you."

Anita's face scrunched up in deep thought. "But don't you love me, too?"

"'Course I do, little one. More than I love your mama's cooking."

"For always and always?"

"Always and always. You're still my chickabiddy, ain'tcha?"

"Uh-huh."

"And you always will be—no matter what."

Her child mind quickly leapt to something else. "So...what kind of fun stuff can we do?"

"Well..." He cast a questioning look at Rosario that showed he hadn't really thought ahead that far. But the woman, clearly enjoying his dilemma, merely shrugged; she would be no help at all.

"Well, sir...how 'bout you and me—" At a soft, whining noise, he glanced down. Hector was lying at his feet, looking up at him with the soulful eyes of a lost orphan.

"You and me and *Hector*...uh...we could all go on a *picnic*."

"Just the three of us?"

"Just the three of us."

She pondered on this for a moment. "Maybe we should invite Toby Applegate, too. He's just a mean ol' boy—but he don't get to do many fun things."

"That's awful sweet of you, poppet," Mankiller said. "Sure, we can bring him along. I'll rent us our very own buggy and bring a basket of food your mama won't have to cook and we'll go out and spend the whole afternoon together. How's that sound?"

Little Anita's response was to throw her arms around his neck and squeeze tightly. The bounty hunter returned the hug fiercely, glancing at the child's mother. There were tears welling up in Rosario's eyes.

He smiled at her and gave her a wink.

Chapter 30

Jason Mankiller hoisted the 50-pound bag of grain over one shoulder with what seemed to be little effort.

He carried it to the nearby wagon parked at the rear of the mercantile store and threw it into the bed where similar bags already rested. As he headed back for another, the local rancher he was assisting passed him, likewise heading for the wagon with a similar load.

The bounty hunter had been performing such chores for the past week, collecting no wages for his labors. He had volunteered his services to the storeowner, thinking that such heavy physical work would be beneficial in restoring the full strength to his body and limbs. It was clearly working, and the storekeeper was mightily grateful for the free assistance.

"Thanks for your help, Mr. Mankiller," the rancher said when the last sack was loaded. With his left hand he mopped the sweat from his brow with a faded kerchief, while pumping Jason's hand with his right.

"You're welcome, Mr. Blake," Jason replied, then motioned toward the loaded wagon.

"When you get back to the ranch, you might oughtta take a close look at that off rear wheel. It's showing some cracks and you wouldn't want to throw it while you're on the road."

"Thanks. I'll do that."

Mankiller was standing and watching the wagon roll away when he saw Newt Carpenter walking toward him. Newt was a cousin to Cash

Carpenter, but more important, he was the chief deputy of Fort Rogers' marshal, Clayton Russell.

"Afternoon, Jason," he said cordially.

"Newt."

"If you got the time, Jason, the marshal'd like to see you over to his office."

"Sure thing. Just let me wash up a bit."

Mankiller walked over to a nearby water trough and began to crank the handle of its pump. He was not wearing a shirt, and as the water flowed he first rinsed his hair, hands and face thoroughly before splashing water on his chest and back to wash away the sweat and grime.

The deputy winced at the sight of the bounty hunter's back. The welts left by the kiss of the whip were still clearly visible, red and raw trails that ran from his neck to the base of his spine. Newt was relieved when Jason pulled his shirt on and hid those and multiple other scars.

When Mankiller entered the marshal's office a few minutes later he saw that Russell, seated behind his battered desk, was not alone. A second, more portly man was sitting on the opposite side with his back to Jason. This man turned at the sound of the door opening, and a surprised Mankiller instinctively reached for his pistol at the sight.

It was "Mayor" Delmar Owens from Low Water!

Owens' eyes widened in unconcealed terror and he threw up his empty hands. "I'm unarmed, Mankiller!" he screeched. "Don't let him kill me, marshal!"

Mankiller already had his Colt cocked and aimed by the time Marshal Russell was able to jump to his feet and place himself in front of the bounty hunter's intended target.

"Ease up, Jason," the lawman said. He spoke the words softly, but with an undeniable tone of authority.

The muscles in Mankiller's face clenched tightly, but at last he exhaled, giving his pistol a twirl around his finger before sliding it back into his cross-draw holster.

"You keep him away from me, marshal!" Owens practically blubbered. "I turned myself in voluntarily and you gotta protect me!"

"Don't tell me my job, mister," Russell growled back. He made a calming gesture toward Mankiller. "The mayor here was just giving me his statement.

"Get on with it," he told Owens.

"It was wrong, what we done to the bounty hunter," Owens admitted.

"But it was more Blue Thorpe's doin' than mine. I swear it."

"Don't sound like much of a confession to me," Mankiller said coldly, taking a menacing step closer to Owens.

"Wait!" the crooked mayor shouted. "If you want a confession—you got it. Everything that's on the wanted poster they put out on me—it's all true! I did it all."

"Go on," Russell pressed. "What brought you here and now?"

"It's him!" Owens stammered, pointing at Jason. "I know what he's capable of; ever'body knows."

"People started packing up and leaving Low Water the day the two deputies sent to take him to prison didn't come back when they was supposed to. When word came that Mankiller was out of the pen—that trickle became a flood.

"The place is virtually empty now." Owens paused to wipe sweat from his face; he was huffing and puffing like a steam engine straining on a steep grade.

"About all that's left in town now is Marshal Thorpe, the hired gunmen he calls 'deputies'—and the men who sat in the jury box at your trial."

"And why ain't you with 'em?" Russell probed.

"Because I don't wanna *die!*" Owens said, slumping in his chair. He cast his eyes at Mankiller for just a second before averting them in shame.

"I've turned myself in and confessed to my crimes; I'll do hard time myself, for sure.

"I know that don't change what I done to you," he muttered, seeming to shrink in stature even as he spoke. "But I hope it'll convince you to spare my life."

"We'll see," was all the bounty hunter was willing to concede.

"Take him back and lock him up," Marshal Russell said, and his deputy hustled to obey. Delmar Owens' shoulders slumped and he began to sob softly as he meekly allowed himself to be led back into the building's cellblock.

"Damnedest thing I ever saw," Russell said, shaking his head. "He ain't but a shell of a man now."

"He wasn't no real sort of man to start with," Mankiller grunted.

"I suppose." The graying marshal sat down and leaned back in his chair, hands folded atop his only slightly bulging belly, and smiled up at Jason.

"Nice to know you've been on your best behavior lately, bounty man," he said.

"What's that s'posed to mean?"

"Oh, nothin'. It's just that you've been here for a few weeks now and haven't been involved in a single *shootin'*. I appreciate that."

Mankiller availed himself of the chair that had been vacated by Mayor Owens. "Maybe folks around here are just finally catching on to the fact that I'm a peace-loving man who don't want no trouble."

"Yeah," Russell replied dryly. "That's probably it."

"What's gonna become of Owens?" Jason asked, jerking his head in the direction of the cellblock.

"I'll get him to sign a statement verifying that he's admitting to his past crimes, then hold him here till the circuit judge comes around."

"Good."

Russell coughed and cleared his throat. "There's somethin' else I wanted to tell you, Mankiller."

"What's that?"

"I took the advice you gave me when last you was here. You know, about taking a room over to Miz Pennington's boarding house."

"Worked out well, has it?"

Rather sheepishly for a man his age, the marshal made a confession of his own. "Me and Martha—the Widow Pennington, I mean—well, we've started steppin' out together. Things are getting pretty serious between us."

"Why, you old hound dog," Jason teased. "Congratulations." He was smiling as he stood to take his leave.

"One more thing," Russell said. "What about the *reward*?"

"What reward would that be?"

"Even though the paper on 'im's kinda old, Delmar back there is still carryin' a $500 bounty on his head.

"Granted, he turned hisself in, but we both know you're the one responsible for it. So by rights you're entitled to lay claim to the reward.

"Maybe you could think of it as compensation for the pain and suffering him and his partner inflicted on you."

"Breathing free air's all the reward I need," Jason said. "I don't suppose *you'd* be willing to accept the bounty?"

"You know I can't do that," Russell replied gruffly, ever the stickler for the letter of the law.

"All right," Mankiller said, taking a minute to think on the matter. "Put in a claim for me on the reward.

"Only thing is, I'll probably be gone by the time the money gets here. Would it be allowable for you to turn it over to Byron Longfellow over at the bank and ask him to deposit in into my account?"

"I could do that."

"Then that's what we'll do." He pointed at the cluttered top of Russell's desk. "And would you mind if I take the wanted poster on Blue Thorpe?"

"Take it. And be careful."

"I almost always am."

"Yeah. So I've noticed."

Once outside the office, Mankiller carefully folded the poster and thrust it into a pants pocket.

He thought it might come in handy should the question ever arise as to why a bounty hunter was tracking down a "lawman."

Chapter 31

"**M**ind if I have a dance with my fiancée?"

A party was in full swing inside the main ballroom of the Hansen House Hotel. Twin chandeliers brightly lit the facility, and both food and drink were in ample supply. A local band was in fine fettle and couples filled the dance floor.

It would surprise some to learn that the host of this soiree was none other than the notorious gunman Jason Mankiller.

Though he'd not made his plans known to anyone, he intended to depart from town the following morning and had decided to go out with a bang.

Jason has already enjoyed a few dances with Sarah Applegate and even a couple of reels with little Anita Mendoza. The child had practically burst with excitement as he held her in his arms and swirled her around and around on the dance floor.

Over her adamant protestations, Sarah had then taken Anita home to put her to bed and allow the girl's mother to spend some time with Byron Longfellow.

Before that, though, Mankiller had exercised his right as party host to take a few turns with Rosario Mendoza himself. After patiently waiting through three numbers, though, Longfellow was now cutting in.

"Sure, sure," Jason allowed graciously. "I've probably worked the poor girl into a bit of a lather, though, Byron. Why don't you let her cool off with a glass of punch while you and me have a quick word."

"All right," Longfellow replied, somewhat puzzled.

"Here's the thing," Jason told him once they were alone. "A week or two from now, Marshal Russell is gonna give you $500 to put in my account. Reward money."

"All right." Longfellow wasn't sure why Mankiller was acting a bit secretive about what appeared to be a fairly straightforward matter.

"Only, I don't want you to do that."

"Oh?" The bank clerk's right eyebrow lifted slightly. "What *do* you want me to do with it?"

"I want you to give it to the Widow Pennington. I tried getting Russell to take it but he turned me down. From what I know of her, Mrs. Pennington's got a lot more practical head on her shoulders.

"He does have sense enough to marry the woman, though. So just tell her she can make the money part of her *dowry*."

"But what if they *don't* get married?" Longfellow asked.

"Then she can use it for her own purposes. I imagine she's had a pretty hardscrabble life on her own and could use a little something extra socked away in a coffee can somewheres. Besides, she took in Rosario and little Anita when they first came to town."

"All right," Byron said, nodding. "I'll make sure it gets done."

As Longfellow walked away to join Rosario, Mankiller turned toward the small bandstand, stopping short when he nearly collided with Jane Starr.

"Now that you've tripped the light fantastic with every *other* woman in town—both young and old—do you suppose you could spare a moment for the woman who nursed you back to health?"

Jason affected a bow at the waist. "Madam, I am at your disposal for the rest of the evening."

"I'll hold you to that," she said, presenting a hand to him.

"But why isn't Cash here with you?" Jason asked as they began a slow waltz.

"He's occupied with his *first* love—a high stakes poker game at one of the saloons across the Deadline." She was referring to that part of Fort Rogers wherein sat the town's less savory establishments devoted to the allures of alcohol, whores and opium.

"Well, his loss is my gain," Jason said with a gallant smile.

This very hotel had itself been a house of prostitution when Mankiller had first arrived in the Texas town. Its original owner, Bertha Hansen, was still the manager and strictly on the up and up.

She waved at Jason from her place at the table holding several bowls of punch (of both the fruit and alcoholic variety). Mankiller's senior partner,

Longfellow was now cutting in.

Sam Dobbins, who now co-owned this establishment along with Jason, stood beside her smiling broadly.

Sam and Bertha had become a couple now, though neither felt the need to make it any more binding with some sort of paper or legal ceremony.

Except for a few short breaks, Jason and Jane danced every dance for the rest of the night. By the time the band played its final note it was well past midnight and the pair was the only couple left on the floor. Jason thanked the musicians and slipped each of them a little extra cash before he escorted Jane back to the Bloody Eye.

He knew it was the last pleasurable evening he would enjoy for some time to come.

Chapter 32

Silently chiding himself for not rising and setting out even earlier the following morning, Mankiller hustled to fill his saddlebags with possibles.

He was not so distracted though that, when the door leading into his suite of rooms was suddenly thrown open, he was not still blazing fast at drawing, cocking and aiming his pistol at the doorway.

"*No, Jason!*"

It seemed as if a force outside himself flung his gun hand to one side and kept his finger from tripping the trigger of his Colt in the same instant in which he realized his unannounced visitor was Jane Starr.

Her own heart pounding like a trip hammer, the woman saw Mankiller's face contort horribly as if he was in great pain. His elbows bent into his midsection as he nearly doubled over. As his body spun away from her, she saw his pistol drop to the carpeted floor.

Closing the door, Jane raced to his side. He was bent over a chair, panting heavily, seemingly oblivious to her presence.

"Jason."

"Don't ever do that again, Jane," he gasped. "I almost...I could have..."

"But you didn't. You could never hurt me, darling. I know that."

"Thank you."

He jerked erect when, in the next breath, Jane slapped him sharply across his upper arm.

"What was that for?" he demanded.

"Because I'm mad at you, that's what for!"

"Because I—?"

"Oh, hell no. I'm in more danger when I deal faro!"

"Then why?"

"Because you didn't tell me last night that you were planning to leave today; I had to hear it from Cash." She kicked at his fallen saddlebags. "And because you obviously intended to leave without even telling me good-bye."

"I just thought it would be easier this way," he said lamely.

"For who—you?" There was no reply he could make to that.

"And for what?" she pressed on. "You're going back to that town, aren't you? Why? Is it so important that you get your ounce of flesh from them?"

"It was more than an ounce of flesh that was ripped off my back, Jane!" he growled through clenched teeth.

She winced at her choice of words and reached a sympathetic hand out to his arm.

"I know, Jason. And I'm sorry, more sorry than I can say. But there has to be another way, a better way."

"There isn't. Someone's got to lay down the law, Jane—or else there'll be no law."

"But why does it have to be you that does it?"

"Because I was the one who was wronged—and the only one who cares enough to make it right."

Recognizing the intractable look in his eyes, Jane turned her back to him, folding her arms in front of her.

"Just don't go getting yourself killed," she said in resignation.

"I don't aim to," he said gruffly, walking out of the room after retrieving his pistol.

Downstairs, as he expected, he saw his partner Sam Dobbins already behind the bar, seeing that everything was in order for the customers that would soon be filtering through the batwing doors. As he saw Mankiller approaching, he poured them both a cup of fresh coffee.

"Leavin' town, are ya?" Sam said, stating the obvious.

"For awhile," Jason replied, sipping at the blistering hot Arbuckles.

"Not sure when I'll be back," he told the bartender. "But I had a little piece of business I wanted to discuss with you before I hit the trail."

"Sure thing. What's that, Jason?"

"I'd like to buy out your share of Rosario Mendoza's restaurant."

Dobbins stiffened slightly. "You ain't getting' tired of havin' me for a partner, are ya, boy?"

"Aw, you know better than that, Sam. It's just that I might not be here when her and Byron get hitched—and I thought I'd just give 'em full ownership of the restaurant as a wedding present."

"Hmm." Sam scratched his head as he gave the idea some thought. "I kinda like that idea," he said at last. "So why don't you and me *both* just give 'em our shares?"

"That'd work out just fine with me," Jason assented. "If you're sure it's all right with you."

"It suits me just fine. I'll get that new lawyer of ours, Frain, to draw up whatever paperwork might be needed."

"Good. If you'll just give me a piece of paper and a pencil, I'll write a quick claim transferring my share to you—then you can see that it all gets turned over to the happy couple."

After signing the simple document, Jason raised his head and looked all about him. "We've done pretty well together, you and me, haven't we, Sam?"

"I'd say so."

"We've done well for ourselves and well for the community. We've come a long way."

"With more yet to come," Sam replied.

"I hope so." He extended an open hand toward Dobbins. "It's been a pleasure being your partner...and being your friend."

Sam frowned slightly even as he gladly took the bounty hunter's hand. "Yer kinda talkin' like you don't expect to make it back."

Mankiller shrugged and gave Dobbins a weary smile. "I'll be back... sooner or later, one way or another."

The bounty hunter was taken by surprise when he stepped out of the saloon and saw Cash Carpenter out in the street, sitting astride a buckskin gelding.

The professional gambler looked slightly the worse for wear, having spent most of the previous night in his poker game; yet he still sported a game if crooked smile.

"Where are *you* bound for, Cash?" Mankiller asked.

"The same place you are, my friend," came the reply in a leisurely Southern drawl.

"Why would you want to do that?"

"Because from what I hear, you are heading right into the teeth of a storm. That sounds like fun to me!"

Jason couldn't help but chuckle, though he quickly grew deadly serious.

"Cash, what I plan to do involves killing. A *lot* of killing." His eyes narrowed.

"And I don't intend to stop until that pestilent hellhole they call Low Water is nothing more than a *bone orchard*."

"So, like I said," the gambler retorted. "*Fun*." Then he too turned serious.

"You used the word *killing*, Jason—but you made no mention of *dying*; which is just what you might do if you go into that place alone."

"The kind of men we'll likely be facing would just as soon gun down two as one," Jason told him grimly.

"But they'd have a harder time of it."

When the gambler failed to flinch under his glare, the bounty hunter finally shrugged.

"It's a few days' ride," he said. "You got anything in the way of provisions?"

Cash seemed to wobble slightly in the saddle as he leaned to one side and withdrew a slender, silver metal case from his pocket.

"Cigarettes," he declared almost triumphantly. "Tailor made, I'll have you know." From the opposite pocket, he pulled a metal flask.

"Liquid nourishment," he said. "And in my saddlebags I have an additional bottle of medicinal snake oil—guaranteed to protect against all ailments of the spleen and liver."

Winking and holding up one finger, Cash then pulled aside one lapel of his coat, revealing the shoulder holster he preferred. A .38 revolver was nestled inside it.

"Being the rugged outdoorsman that you are," he concluded, "I assumed you would provide the rest!"

Mankiller made a noise that was a blend of a laugh and a grunt. "C'mon, gambler," he directed, setting out at a brisk walk for the nearest livery stable.

As the gambler surmised, Jason had indeed already made provision for the trip. He had purchased two horses the previous day: one for riding and one for carrying packs of supplies for the road. After saddling the one he inspected the packs on the other to insure all were secure and would not unduly chafe the beast.

"Last chance to change your mind," he said to Cash as he walked his horse out of the stable.

"Whither thou goest, I shall go," came the overly dramatic reply. The gambler slapped the heels of his boots into his steed's flanks, setting off in a bouncing trot after Mankiller.

The bounty hunter slowed his mount to a walk as he passed the office of the *Diligence* newspaper and saw the publisher and editor Ezra Vail standing on the boardwalk.

The newsman gave Mankiller a cold stare of contempt. In return, Jason tipped his hat to Vail in a chivalrous gesture.

"Hold the presses for a front page story, Mr. Editor," Cash shouted as he trotted by.

"We're on our way to *glory!*"

Chapter 33

Dusk was beginning to descend upon the nearly deserted streets of the cursed town of Low Water.

On the boardwalk outside the marshal's office, Deputy Dan Green stood watching the sun make its final fall. A movement caught his attention and he shielded his eyes with one hand. This allowed him to make out the tall, wiry figure of Dex Roundtree walking toward him.

The hired gun had only been in town a couple of weeks, but that was long enough for Green to take a dislike to him. Wisely, he kept that feeling to himself; it was said of Roundtree that he had more victims to his name than he had teeth.

"Where's Marshal Thorpe?" the killer asked the deputy as he stepped up beside him on the boardwalk.

"He's holed up in his office with that crony of his, same as usual," Green replied. "I think he's scared."

"Aren't you?" Roundtree said, making no effort to hide the contempt in his voice. Green made no reply as Roundtree pulled out the fixings and rolled himself a cigarette.

"Don't look like this town was much more than a wide spot in the road even *before* everybody pulled up stakes," he commented after exhaling a puff of smoke.

"Yeah," the deputy concurred. "The last few were in such a hurry that they left half of their belongings behind.

"It won't take long to fill it back up, though—just as soon as we put Jason Mankiller under."

"You seem mighty sure that's what's gonna happen here," Roundtree said, his lips curling around his smoldering cigarette in a sneer.

"Why shouldn't I be?" the deputy retorted. "We got the twelve men who put Mankiller in the pen: we got the marshal, me and another deputy; and we got you and your four cronies to sweeten the deal.

"Twenty against one? I'll take them odds any day of the week!"

"How can you be sure the bounty hunter will show up *alone*?" Roundtree asked.

"Huh?"

Roundtree made a scoffing sound, realizing it had never occurred to the not overly bright deputy that Mankiller too might recruit other guns to back his play.

Green jumped nervously as he suddenly heard the sounds of a wagon coming from the south side of town. He and Roundtree cautiously stepped off the boardwalk into the street, watching closely as it drew near them.

The wagon carried a large, cylindrical tank and was driven by one man—a man whose clean-shaven face was unmarked by tattoos and who therefore was definitely not Jason Mankiller.

"Good evening, gentlemen," Cash Carpenter said cordially as he pulled the wagon to a halt in front of the two gunmen. With a casual air, he looked around him.

"Appears to be a nice, quiet little town you have here."

"Wotta you want?" Roundtree asked gruffly.

"Why, not a thing. I'm merely passing through, on my way north to deliver water to a crew stringing telegraph lines."

"You'd best be on your way, then."

"I beg your pardon?"

"You heard me. If you got no business here, you'd best just keep right on rolling."

"There's no need to be so inhospitable, sir," Cash said, feigning mild indignation. Nonetheless, he flicked his reins and continued on his way.

The two gunmen stepped farther out into the street, watching as the tanker ponderously rolled into the gloom. From across the street, Henry Warner, one of the townsmen who had served on Mankiller's jury, walked out to stand beside them.

"Who was that?" he asked.

"Nobody," Dan Green replied.

That's when the first shot rang out.

The heavy slug struck Warner squarely in the chest, shattering his breastbone before tearing out a large part of his heart. He lifted slightly off his feet before slamming to the street. He was dead before the dust he'd stirred up had time to settle.

Green and Roundtree both dived back under the cover of the awning above the boardwalk. Roundtree fired two shots into the air as an alarm to his fellow gunmen scattered about nearby.

"Mankiller's come to call, boys!" he shouted loudly. "Keep yer wits about ya!"

Atop a grassy knoll just to one side of the south end of Low Water, Jason Mankiller studied the scene below through a military spyglass. From the sounds and movements he could detect, he surmised that there were killers aligned on both sides of the town's main street, but clustered in the buildings closest to its center.

For the next half hour, he sent sporadic shots into some of those buildings; not expecting to hit anyone but simply to keep them tied down and on edge until the sun sank fully below the horizon. The flashes of ineffectual return gunfire also helped him pinpoint which buildings hid gunmen.

Once full dark lay blanketed over the street, it was time for him to move on. In addition to a lever action Winchester rifle and the usual Colt he carried in his cross draw holster, he had a second pistol stuck into the back of his belt. A leather bag filled with additional ammunition hung from a strap crossing his chest and back.

He hoped that before long the bag would be nearly emptied.

Chapter 34

Circling stealthily to the west, Mankiller entered the back of what he thought was the southernmost of the buildings housing the waiting assassins. He had a bullet in the chamber and the hammer cocked on his rifle as he deliberately slid toward the front of the building.

There he saw two gunmen, standing at separate windows and staring off into the darkness. Mankiller struck without warning.

His shot struck one of the gunmen in the back of the head. As if a mallet had struck him, his head flung forward out through the glass of the window.

The second gunman spun around, but before Jason could take aim at him, he was struck by a fusillade of shots fired by his own cohorts in the building directly across the street. Mankiller threw himself to the floor to avoid being hit by any of the wildly flying slugs.

When the shooting died down, Jason leapt to his feet. He didn't head back the way he had come, though, but rather raced up a stairway that led to the roof. Without breaking stride, he ran across the rooftop and launched himself through the air. After landing and rolling atop the roof of the adjacent building, he used its back stairway to make his way back down to street level.

In one of the buildings located on the east side of the main thoroughfare and slightly to the north of where the gun battle had now been joined, two more armed townsmen peered out into the dark.

"You reckon that's Mankiller?" one of them asked.

"Mebbe. If it is, mebbe they already got 'im; the shooting's stopped."

"I sure hope so. I don't mind telling you, man to man, I'd just as soon not have to face up to that killer."

"Me, neither."

One of the men straightened, tilted his head back and sniffed loudly. "Do you smell somethin' kinda *funny*?" he asked.

"That is a hell of a thing to say about a man's after shave," a soft Southern voice said from behind them.

The townsmen spun to find Cash Carpenter standing with his pistol on them. Fearing they were dead men at any rate both raised their weapons and opened fire on him.

In response, the gambler rapidly fanned the hammer of his pistol four times. One shot flew wild, one struck an opponent in the belly and two more slammed into the second gunman's chest.

Both men collapsed on the floor, but only one was dead. The man who was gut-shot had dropped his pistol but was now trying to retrieve it. Cash stepped up close to him and put a bullet through his brain. He thought of it as almost a mercy, since the wounded man was otherwise bound to have died slowly and horribly from the hole in his stomach.

The gambler himself let out a low groan. One of the shots fired at him had blazed a blistering trail across his upper left arm.

The wound wasn't serious, but Cash cursed himself for a fool as he reloaded his pistol. He shouldn't have given them any warning, he knew, but rather should simply have opened fire on them before they knew he was there.

It was a careless mistake he did not intend to make a second time.

The odds against him and Mankiller were less now, he thought as he slid his pistol into its holster, but still strongly against them. He knelt to pick up the gun of one of the men he had slain, ejected its spent shells and replaced them with fresh loads before slipping the gun into his own belt.

He retreated to the back of the building and stepped outside—only to feel a steely hand clamp over his mouth to stifle any outcry!

Chapter 35

"It's me!" Jason Mankiller hissed into Cash's ear and the gambler ceased to resist.

"I liked to soiled myself!" Cash huffed.

"Well don't. The smell will give you away."

"I'm sure some would call your ability to make jokes in the face of death a virtue," Cash replied, quickly pulling himself back together. "I am not one of them."

Still, Jason was smiling. "I'm sure you heard all that promiscuous shooting awhile ago."

"I did. Sounded like you had taken a proverbial stick to a hornet's nest."

"You could say that. Near as I can tell, most of the shooting was coming from the place that used to be a saloon."

"And it might still be," Cash observed. "Are you thinking their guns might not be the only things that are loaded?"

"Could be. Take a bunch who are lowlifes to begin with; alcohol might be a way to fight off the boredom of waiting for me to finally show up."

"Which means they might not only be impaired—but bunched up together for us."

"Could be. I aim to find out. You still with me, Cash?"

The gambler gingerly rubbed the spot on his shoulder where the bullet had grazed it. "All the way to glory," he said flippantly.

The current occupants of the saloon had heard no further gunfire for some time, which only made the nine of them even more jittery than before.

Several of them were gathered at the bar, again helping themselves to doses of liquid courage. The former owner of the establishment had been one of several townsmen who had vacated the city limits with such haste that he hadn't bothered trying to take his inventory with him. These wannabe gunmen were taking full advantage of that fact.

"You smell somethin' funny?" one of the men at the bar said, sniffing the air.

"Prob'ly just the rotten snakehead in this hooch," one of his comrades replied, taking a swig directly from the bottle he was now holding.

All grew drunkenly alert, however, when half a dozen shots rang out in the night. The retorts had barely faded when, quick on their heels, a low rumbling sound took their place.

"It's our horses!" one of the gunmen yelled frantically.

Every horse had been turned out of the livery stable, and the gunshots had prompted them to become a small but panicked stampeding herd that came racing down the town's main thoroughfare.

Through the dark and the dust and the bunched equine bodies, none of the men in the saloon could see Jason Mankiller running right behind the hindmost of the horses.

As the herd passed the saloon, he peeled off from it and rambled straight toward the saloon. He fired wildly through one of its windows to call the attention of the men inside—then hurled himself straight through the glass of another window to one side!

At virtually the same instant, in response to the shot through the window, Cash Carpenter burst through the back door of the saloon.

This time, Cash did not hesitate, did not wait for the man to turn around. He fired, saw his target topple over sideways. The gambler quickly stepped over him.

In the front of the saloon, the stunned gunmen stood as statues as Mankiller hit the floor across the room from where most of them stood. He rolled several times before reaching a poker table, which he flipped over to form cover for himself.

The gunmen's collective stupor broke when Jason popped up with a pistol in each hand, firing randomly in their direction. No one was hit, but they all now scurried for cover of their own.

Back down behind the cover of the table, Jason quickly slammed fresh rounds into his pistols. A dull pain reminded him of the risk he had taken by hurtling through the window; a small shard of glass was now protruding from his lower left arm.

He plucked out the shard and, seeing it had penetrated the skin deeply enough to draw blood, quickly wrapped his neckerchief around the wound.

When he had first jumped up and started firing, Mankiller noted that three of the men at the bar, possibly the most inebriated, had appeared to simply drop down to their haunches beside it rather than seeking any true cover. Using one shoulder, Jason pushed the poker table that was his protection forward.

Lying on his side, he could now see all three of the stunned gunmen. Fear had sobered them somewhat, but their expressions showed them to still be somewhat addled.

Holding his guns sideways, the bounty hunter opened fire. All three targets crumbled flat on the floor without ever having gotten off a single shot.

Mankiller rolled the poker table, while remaining crouched behind it, toward the bar. The movement brought fire and he could hear slugs banging against the tabletop. Two shells actually penetrated it, but failed to find any fleshy target.

When he was close enough, he dived away from the cover of the poker table to a spot behind the bar. Not only would its sturdier construction provide him with better protection, it would also prevent his opponents from knowing where along its length he might pop up at any given moment.

His first move again, though, was to fully reload his weapons. He was afforded the luxury of time to do this by Cash Carpenter, who pinned down the remaining gunmen with shots fired from his position behind the doorway leading into the main room from the back of the saloon.

Caught in something of crossfire, one of the townsmen broke and ran for the front door of the saloon. No bullets flew after him, but his action proved fatal nonetheless.

Given the heavy barrage of gunfire coming from inside the saloon, those men positioned in other spots across the street were not prepared to take any chances. Seeing a dark figure, backlit by the lights of the saloon, come bursting out—they all opened fire.

Most would never realize it was one of their own that had been cut down by the hail of lead.

"Rush the bar!" one of the remaining gunmen inside the saloon shouted hysterically; his position as one of Marshal Thorpe's surviving deputies made the others committed to following his commands. It did not occur to him that his target was close enough to hear him as well.

Mankiller leaped to his feet behind the bar; thus the lower half of his body was still afforded its protection while his opponents were caught exposed and in the open as they charged forward.

Eyes narrowed and focused, he began to methodically cock and fire the guns held in both hands. He saw some of his foes jerk in a death dance.

At the same time, Cash Carpenter stepped fully into the room, triggering his pistol quickly but not rashly. When the hammer at last clicked on an empty chamber, he merely dropped the gun to the floor, pulled the second pistol from his belt and resumed firing.

Mankiller felt heat as a slug sizzled along his right cheek. Another piece of lead tugged at his shirt; but he never flinched as he coolly selected likely targets and continued firing away.

So heavy was the gunfire coming from all sides of the saloon that a thick pall of black powder smoke quickly filled the room.

Mankiller continued to blast away until both guns were empty. An oppressive silence immediately descended, but he took no chances and quickly reloaded each pistol.

With the shooting ended, the dark smoke began to rise and dissipate. As it cleared, Mankiller could see that all those who had faced him were now lying sprawled about on the floor.

The only other person still erect was Cash Carpenter, who walked slowly toward him, leaning on the bar. The gambler looked somewhat dazed, unaccustomed as he was to such carnage.

A soft moan escaped from the lips of one of the fallen gunmen. Without hesitation, Jason walked over and coldly shot him again.

"Was that really necessary?" Cash asked breathlessly.

"A wounded animal can still kill you," the bounty hunter replied calmly. "A dead one can't."

As if on cue, another of the gunmen rolled over—and Cash and Jason both shot him, firing virtually simultaneously.

"Days of glory," Cash muttered softly.

"Just don't get to liking it," Jason warned.

"Small chance of that," Cash replied, then sagged weakly against the bar.

Mankiller hurried to his side, helped him lower himself to the floor. As the front of the gambler's coat fell to one side, Jason saw a spreading bloodstain on the right side of Cash's shirt, down near his waist.

Jason breathed a sigh of relief when he rolled Cash slightly and saw a corresponding stain on the back of his shirt, indicating the slug had passed completely through rather than lodging inside his body.

Likewise, the blood coming from the wounds was oozing rather than pumping; most likely meaning no major artery had been nicked or severed.

"It's a good thing you lead such a soft life, card sharp," Jason joked grimly. "It's given you a nice little roll of fat to deflect lead from hitting any vital organs."

"So I'll live?" Cash said blandly.

"Wouldn't have it any other way," Jason replied. "If I brought you back to Fort Rogers dead—Jane would kill *me*."

As carefully as possible, Mankiller unbuttoned and removed his friend's linen shirt and tore it into long strips to use for bandaging. He intended to do no more than affect a temporary patch over the wound; with an unknown number of assailants still after them, there was no time for anything more.

Before wrapping the gambler's midsection, he pulled a bottle of bourbon from behind the bar. Seeing what he intended to do with it, Cash snatched the bottle from Jason's hand.

"At least allow me the opportunity to fortify the *inside*," Cash drawled, "before you waste the rest of this lovely nectar on the *outside!*"

Mankiller smiled as the gambler took a deep swallow. He then took the bottle back, raised it in a toast, began to tip it toward his own lips—and instead tipped it forward so as to send its remaining contents gushing over Cash's open wounds. The gambler cried out and clutched at the bar's foot rail, nearly passing out from the intensity of the flaming pain.

After firmly wrapping the affected area, Mankiller helped Cash get to his feet and directed him to a seat at one of the poker tables. He poured the gambler another stiff drink; as he consumed it, Jason reloaded both of Cash's pistols and set them on the table within easy reach.

"What's our next move?" Cash asked. His voice was shaky but the drink seemed to be returning a little of the color to his cheeks.

"*You* have no move," Jason replied sternly. "For you, this fight is ended."

"Like hell it is!" the gambler declared vehemently, moving to rise up out of his chair. Jason had no trouble pushing him back down.

"There has to be *something* I can do to help," Cash insisted.

"Maybe there is," Mankiller replied. He had just spied a rifle one of their slain opponents had dropped on the floor.

He quickly fetched it, made sure it was fully loaded and that the lever action worked properly, then brought it back to where Cash sat.

"Do you think you can make it up to the roof?" he asked the gambler, pointing skyward with one finger.

"I'm sure I can."

"Good. Then we're going to do something these lowlifes apparently weren't smart enough to think of—put an armed lookout up high. You cover me from up there. I'll be going out the front in a few minutes.

"After that, if you see anything that ain't me move, anything at all—you shoot it."

Chapter 36

Slowly but steadily, Cash Carpenter rose to his feet, walked to the stairwell and began his ascent to the saloon's second floor. From there, he should have little trouble reaching the building's roof.

Below, Mankiller patiently waited until he felt sure the gambler had time to reach his roost. He then did something else those arrayed against him should have done—extinguishing all the lights inside the saloon.

Watching through one of its darkened windows, he saw a few moments later the lights of another building go out across the street and down a few doors.

The bounty hunter smiled. The dousing of those lights confirmed that one or more of his remaining enemies occupied the building. As nearly every other building in town was already darkened, it might also indicate that their numbers had almost dwindled away to nothing.

He did see one other small building from which a faint light flickered. If memory served him correctly, it was the office of Low Water's outlaw "marshal."

He would make it his final target.

Mankiller turned away from the window and quietly padded up the stairs of the saloon. "Cash?" he called out softly, poking his head cautiously through the opening to the roof.

"Yes?" came the equally hushed reply.

"Did you see that building across the street go dark?"

"I did."

"All right. Here's what I want you to do. Give me a five-minute head start, and then start peppering the front door and windows of the place. Keep it up for three minutes, then stop.

"There'll be some shooting from inside commence about then. When it stops, watch for me to come out of the front."

"Five minutes, then three. I'm good as gold."

Knowing that to be true, Jason dropped back down out of sight, leaving the gambler alone with his thoughts.

Though even younger in age than Mankiller, Cash Carpenter had known his share of violent actions. He had faced Indians, drunks, malcontents, and sore losers—but had never before found himself in a situation so intense as this one.

And never as alone and exposed as he felt at this moment. Yet he knew Mankiller almost always played a lone hand; he had intended to do so on this occasion, regardless of the odds against him.

Such a determined state of mind required incredible bravery, or perhaps some form of insanity; at the very least, a bit of a death wish. None of these inflicted the gambler to such an extent.

Cash glanced at his pocket watch repeatedly; the time seemed to be crawling by. He realized his heart was beating at a rate even faster than the ticking timepiece. He also noticed how sweaty the palms of his hands became and wiped them furiously along the legs of his trousers.

Then his mind cleared as he rose up over the false front of the saloon and began to rapidly pump rounds into the building across the street.

The target of his assault had previously been a mercantile store. The owner of the establishment *had* taken the time to load as much of his merchandise as he could fit into a single wagon before he fled from Low Water.

He had felt compelled to abandon a fair amount of his inventory, though, and the gunmen who were now the sole occupants of the town had been freely helping themselves to it.

Three of them had been inside the abandoned store when all hell began to break loose a short time earlier and all were now crouched low against its front wall, below the level of the now shattered windows.

They were as dumb as most of their comrades, Jason Mankiller thought as he quietly entered the rear of the store; it had never occurred to them to watch their backs. Again, he gave no warning before opening fire with both pistols.

One of the kneeling gunmen went down instantly with a bullet in the back; a second managed to rise to a crouch and spin partially around before a slug slammed into him just above his belt buckle. A second struck him near his groin. Before toppling to the floor, he managed to touch off a shot of his own, but the slug bore harmlessly into the boards at his feet.

"Don't shoot!" the final townsman screamed, throwing his pistol away. "Please God—don't shoot!"

Mankiller held his fire but kept one pistol aimed at the man as he slowly walked toward him. With little light filtering in through the shattered windows, Jason was nearly on top of the quivering man before he recognized his face.

The man had been seated on the front row of the "jury" that had unjustly convicted the bounty hunter and sent him to Pima Prison.

"Guilty," Mankiller said softly.

The townsman's eyes had only a second to widen before the .45 slug burrowed through the front of his skull and closed them forever. The back of his head slammed against the wall and left a bloody smear on it as his body slid to the floor.

Mankiller had no more interest in him; he walked over and nimbly hopped up atop the store's front counter. Taking his time, he methodically reloaded both of his firearms.

Based on the scouting of the small town he had done before firing the shot that initiated this melee, and on the number of horses he had driven from the livery stable earlier, the bounty hunter calculated that he and Cash Carpenter between them probably had eliminated most of those who had lain in wait for them in Low Water.

He estimated there were no more than two or three of them remaining. They were most likely in or near the office of the marshal—including Thorpe, the crooked lawman, himself.

With one freshly loaded gun in hand and the other behind his back, Mankiller cautiously eased out of the mercantile and onto the wooden sidewalk outside. His off hand gripped his hat and he moved it back and forth several times from under the awning to alert the hidden Cash that he was alive and coming out.

Even as he made the signal, his eyes remained fixed on the boardwalk; two shadowy figures stood together near the front door of the marshal's office and jail.

One of the two split off and vanished into the doorway of the office. The second man made no such sudden moves but instead nonchalantly stepped off the boardwalk and out a few feet into the street.

"That you, Mankiller?" the man called out. The bounty hunter made no reply.

"Join me out of the street," the dark figure challenged. "My gun's holstered and my hands are empty."

Carefully, as always wary of a possible trap, Jason too stepped out onto the street. Unlike the gunman, though, he continued to hold his revolver in hand.

"I'm Dex Roundtree," the gunsel boldly announced. "You may know me."

"I know the name," Mankiller finally spoke. "And the reputation that goes with it."

From what he'd heard, Roundtree was a man of highly flexible morals; equally willing to work for or against the law as circumstances and money dictated. He was known to be a man who hired out, and not cheaply.

He was also fast with a gun and not the least bit averse to killing.

"What do you say, Mankiller?" Roundtree again challenged. "A fair fight, just you and me." Even in the diffuse light escaping from the nearby jail, Jason could see the other man smile.

He felt sure Roundtree was playing it straight, but that didn't mean one of his cohorts wasn't skulking in the dark waiting to take down the bounty hunter from hiding. If so, though, they would most likely already

Mankiller cautiously eased out of the mercantile.

have sent a shot his way.

Saying nothing, Mankiller holstered his pistol and assumed his customary sideways stance, making himself as small a target as possible.

"I've been curious to know which of us was the fastest," Roundtree said eagerly—then went for his gun.

A shot rang out in the dark and a bullet slapped into Roundtree's chest before he had even gotten his revolver fully cleared of its leather.

The slug staggered him back a step or two, but also left him puzzled. Though his vision was already dimming, he could clearly see that Mankiller also had his pistol only partially drawn. He then pitched over and fell heavily into the dust of the street.

Mankiller, now with gun fully in hand, slowly approached the fallen gunslinger. Though Roundtree's eyes were still open, it was clear at a glance that he would soon breathe his last.

"I reckon all we'll ever know for sure now," Jason said to the dying gun hand, "is which of us is gonna get to *Hell* first."

Roundtree made a gurgling sound, then expired.

Jason turned away from him, looking up and back. On the roof of the saloon, he saw Cash Carpenter sagging against its façade, waving at him weakly.

The gambler had also been familiar with Dex Roundtree and his reputation as a fast hand, and saw no reason to put it to the test. It was Cash's rifle that had delivered the killing blow.

He waved once more to Jason, then dropped down out of sight as his legs gave way beneath him.

The gambler would have to wait for any assistance from Mankiller; there was still the matter of the shadowy man he had seen scurrying into the marshal's office earlier.

Pistol cocked and ready, the bounty hunter kicked open the front door of the jail. Stepping inside quickly and slightly crouched, his eyes took in the entire office at a glance.

A movement tugged at his vision and he spun to see an open safe sitting in one corner of the room. A man had been kneeling behind its open door, rummaging through its contents; but he now leaped to his feet. Mankiller recognized him as being one of Marshal Thorpe's deputies.

Knowing it was probably futile, still Dan Green went for his holstered gun. He never had a chance. With his own pistol already drawn, Mankiller had time to take careful aim and fire even as the deputy's gun cleared its confines.

Green's revolver flew unfired from his hand as a .45 slug tore into his right shoulder. He fell back against the nearest wall before sliding to a sitting position on the floor.

Too savvy to lower his guard completely, Jason continued to cast his eyes back and forth, alert for further danger, even as he slowly strode to stand over the fearful, wounded deputy.

"You gonna kill me?" Green asked in a hoarse, muted voice.

"Probably," Mankiller replied coldly.

Chapter 37

"Where's Thorpe?" Mankiller asked curtly, bringing the barrel of his pistol around so that the fallen deputy was staring right down its bore.

"It appears he ran off," Green hissed, bitterness evident in his pained voice. "Though not 'fore he took time to clean out the safe."

Sensing that the man had no good reason to lie to him, Jason holstered his revolver.

Without a word, he grabbed the collar of the wounded deputy's shirt and used it to drag him across the floor. Green groaned in agony, but the bounty hunter paid no heed.

Snatching up a ring of keys as he passed them, Jason roughly dragged Green into the nearest empty cell at the back of the building. Dropping him, he slammed the cell door shut and locked it.

"You ain't gonna just leave me in here bleedin', are ya?" Green called out as Jason turned and walked toward the open door of the jail.

Mankiller made no reply.

Rolling onto his stomach, Green slowly crawled over to the cell's lone cot, pulling himself up and throwing himself face up upon its thin mattress. He didn't know how long he lay there, panting in rhythm to the throbbing in his shoulder before he heard an odd crackling sound coming from somewhere outside.

He swung his legs over the edge of the cot, slung them over and rose to a sitting position. A mild dizziness prompted him to remain seated for several moments. At last, though, he pushed himself up to his feet and shuffled over to the cell's solitary, barred window.

The main town proper of Low Water consisted almost entirely of its long main street. But there were other buildings—mostly the small cribs used by whores but also a few small houses—scattered about the nearby environs east and west of that central thoroughfare.

The ones Dan Green could now see from his limited vantage point—were all on *fire!*

Fearful now that the same fate might lie in store for the jail, he hobbled over to the locked door of the cell in which he was imprisoned.

"Let me outta here!" he screamed at the top of his lungs, vainly trying to shake his cell door open.

After what seemed like an eternity, he heard the door of the outer office open and close, followed by what sounded to be someone rummaging through the marshal's desk drawers.

A minute later, a somber Jason Mankiller walked back into the cellblock. A pair of handcuffs dangled from the fingers of his left hand, swinging freely back and forth with the movements of his stride.

"Turn around," he directed the captive deputy. "Put your hands behind your back and back up toward the door."

Seeing no other viable choice, Green did as he was told. Mankiller slapped the cuffs on him, then opened the door and led him out of the cell.

"Outside," the bounty hunter ordered.

Once out on the street, Jason looped a long length of rope around the handcuffs holding Green, then tied the other end to a hitching rail, allowing the deputy enough line to walk a ways out into the street. The frightened deputy saw no movement on the thoroughfare; even the body of the slain Dex Roundtree was not in sight.

"What's that smell?" he asked Mankiller, again detecting an odor he had noticed just as the shooting began earlier but had since given little thought.

"Kerosene," the bounty hunter replied.

He didn't bother to explain more to the deputy. No need to tell him that the tanker Cash Carpenter had driven into town, which had sat for a minute right in front of the eyes of Green and Dex Roundtree, had been filled with the fuel oil rather than with water.

After driving the tanker to the north end of Low Water—which was *uphill* from the rest of the town—Cash had emptied its considerable contents first on one side of the main street and then the other. From there it had flowed under the front boardwalks from one end of town to the other.

"I told you," Mankiller said harshly, his face close to that of Dan Green. "I told *all* of you what would happen on the day I came back to this stinking pustule." His eyes fairly glowed in the darkness.

"Now you're going to see me keep my word."

Turning on his heels, Mankiller strode to the center of the street, where Cash Carpenter now appeared and joined him. In the aftermath of the gun battle, Jason had helped the gambler down from the roof of the saloon and taken the time to more fully and carefully dress his wound.

Now, much revived, Cash stood holding two small, flaming torches: one of which he handed to the bounty hunter. Mankiller nodded as the two silently split, walking to opposite sides of the dusty street.

Each thrust his torch into the rivulets of kerosene running under the dry, wooden sidewalks. When the ignited kerosene flared up it spread its fire up and down the length of the street. The boardwalks quickly burst into flames that hungrily lapped at the vulnerable buildings butting up against them.

The shackled Deputy Green watched helplessly, horrorstricken by the tails of fire that spread along both sides of the thoroughfare from one end of the town to the other.

With not a single structure of brick or stone within its limits, in just a matter of minutes the entire town of Low Water was ablaze!

The night sky became bright as day and the crackling, cackling howl of uncontrolled fire drowned out all other sounds. Green cowered fearfully in the street as waves of heat from the burning buildings—including the marshal's office just yards behind him, washed over him in blistering torrents.

He cried out in alarm as a nearby building seemed to explode. When the mercantile had been abandoned, one item left behind had been a small keg of *gunpowder*. Flaming fragments of one of the store's walls blew out onto the street where they continued to burn.

Above a myriad of other smells, a particularly sickening odor assailed Green's nostrils. When he realized this must have been emanating from the roasting bodies of Dex Roundtree and the other fallen gunmen, the deputy bent over and violently vomited out the contents of his stomach.

He had fallen to his knees, helplessly crying like a baby, when a shadow of movement caused him to lift his head. It was cast by Jason Mankiller, who was approaching him leading a horse. Retrieved from among those he had stampeded earlier, the roan had no saddle. Mankiller had tied a simply hackamore to its head, which he held tightly to prevent the fearful animal from retreating before the flames.

"You finally gonna kill me now?" Green sobbed hysterically. Mankiller stared coldly and silently down at him for an uncomfortably long time.

"You deserve to die, same as the others," the bounty hunter pronounced at last. "But I've got a better use for you." He leaned down close to the flinching Green, who could not meet his gaze.

"I'm gonna let you live, deputy…because I want a *witness* to all this.

"Wherever you go…for as long as you live…I want you to tell this story. I want you to tell anyone who will listen what happened to Low Water.

"And I want you to tell them who did it!"

Green nodded numbly. Mankiller loosed him from the handcuffs and practically flung him up onto the barebacked horse.

"Don't ever forget," he reiterated to the deputy. "And don't let anybody else forget—else you'll still answer to me."

Mankiller then slapped the horse on the rump and sent it galloping off into the night.

One-time deputy Dan Green would die a broken and penniless derelict in an indigent ward in Tacoma, Washington in the fall of 1912.

The last words he ever spoke, from his deathbed, were of the total and merciless destruction of the town of Low Water—at the hand of the Man Who Cries Blood.

Chapter 38

A few small fires were still burning in Low Water the following morning; but all of its buildings were now nothing more than ashen piles of smoldering ruin. Gray-black smoke also lingered, too thick to be dissipated by the light breeze blowing from the north.

Jason Mankiller helped his friend Cash up onto the seat of the now empty tanker wagon. Half of their provisions rested beneath the seat; including items he had salvaged from the mercantile store before putting the torch to it.

"Are you sure you'll be able to handle this rig and take care of yourself alone?" Jason asked for at least the third time. He had seen the gambler wince with pain as he assisted him up.

"I'm not only fit enough for that," Cash tried to allay his concerns, "I'm telling you I'm fit enough to carry on with you." Mankiller had told him of his own plan to track down the fled Marshal Thorpe.

"I know you mean well, Cash," Jason said softly. "And I know you'd give it your best. But you've done more than enough already."

"We did raise some glorious hell here, didn't we?" Cash said with a wan smile, gazing out over the carnage they had wrought.

"We did that. And it will be long remembered," Mankiller replied, nodding.

"For now, though, I want you to get this rig back to the town where we rented it. Make sure the liveryman has taken good care of the horse you left with him.

"You be sure to see a doctor there as soon as you can, too. Get that wound of yours took care of proper." He patted the gambler on the leg and smiled up at him.

"Stay there as long as you need; get rested up and healed before you head on to Fort Rogers. Maybe play a little poker."

To Cash's surprise, Mankiller pulled from a pants pocket a fairly large roll of bills. He peeled off several of them and pressed the money into the gambler's hand.

"This should be enough to take care of all your needs," Jason told him.

"More than enough," Cash replied, looking quizzically at the roll resting in his palm. "I don't recall you having quite this much money on you before, Jason. Where'd it come from?"

"Oh...just think of it as a contribution," Mankiller replied vaguely.

"A contribution from *who*?"

The bounty hunter shrugged. "From the fellas that tried to kill us last night. Seems somebody paid Roundtree and some of the others a fair amount of money for their services."

Cash pressed no further, assuming correctly that Jason had stripped the bodies of all the slain gunmen of anything of value before lighting the town up.

"Once I get back to Fort Rogers," the gambler said, moving quickly to another topic, "what do you want me to tell *Jane*?"

Mankiller shrugged again. "Tell her I'm well—and that I'll send her a wire when this is all over."

"A wire?" Cash repeated, frowning. "Aren't you coming back to Fort Rogers yourself when this is all settled and done?"

"No," Jason replied, staring off into the distance. "Not right away, anyway.

"I think I'll drift up north. Denver, maybe."

"You *are* expecting to survive what comes next, aren't you?" Cash said rather suspiciously.

"If I wasn't," the bounty hunter replied with a wink, "I'd be racing you back to Texas!"

He stood watching for several minutes as Cash drove away. Then, leading his saddle horse and his packhorse by their reins, he walked around to the backside of the blackened ruins that had been the office of the crooked Marshal Thorpe.

Mankiller's hope was that in the light of day he would be able to find sign of the path Thorpe had taken when he fled from Low Water the night before. His hopes were realized when, in the soft soil twenty feet behind the jail, he did detect a set of horseshoe prints, heading in a general northwesterly direction away from the town.

In actuality, he found *two* sets of tracks, moving together. He speculated that the marshal may have planned ahead of time to skip out on the other gunmen and leave them to face Mankiller alone when the showdown finally came.

If so, the second pair of prints quite likely belonged to Thorpe's own extra pack animal. One set of hoofprints pressed slightly deeper into the soil, indicating the second horse was carrying a heavier load. That would support the theory that it was shouldering provisions.

Mankiller felt confident as he mounted his own steed. Both his horses were rested and well fed; he had plenty of provisions and what he believed would be sufficient water. A lifetime of hunting had made him adept enough at tracking that he bore little fear of losing Thorpe's trail.

With a light tap of his boot heels against the ribs of his mount, the bounty hunter set off at a mile-eating lope.

Chapter 39

Former marshal Blue Thorpe sat alone near a small campfire as night fully closed around him, staring down forlornly at the shiny object he held in one hand.

It was the badge the equally crooked mayor of Low Water had pinned to his vest with much ceremony many months ago. Then, besides being the symbol of his office, it had been his ticket to even more ill gotten gains than he had reaped while being more honestly outlaw.

Now...it was just a worthless piece of tin that seemed to be mocking him.

Growing angry, he flung it away into the darkness.

Thorpe had chosen to make his camp on the bank of a swiftly flowing stream rushing coldly from the higher elevations toward which he was headed. He cursed himself under his breath as he realized the hand holding a steaming cup of coffee was trembling slightly, and not from the chill in the air.

He jerked erect at a slight sound coming from out in the dark, dropping his cup and reaching for his holstered pistol. The disgraced lawman's breathing was ragged as he peered out into the night. His eyes could not pierce its veil, nor did he hear any further sound.

After an interminable time, he slowly holstered his firearm and bent over to retrieve his fallen cup.

When he straightened back up—he saw Jason Mankiller standing just inside the far edge of his campfire's glow. The bounty hunter's own pistol was drawn and aimed menacingly at Thorpe.

Thorpe again dropped his cup and very slowly extended both arms out to his sides, wiggling the fingers to show they were empty.

"You think I *care* whether you draw on me or not, Thorpe?" Mankiller snarled, ominously cocking his revolver.

A shot rang out loudly in the night—but it had *not* come from Jason's gun!

Mankiller felt something hit him hard and high on the back of his left shoulder. The force of the lead slug caused him to spin and fall heavily to the ground, sending his pistol skittering off into the darkness.

He rolled onto his side, clutching at the shoulder that was quickly growing numb. As he did, he spied a previously unseen third man come walking out of the underbrush and into the light of the fire; a man who had obviously been lying in wait for him.

As the portly figure drew closer on shaky legs, Jason was stunned to see that it was Holden Mayhew—the corrupt former warden of Pima Prison.

"Didn't count on this, did you, bounty man?" Blue Thorpe gloated, rising to his feet. "Else you might not have been so careless in lettin' yourself be seen followin' my trail."

"You two have been in cahoots all along?" Jason asked, panting heavily as blood spread wetly from his wound. Too late, he realized that the second set of hoof prints he had assumed to be those of a pack horse had instead been from the mount ridden by Mayhew.

"All along," Thorpe confessed, taking pleasure in the talking. "Me and 'Mayor' Owens kept Mayhew here supplied with free labor—and he shared the spoils with us. So when things got a little too hot for him in Pima—he just sorta naturally drifted over to Low Water." He turned away from

Mankiller and toward his coconspirator.

"Finish him off," he ordered Mayhew.

But he saw that the disgraced warden now looked hesitant, even fearful. Now that his intended target was *facing* him, even if prone on the ground, Mayhew's resolve weakened and the gun holding his pistol shook.

"Aw, hell!" Thorpe snapped. Spinning back toward the wounded bounty hunter, he drew his own pistol and fired.

Chapter 40

Thorpe was not lacking in the least in murderous intent, but he fired his gun without taking time to aim carefully; he had also grossly underestimated the cunning and survival instincts of his intended prey.

Mankiller rolled to his right, causing Thorpe's slug to do nothing more than kick up dirt. Nor did he stop rolling until he was clear of the circle of light cast by the nearby campfire.

"Shoot him!" Thorpe screamed. Mayhew jumped as if prodded, then began to furiously trigger his pistol. Thorpe likewise blasted away indiscriminately.

This too was a mistake on their part, as they stood still and fired blindly into the darkness rather than chase after their prey and by so doing give themselves a more sure shot. In the surrounding darkness, their slugs flew wildly off target—and by not chasing after him they were unable to prevent Mankiller from spinning off the bank of the adjacent stream and hurtling into its cold embrace.

The shock of the frigid water coupled with the sharp pain radiating from his shoulder was nearly enough to cause the bounty hunter to black out. As it was, he was barely able to bob to the surface and suck in a deep gulp of air before the swift current pulled him back down under.

Hearing the loud splash as Jason's body struck the water, Thorpe at last ceased firing and set out toward the stream's bank. Mayhew, puffing from the unaccustomed physical exertion, plodded up beside him. More time was lost as, having expended their full loads, both men had to reload their pistols. Standing shoulder-to-shoulder, the two of them fired rapidly and errantly into the water below as it rushed past them on its way downstream.

Trusting in his ability to hold his breath as long as needed, Jason had allowed himself to sink nearly to the bottom of the stream even as it rapidly pushed him along, away from the two murderous outlaws.

Some of the bullets being blindly launched at him simply skipped off the surface of the stream like flat rocks. Those that managed to penetrate the surface were utterly off target and quickly slowed to the point of being totally ineffectual.

Mankiller remained underwater as long as he was physically able, hoping that his foes were not pursuing along the shore as he drifted downstream. At last, though, when the burning sensation spreading through his lungs began to feel almost like a red-hot branding iron being pressed against his chest, he bobbed back to the surface of the stream.

The next few moments were the most frightening, as the unavoidably loud gasping sounds made as the bounty hunter sucked air into his depleted lungs would surely give away his position to anyone who was nearby.

No shots rang out, however; nor did he see any figures along the close by bank of the stream. While both Thorpe and Mayhew were cold-bloodedly merciless to their cores, they lacked the instincts of a true stalker, Jason decided.

Floating on his back, he allowed himself to be carried even farther downstream before at last taking a chance and swimming ashore.

Fully catching his breath as he sat on the grassy, slightly sloping bank, Jason only now had the chance to more clearly examine his wound. Lightly feeling around on the front of his shoulder, he found no evidence of an exit wound, which meant Mayhew's bullet was still inside him.

He rotated and moved his left arm up and down and round and round. Doing so hurt like Hades, but he felt fairly sure the slug had broken no bones upon entering his body.

By reaching across and back with his right hand, he quickly found news both good and bad. He could feel the hole left by the bullet's entry; it appeared to have fortuitously passed between his shoulder blade and collar bone without striking either with anything more than a glancing blow.

The bad news was that his hand came away sticky and wet. The wound was still bleeding.

He ripped a patch of cloth from the tail of his shirt and used it to plug the hole as best he could by touch alone. Roughly estimating how far he had been carried downstream, he pushed himself to his feet and managed to retrace his trail to where he had left his two horses.

Before approaching them, he remained in hiding for nearly half an hour, scanning for any sign that Thorpe and Mayhew may also have found them and be lying in wait. When finally he approached the animals, nothing untoward happened.

Mankiller did not linger there long, but took the time to dig out his second pistol from one of his saddlebags. Checking its loads, he painfully pulled himself astride his mount and set out to return to the campsite of the outlaws.

He took pains to approach from a different direction this time and scouted thoroughly its perimeter to stave off any possibility of another ambush. At last satisfied, he strode directly into the site, finding it to be empty.

Their fire had been allowed to burn out and the remaining embers were only mildly hot to the touch; there was no trace of either the men or their horses. They had clearly fled into the night, hoping no doubt that Mankiller had drowned or bled out but unwilling to bet on either.

Deciding it was wisest not to attempt to follow them in the dark, yet also not wishing to risk that they might still be close by, Jason set out to find a suitably secluded spot to make his own camp. An outcropping of rock projecting from a hillside would provide a sufficient concealment for the small fire he built.

Beginning to shiver in the chill air of the autumn night, Jason stripped off all his clothes and hung them atop bushes to dry. He used a blanket to dry himself before changing into a fresh pair of trousers and socks. He remained bare-chested for now; there was still the matter of attending to his bullet wound.

Even as he warmed himself beside the fire, he used its flames to heat the blade of a hunting knife to a red-hot glow. There was no way he could remove the bullet from his shoulder on his own, but he was determined to at least stop the bleeding.

Finding a short, sturdy stick, Mankiller clenched it tightly between his teeth. He withdrew the glowing knife from the fire with his left hand, using his right to re-familiarize himself as to the exact spot where the wound in his back was located. Quickly transferring the knife to his right hand, he reached over his shoulder and pressed the blazing steel to his flesh.

Even with the stick in his mouth, the groan of pain that issued from his lips was nearly as loud as the sizzle of the hot blade cauterizing his wound. The smell of his own burning flesh assailed his flared nostrils.

When he had taken all the pain any mortal man could bear, he pitched over sideways onto the ground, having passed out cold.

The gray color of pre-dawn greeted his eyes when next he opened them. Moaning softly, he pushed himself erect. With his hand he examined his wound. It would take time for the burnt flesh itself to stop hurting and start healing; but the hole in his shoulder had closed and he felt no pain from the bullet lodged inside him.

He fanned the embers of his fire back to life and took the time to fix a small pot of coffee. He also heated several fatty strips of bacon over a long stick held over the fire. The meat would help restore his lost blood and renew his depleted strength; strength that was already weakened by his hellish stretch inside Pima Prison, despite his restorative sojourn back at Fort Rogers.

Mankiller knew he would need all the strength and stamina he could muster for what still lay ahead.

Chapter 41

The jumbled piles of boulders dotting each side of the narrow, winding trail had probably been deposited there by some antediluvian geographic upheaval eons ago. They were one of the many marvels to be found in nature.

The two fugitives slowly winding their way through this maze of stones on horseback had no interest in such things.

"He's got to be dead," Holden Mayhew said yet again, glancing anxiously back over one shoulder. "There's no way he could have survived!"

"Who you tryin' to convince, Warden," Blue Thorpe replied in clipped tones, "me—or yourself?"

"But it's true, isn't it?" Mayhew stammered. "There's no way he could have survived?"

"Just like there was no way he could survive yer prison, huh?" Thorpe replied.

"Oh, Lord!" Mayhew gasped. Looking again at his back trail, he let his horse nearly collide with that of Thorpe when the latter suddenly pulled to a halt.

"Jesus..." Thorpe whispered.

A short distance ahead of them, a shaded figure had stepped out from behind one of the boulders standing like sentries on each side of the trail. From out of their shadow, pistol in hand, Jason Mankiller slowly walked toward them.

"It's not possible!" Mayhew squealed. "Even if he survived—he couldn't have gotten ahead of us!"

"Yet there he is," Blue Thorpe drawled laconically. "Big as life—and twice as deadly."

Had he a moment to think about it, Thorpe might have figured how it was that the bounty hunter had managed to get ahead of them on the trail. Mankiller had left his packsaddle and provisions behind, carefully cached out of sight, when he set out in pursuit of the two outlaws.

That way, when his mount grew tired, he simply stopped long enough to transfer his saddle to the second, less tired horse and continued on without the need to stop and rest either animal.

Both were fresher than the outlaws' poor steeds, which had been pushed with almost no respite since they had fled from Low Water. Moving in this fashion, Jason had not only been able to catch up to his prey but to swing wide around and find a likely place to lay in wait ahead of them.

There was no mistaking the murderous look in his eyes as he steadfastly approached them afoot now, never saying a word. One of the outlaws, at least, knew in the instant that surrender would not be an option.

"When he gets closer," Thorpe whispered to Mayhew from the corner of his mouth, "you draw first."

"Me? Why me?" the overweight and disgraced bureaucrat squeaked.

"'Cause I'm faster than you are," Thorpe explained impatiently, "but not near fast enough to beat a man who already has his pistol drawn.

"When he sees you go for your gun, he'll have to shift his focus from me to you. That should give me just enough time to pull leather and plant a bullet in his brisket!"

By the time Mankiller's pace had brought him to within twenty steps of the outlaws, neither of them had yet made a move for his own gun. Just as Thorpe began to think his portly partner was too petrified with fear to make a move, Mayhew's hand flashed toward his holster.

But unlike the way Thorpe had surmised, the bounty hunter ignored Mayhew and kept his gun aimed at the crooked lawman—whose revolver barely had time to clear its holster before an ounce of lead crashed into the center of his chest. As if a giant, unseen hand had reached down and grabbed him, Thorpe was plucked from his saddle and sent flying back over the rump of his horse.

Before Thorpe had fully lifted off the saddle, Mankiller swiveled toward Mayhew. The warden had his pistol in hand; it was even loosely aimed toward Jason. But he was far too frightened to take clean aim or even to pull the trigger.

No such paralytic malady afflicted the bounty hunter; he coolly cocked his pistol and drew a steady beam on the quivering warden. This seemed to spark Mayhew into action, but not directed at Mankiller.

Instead, he raised his pistol, pressed the end of its barrel up under his ample chin—and pulled the trigger.

The slug—along with bone and bloody red and gray brain matter—exploded up and out of the top of his head. Mayhew's arms fell to his side and, eyes staring blankly from their sockets, he wobbled in the saddle before toppling over sideways off his horse and onto the ground.

Remaining on the alert, Mankiller walked over to make sure Mayhew was dead. Assured that he was, he knelt down and rifled through the warden's pockets, removing cash, coins and a mighty fine gold watch.

He then grabbed the heavy corpse by the ankles and callously dragged it off the narrow path. Finding a likely crevice, he gave the body a short shove of his foot to send it toppling over the edge. He spoke no words; he'd be damned before he'd expend the effort to try to cover the remains in any way.

After all, he reasoned...coyotes and buzzards needed to eat, too.

In no great hurry now, he returned to the initial spot of the ambush and was mildly surprised that Blue Thorpe was still alive, if just barely.

The single shot had done Thorpe in, penetrating the chest cavity before hitting and shattering his spinal cord. All the outlaw could do now was lie in the dust and twitch spasmodically.

Thorpe's facial muscles were able to register a look of raw hatred as the bounty hunter came to stand over him.

"We...we shoulda...we shoulda hung ya...when we had the chance," the crooked marshal managed to snarl.

"That's what I told you, Thorpe," Mankiller replied dispassionately, raising his pistol and cocking the hammer.

Chapter 42

In his office in the middle of the town of Ordway, Colorado, Marshal Roy Lee sat dealing with one of his least favorite duties as head lawman: paperwork.

When the door leading in from the street opened, Lee initially paid scant notice. Most likely it was a citizen who felt some minor, petty nuisance required immediate action on Lee's part. This time, though, the first glance was enough to make the experienced lawman drop his pencil and sit up straight.

The man standing before him presented an almost pitiful sight. He was bedraggled and covered in trail dust. He seemed desperately weary and his left arm hung by his side at a slightly awkward angle.

But the tattoo of a red teardrop on the man's gaunt left cheek told Lee this was no simple saddle tramp.

"Can I help you?" the marshal asked.

In response, Jason Mankiller reached into a coat pocket and withdrew a folded sheet of heavy paper. Stepping closer, he unfolded the flyer and after smoothing it out slid it across the desktop toward the seated lawman.

"A reward poster for a Blue Thorpe," Lee read aloud, looking up at the bounty hunter with hooded eyes. "You lookin' ta find 'im?"

"I already found him," Jason replied. "I got him right outside."

Marshal Lee exhaled deeply as he rose from his chair. "Sittin' on a horse...or layin' acrosst it?"

Mankiller said nothing, simply turning and walking back outside. Snatching up the wanted poster, Roy Lee followed him. A small crowd had gathered around the body lying stretched over the top of a horse tethered to the hitching rail in front of the jail.

"Move along, folks," Lee said with firm but not strident authority. "Nothin' more ta see here."

Stepping up to the horse, Lee lifted up the head of the dead man. The line drawing of his face on the wanted poster was an excellent likeness.

"Looks ta be in order," Lee said. "'Course, it'll take a few days, mebbe a week to process your claim before I can pay out the reward."

"That's fine, Marshal," Mankiller allowed. "I can sure use the time to get cleaned up and rested up."

"The Continental's a decent hotel," Lee told him, then gave him and his disheveled appearance a questioning look. "You got enough money ta last ya till the reward comes through?"

"Thank you for asking, Marshal. I'll make out fine."

Mankiller did not reveal to the lawman that he would be more than fine. He'd left Holden Mayhew's body to rot in part because he knew of no reward he could collect for the disgraced warden's truly worthless carcass. But Mayhew had carried off a significant amount of cash when he fled from Pima Prison.

Jason had found Mayhew's saddlebags bulging with money. The same had been true of the late Marshal Blue Thorpe. Those ill-gotten gains now rested comfortably in Mankiller's own saddlebags.

He also intended to sell his two horses along with the mounts and gear of the two outlaws he had slain back on the trail, so money would be no object for quite some time. The pending reward for putting Thorpe under would simply be icing on this cash cake.

"How 'bout a doctor?" Jason next asked of the marshal. "There a reasonably qualified sawbones hereabouts?"

"Yeah. You'll find his office just a few doors down from the hotel."

Mankiller nodded. The bullet he was still carrying in his left shoulder was not life threatening unless it took a notion to start moving around inside him, but its presence would be a continuing hindrance to his range and power of motion; as such, it needed to be removed.

"Anything else?" Marshal Lee asked.

"Just one thing," the bounty hunter replied. "This town big enough to have a telegraph office?"

"It is; just about anyone can direct you to it."

"Good." Thinking of Jane Starr back in Fort Rogers, a weary smile turned up the corners of Jason's mouth.

"There's a little lady I promised to send a message to."

-THE END-

ABOUT OUR CREATORS

WRITER

R. A. Jones is a native of Oklahoma (originally Indian Territory) where he still resides. R. A. has been a freelance writer and editor for the past thirty years.

His credits include newspaper and magazine columns, articles and short stories. He has been a movie reviewer and commentator in newspapers and on radio. He assisted actor Gary Lockwood (Star Trek; 2001: A Space Odyssey) in the writing of Lockwood's autobiography, *2001 Memories: An Actor's Odyssey*. With Michael Vance, R. A. co-wrote the syndicated comic book and comic strip review column *Suspended Animation* for five years.

The readers of *Comic Buyer's Guide* magazine voted him "Favorite Writer About Comics" in 1985, and in 2006 he was inducted into the Oklahoma Cartoonists Collection Hall of Fame.

He has scripted more than 100 different issues of various comic book titles in his career. Among the more noteworthy are Wolverine and Captain America for Marvel Comics; *Harlan Ellison's Dream Corridor* for Dark Horse Comics; and Star Trek: Deep Space Nine for Malibu Comics. He also co-wrote, for Image Comics, *Bulletproof Monk*, which served as the basis for the 2003 movie of the same title.

His comic book stories, "Cold Hard Facts" and "Three On A Match" which originally appeared in the magazine *Metal Hurlant*, were short films in France.

His novels include *Deathwalker, Global Star* (written with Michael Vance and Mel Fox), *The Equation* (co-written with Michael Vance), *The Steel Ring*, a superhero book based on characters from one of the earliest publishers of comic books, Centaur. He also wrote the Western thriller, *Gun Glory* and the sequel *Comanche Blood,* both are previous adventures of Jason Mankiller.

INTERIOR ILLUSTRATOR

NEIL T. FOSTER - studied art at Bolton Art College in England before moving to Australia in 1980. Neil contributed interior art and painted covers for the underground comic Captain Koala as well as various CD and video game covers before bringing Planet of the Apes back into comic form for fans with the web published Beware the Beast. Neil has provided illustrations and covers for various horror and fantasy magazines including 10 years worth of pictures for sci-fi/fantasy magazine Tales of the Talisman. He currently lives in sunny Queensland.

COVER ARTIST

CHRIS RAWDING—is an eminent artist, educator and outdoor enthusiast. He has been a keen artist from his early days living on the South Shore of Massachusetts where he currently resides with his two sons. After attending the Museum School of Fine Arts and receiving his Bacherlor's in Commercial Illustration from the Art Institute of Boston, he now specializes in digital illustration, caricature design, branding and book illustration, as well as, screen printing and log design. His distinctive comic art style combined with his creativity and passion takes the subject matter to another level and uses color that don't exist in the real world, but makes them believable and turns them into edgy, eye-catching designs. As an eclectic visionary his gallery includes; pop culture, steampunk chic, superheroes and famous phantoms. For the past 20 years, he likes to take rish and pushes his concepts beyond the ordinary with a knack for modern, bold and organic design. (www.rawding.daportfolio.com)

Previously in the Mankiller saga:

During the Civil War, young Jason Mankiller had a tattoo painted on his left check; that of blood drops falling from the corner of his eyes. Since that time, earning his reputation as a bounty hunter, he is known on the Texas frontier as *The Man Who Cries Blood.*

In this second tale, Mankiller is on the trail of three vicious Comancheros who have been stirring up trouble between the Comanche and the white settlers of Fort Rogers. Even though the skilled hunter has the friendship of the notorious half-breed Comanche Chief, Quanah Parker, it is still left to him to find the renegades and prevent more bloodshed.

Once again writer R.A. Jones weaves a thrilling adventure set against the backdrop of post-Civil War Texas, bringing to life the pioneer men and women who crossed a vast wilderness to create a new chapter in American history. Comanche Blood is a part of their story.

HE RODE A
GUNFIGHTER'S
TRAIL

R.A. Jones

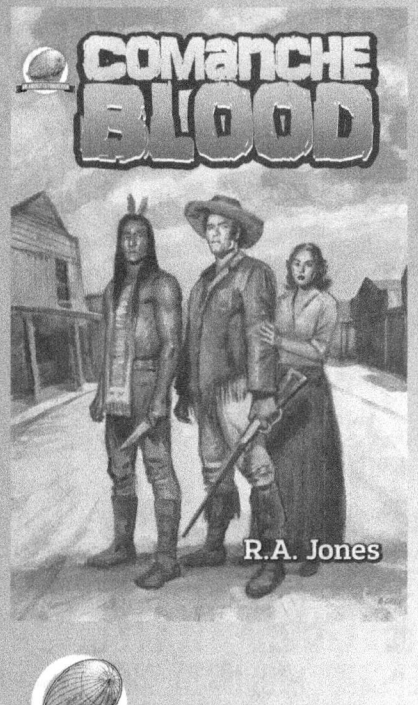

R.A. Jones

Young Jason Mankiller never believed his surname was an omen of his future until the Civil War broke out and he joined the Union Army. Fate took him to the fields of Gettysburg. By the time the battle ended, he was sitting atop a small rise surrounded by the bodies of dozens of Confederate troopers. Days later, while drunk, his fellow soldiers had tears of blood tattooed onto his face. From that day forward, the Man Who Cried Blood's reputation spread far and wide.

Ten years later, Jason Mankiller is in Ft. Rogers, Texas, hoping to find a job and bury his past. But the blood tattoo won't let him escape the gunfighter's trail. Writer R.A. Jones delivers an old fashioned western adventure in the grand tradition of Max Brand and Louis L'Amour. Here are pioneering men and women facing the birth of a new American destiny that will demand their blood, sweat, tears and sacrifice. For Jason Mankiller, that promise of a better life will be claimed at the end of a smoking gun.

www.ingramcontent.com/pod-product-compliance
Lightning Source LLC
Chambersburg PA
CBHW051124260626
47170CB00005B/1661